A Wicked Enchantment

"You followed me."

Even in the darkness she could see him lift a wry black brow. "How very astute of you to notice."

"Yes, well, I truly wish you hadn't. Just right now I wish to be left alone."

The brow dropped. "Indeed. Off to lick your wounds, my lady?"

He invaded her space, not because he moved toward her, but because of the sensual way he looked at her. Even in darkness she could see his eyes flame. "Or are you afraid of me?" And this time he did lean toward her.

"Why should I be afraid of you?"

He shrugged broad, powerful shoulders. "No reason."

Her heat increased. Ah, but she was afraid of him, though she refused to let him see it.

"And I repeat, sir, what concern is it of yours if I run away or not?"

"Because I refuse to let you do so."

Other Romances by
Pamela Britton

MY FALLEN ANGEL

PAMELA BRITTON

ENCHANTED BY YOUR KISSES

HarperTorch
An Imprint of HarperCollinsPublishers

This is a work of fiction. Names, characters, places, and incidents are products of the author's imagination or are used fictitiously and are not to be construed as real. Any resemblance to actual events, locales, organizations, or persons, living or dead, is entirely coincidental.

HARPERTORCH
An Imprint of HarperCollins*Publishers*
10 East 53rd Street
New York, New York 10022-5299

Copyright © 2001 by Pamela Britton
ISBN: 0-06-101430-3

First HarperTorch paperback printing: March 2001

Printed in the United States of America

Visit HarperTorch on the World Wide Web at www.harpercollins.com

10 9 8 7 6 5 4 3 2

*For Michael
and the precious gift you gave me—
Codi Jaunita Rose Baer—
our little miracle*

I love you both so very, very much!

Acknowledgments

People say that you find out who your true friends are in a time of crisis. I realized in 1999 that I truly have the best friends a gal could ever want. You all make me cry when I think of the support you gave me through my tough times. If this book could have two dedication pages, this one would be yours. You all know who you are, even though I'm going to try and list you. Know that this book would not be in existence without your help. You brought me laughter at a time when I didn't think I could laugh anymore. You let me cry on your shoulder when I needed your support. But most of all you gave me your love. God bless you all.

Michelle Pomar, Jennifer Skullestad, Cherry Wilkenson, Rose Lerma, Susan Edwards, Nanet Fisher, Patty Mahaney, Lori Mattocks, Amy De-Carlo, Linda Simi, Robin Richert, and Julie and Melissa Craycroft. And to my on-line buddies: Caroline Fyffe, Tracy Cozzens, Adele Ashwoth, Susan Grant-Gunning, Brenda Novak, Terri

Weedeman (may you rest in peace), Rose Daven-port (for the quick read) and my new editor, Monique Patterson. Your help on this manuscript was invaluable, hon. Thank you so much.

Spammy

PART
ONE

Man is the hunter; woman is his game.

TENNYSON

Prologue

England, 1781

Losing one's virtue, Lady Ariel D'Archer decided, was not the glorious experience she'd expected it to be.

Of course, she hadn't exactly lost her virtue yet, but they were close. At least Ariel thought they were.

"Ariel," Archie moaned, his lips trailing wet, slobbery kisses down the side of her neck, his breathing loud in her ear. Too loud. He sounded like a team of horses.

Ariel stared up at the ceiling of the room they occupied, trying to understand where exactly things had gone wrong. Certainly she loved Archie. His stolen kisses in her family's garden had proved that. But something had changed since the time she'd agreed to meet him at the inn for a secret tryst. Something, she feared, that had to do with the way his elbow dug into her side. Or the way his weight pressed into her body, nearly suffocating her.

"Archie," she managed to gasp as more of his weight pressed her into the feather bed. "I can't breathe."

"I know, my love," Archie answered, in between more kisses, his lips moving lower and lower. "You steal my breath away, too."

Steal his breath away . . . "No," she croaked, for the lower his lips traveled, the more of his weight he put upon her. "I truly cannot breathe."

"Yes, yes, my love. I know." His hand moved. Ariel realized in an instant why. The mint-green dress she wore slid around her breasts, exposing the chemise beneath.

"Archie," she gasped, shocked.

"Ariel," he answered with a groan.

But her surprise was forgotten with the need to breathe. "Move, please," she begged. She tried pushing him off her.

"I am moving," he moaned. "My whole world is moving." His lips latched onto her through the fabric of her chemise. Ariel didn't think that could taste at all good, then she realized she really needed to do something. She'd begun to see spots.

"Archie," she cried, heaving with all her might.

He grunted, moved. Ariel inhaled a deep gust of air. Oh, heavens, that felt better.

His hand moved to her skirts, the edge of the fabric slowly lifting. He kissed her as he did so.

Ariel waited for the feeling to come to her, that marvelous feeling Archie's kisses always seemed to evoke. But it'd disappeared somewhere between their carriage ride here and his pressing her down upon the bed. Suddenly she wasn't at all sure they should be doing this, at least not before they were wed. Archie just seemed so . . . so *exuberant.*

But that was as it should be, she told herself. Wasn't it?

"Oh, Ariel. My darling Ariel. I cannot wait to have you."

His hand moved her skirt up higher, stroking the bare skin above her petticoats. A hangnail scratched her. She jumped. Archie didn't seem to notice. He was too busy sucking at her flesh like a calf searching for its mother's nipples.

And then he found her nipple.

"Archie?" she questioned, wondering if all men did such things. "Archie 'tis my nipple."

"Aye, and a beautiful one it is, too."

"Thank you," she murmured, somehow sensing that was not the proper response.

His hand moved to the apex of her thigh.

"Archie," she gasped his name again.

"I know, my love. I know. Soon we will be one. Soon I will be inside you." He began to press himself against her. Rhythmically. Rub. Rub. Rub. Ariel blushed upon realizing he did exactly what Lady Haversham's poodle did to her that day in the lady's sitting room. This couldn't be right, could it? And what exactly did he mean by inside her? She'd seen animals do obscene things like that, but surely humans didn't do the same.

He lifted himself off her. Ariel breathed a sigh of relief. He began to fiddle with his breeches. Ariel watched, wondering what he was doing. And then her eyes widened. She felt her face flush as he pulled his breeches down.

Gracious, heavens, humans did mate like animals.

"Hold tight, my love," he gushed, his hands reaching for her.

"No, sir, you are the one who will hold tight."

Ariel jerked, surprise, shock and a good amount of relief filling her at the sound of the voice. "Papa!" she gasped, covering herself with her arms.

"Pull your dress up, Ariel," he said. The musket he held was aimed at Archie. Ariel gulped. Her father did not look pleased. Not at all. That he was furious there could be no doubt. He wore no uniform, but he still looked every inch the admiral. Blue eyes pierced her like they were a sword. A tick . . . His jaw ticked, his aged skin was pale, his cheeks were flushed with rage. Still, not for eighteen years had she been his only daughter. She met his gaze bravely, not ashamed of what she'd been about to do. Well, perhaps a tad.

"Put yourself away, sir, before I put it away for you." He waved the musket. "Permanently."

Archie seemed to pale. He didn't look at her as he quickly did as asked.

"Papa, we're to be married," Ariel felt the need to explain.

"Quiet, Ariel. I will discuss your impending marriage with his lordship. Leave the room."

Ariel did as told, eyeing her father as she passed, but his blue eyes didn't leave Archie. Truth be told, she felt rather glad for that. Her father could pierce a person with darts from his eyes. And if she was honest with herself, she was rather glad for the interruption. She needed time to analyze what had happened between her and Archie, or rather, what had almost happened.

She swallowed, squeezed past her father, who all but blocked the doorway. With shaking hands she closed the door. Her maid stood outside the room, but she was too engrossed in her own thoughts to be angry that her trusted confidant had gone to her father. Archie loved her. What they'd been about to do was a natural result of that love. So his caresses didn't stir her blood like his kisses had earlier. And it seemed a bit more, well, messier than she'd imagined. Women all over the world had to endure such messiness else there would be no children born.

The door to the parlor across the hall lay open. Ariel settled herself in a chair to wait. Her father would no doubt be angry that she hadn't waited until she and Archie were married, but Archie would assure him that they would be wed. She forgot about wet kisses and heavy breathing as she recalled the way he'd singled her out from the beginning of her debut. That the most handsome man in London had wanted her was something Ariel still couldn't believe.

The door crashed open. Her father stood there. "Come," was all he said.

"What of Archie?"

Was it possible, or did her father look even more angry? "He will not be accompanying us home."

"You haven't killed him, have you?" Ariel gasped.

"No, I have not, more's the pity."

Ariel felt the first inkling of apprehension, especially when Archie did not even bid her good-bye.

She watched for him, craning her neck around as her father's coach and four rumbled away a few moments later.

"He will not be coming after you, Ariel."

She whipped back around to face her father. "But of course he will, Papa. He loves me."

"No, he does not."

She shot him a look of impatience. "But of course, he does," she argued. "He's told me at least one hundred times."

"Ariel," her father said sternly, "Men will say whatever it takes when they want to steal a woman's virtue."

"He was not stealing it."

"No? Then you are a fool, Daughter, for the

man does not love you. He told me as much tonight."

"You're mistaken." She tilted her chin proudly.

"No, I am not."

But Ariel refused to believe otherwise. Archie was not a lecherous villain out to steal her virtue. No man could pretend a look of love such as she'd seen on his face.

But when her lover did not come for her the next day, or even the next, she began to have her doubts. And when her father came to her room to speak to her, those convictions wobbled even more.

"Ariel, I need to know if you want me to force him to wed you."

"Force?" she croaked.

He nodded. "Aye. Though he might rebel at the notion, I have ways to make him do exactly as I want."

"You will not need to force him," she said firmly, her eyes meeting his bravely.

"Yes, I will," he snapped. "It is time you stop fooling yourself about this. He has no intention of marrying you, not when he is about to wed Lady Mary Carew."

Disbelief filled her. "Lady Mary is a friend. He told me so."

"He lied."

"No, Papa. That I refuse to believe." And she did. Archie would never lie to her.

"Then you are naive. The man is a wastrel. All

society knows it. That I've raised a daughter too empty-headed to realize that is a source of great shame. Thank God no one witnessed this debacle other than the innkeeper."

She felt her cheeks color. Her hands clenched. "You are wrong, Papa. He loves me, no matter what you say."

No one dared tell the earl he was wrong, least of all his daughter. He advanced upon her. For the first time in her life she thought he might strike her. She braced herself for it, even welcomed it. She would show him how brave she could be. She was not empty-headed. She was like him. Strong and powerful. Archie loved her. She would stake her life upon it.

"I pray you are correct, Daughter, for if you are not, it will not go well for you. I will not help you to restore your reputation. Either choose Archie now or have no one at all."

"You will not need to force him."

But days later Ariel realized how wrong she was. Worse, word had somehow filtered out that Lady Ariel D'Archer, daughter of the earl of Bettencourt, had been found in a compromising position with Lord Archibald Worth.

She was ruined.

Her father, a man never given to talking much, refused to speak to her at all. And as days passed into weeks, she realized that nothing could change the path her life had taken. People she'd once thought of as friends now turned their back on her. Family members who once called to visit now shunned her like a bad disease. Even her father's maids raised their hands and tittered whenever she walked by. All alone she was. And betrayed. So betrayed.

Four weeks after her ruination Archie married Lady Mary Carew.

Ariel cried until she could cry no more. She vowed then and there that she would never again be so foolish.

I

Two years later

If being ruined meant she could avoid balls, Lady Ariel D'Archer much preferred to stay ruined.

Forever.

"Are you sure you will be alright if I leave you alone?"

Ariel turned to her cousin Phoebe, the one and only cousin who still deigned to talk to her, and pasted a bright no-no-no-I'm-having-a-glorious-time-can't-you-tell smile upon her face as false as old Lord Hampton's teeth. "Quite, my dear. Now do go before your darling husband grows impatient and dances with someone else."

Phoebe frowned up at her, almost as if she could sense her lie. "I am sorry I made you come tonight, Arie." She looked at the people surrounding her, innocent blue eyes clouding, freckled nose wrinkling. "I did believe people had forgotten."

Forgotten the scandal that had caused Ariel's withdrawal from society two years ago? Not likely, Ariel thought. Society fed on such *on dits*. That she was the daughter of an earl made no difference. Ruined was ruined, as Ariel had tried to tell her naive cousin. But she hadn't been able to resist her beloved cousin's pleading tone and so had accompanied her to town. Now, as she stood at the edge of the dance floor, she wondered at the wisdom of her choice. 'Twas obvious she shouldn't have come. Thank goodness her father didn't have to witness her humiliation. Then again, if her father had been in town, he'd no doubt have forbidden her to come at all.

"If you like, I could have John bring the coach around."

"Leave?" Ariel asked, black brows lifting. "And miss all this?" She motioned to the heavily decorated room. Flowers dotted every available surface, huge vases of them; no doubt some poor gardener was lamenting the loss of his precious blooms. The scent of those petals filled the air, barely but not quite masking the smell of overheated bodies, scented gowns and the candle wax that spotted the floor and guests. "Perish the thought."

"Are you quite sure? It would be no problem for John to come back for Reggie and me."

Ariel turned to her longtime friend and shook her head. Powder from her wig poofed around her like mist from a bag of flour. Gracious, but she'd forgotten how annoying society's fashions could be. Her own silly wig itched her near to distraction, the single gray curl that rested near her neck making her long to scratch beneath it.

"I'm quite content to stand here, my dear," she answered. *Next to standing on a bed of hot coals, this would be my second favorite thing to do*, she silently added. "Now go. Reggie has been patient enough."

But her cousin still looked unconvinced. Ariel took matters into her own hands by spinning her around and giving her a gentle shove toward the bespectacled man waiting by the dance floor. He gave her a tight smile. Ariel returned it.

"Go," she repeated.

Phoebe went, though not without one last backward glance. Her gray wig looked askew, Ariel noted. Ah, well, the whole night felt askew.

Her cousin so wanted this night to be a success. Ariel should have known it would go differently.

She watched Phoebe go, sighing. She tried to tell herself she didn't look as conspicuous as a tick on the bum of a pig. Still, she took a small step back, the potted palm next to her affording her a bit of concealment, though not as much as she suddenly wished for. She should have stayed in the country. Truly, after the first few months of her exile she hadn't missed society one iota. Who would miss pasting black patches upon one's skin? Or drafty hooped skirts? Or so much powder in one's hair, one looked like a giant breast of chicken just as it was shoved into the baking oven? No. No. She'd not missed it. Not at all.

But it was hard to ignore the scandalized looks frequently shot her way. Still, somehow she managed to maintain the indifferent mask she'd practiced in the mirror. It wasn't fair. 'Twas not as if it was she who had been at fault. She had not been the lying cad, the one who'd tried to seduce an innocent girl. And yet society did not care. They knew only that she'd been found in a compromising position with a man who was not her husband. That Ariel had believed with every innocent beat of her heart that Archie would, indeed, come up to scratch mattered not at all. He hadn't loved her. Hadn't even wanted to marry her afterward.

Fie on them all.

"For someone so fair you look remarkably blue-deviled, my lady."

Ariel started, turning toward the baritone voice. For a moment she found herself gawking, then that practice session in the mirror came to her rescue. She straightened. Truly, he was the most sinister-looking man she'd ever seen, yet handsome—fan-yourself-with-your-hand handsome. He had a scar across his cheek that ended near the corner of his left eye. He looked like a panther who'd been in one too many fights.

Dressed all in black he was: black coat, black breeches, even a black diamond winking from his black cravat.

She blinked, telling herself to stare was rude.

Yes, but what a sight to stare at.

"Which really is a pity," he continued, his silver eyes glowing. Those eyes were remarkable, truly his best feature, a myriad colors all coalescing into one. "For such a pretty face should never have a frown upon it."

And Ariel went back to staring, for when he smiled, the scar drew tight across his face. The sight fascinated her, although she supposed some women would have swooned at the sight he made. He wore no wig. That was unusual, too. More unusual still was the way he wore his hair. The ink-black strands were pulled into a tail so tight that it stuck out behind him. No powder. No hair ribbon. Just a leather thong.

"I'm sorry, do I know you, sir?" It must have been her time in the country that made her feel suddenly gauche and tongue-tied as she waited for his response.

"No, my lady, I do not believe we've been introduced."

No, indeed, for she would remember such a man. He looked devilish with an odd half-smile lighting his face. Ariel swallowed, suddenly wanting to escape his presence. "Then I do beg your pardon." She curtsied. "We should not be conversing."

He threw back his head and laughed, the scar

brought to ominous, disturbing attention. People stared, Ariel realized, and not just at her. She looked away, trying not to let him see how much he disturbed her with his strange face and all-black attire.

"Do you think, my lady, that talking to me will harm your reputation?"

She drew back, though she told herself not to react to his words. So he knew of her past? Well, she supposed the whole ballroom knew. Half of London probably, too. No reason to feel hurt.

"Funny, I did not think you so naive," he added.

She straightened her shoulders. "I will agree, sir, that my reputation is a bit tarnished, yet despite what they say, I *am* a lady. As such, I intend to act like one."

She moved to leave, glad to be departing from his disconcerting company. A hand on her arm stopped her. The contact jolted her, so much so that she found herself snapping, "I beg your pardon."

"Don't go."

She looked at his hand pointedly. There was a ring upon it. The stone was unusual. Green with what looked to be faint red spots upon its surface. But then he removed his hand. The ring dipped out of sight. She could still feel where he'd touched her through the silk of her lavender gown.

"I meant no offense. I merely wanted to make your acquaintance."

"Well, now you have made my acquaintance, so I bid you good-bye."

"No," he said quickly, his eyes pleading. "Do not go. I sense that you are as lonely for company as I am."

She stiffened. "I am not lonely."

"Ah, but I think you are."

Suddenly she didn't care that she risked hurting his feelings by being blunt. "I do not care for company right now, sir. Now, please leave before you cause even more of a stir."

"Have we caused a stir?" He looked around, then faced her again. "I see we have."

"How fortunate that your eyes work when it appears your ears do not."

He smiled, the unsettling half-smile returning again. "Yes, well, despite my scar I'm told my mouth works very well, too."

She felt jolted that he would so openly acknowledge his blemish. But if he didn't care, neither should she. "My mouth works, too, and it's telling you to go."

"But I don't want to leave. 'Tis much more fun conversing with you."

"Very well, then I will leave." She turned on her heel.

He stopped her. Again. She glared. He released her.

"Are you afraid to talk to me?"

She lifted her chin. "I am scared of nothing, least of all you."

"Really, then I wonder why you looked about ready to flee the ballroom a moment ago."

"I was not going to flee."

"Poppycock, my lady. You were."

"And if I was, what concern is it of yours?"

He shrugged. "I merely wonder why you would ever give them the satisfaction of seeing their arrows hit true and why you would give them the added satisfaction of running away."

He saw too much. "What do you mean, sir?"

His lips tightened, his eyes turned challenging. "You know very well what I mean."

Yes, she did, but she would not acknowledge it to him for all the guineas in the world.

"Dance with me, my lady. Show them you're made of sterner stuff."

She blinked up at him. "Who are you?"

He didn't respond immediately, almost as if he weighed whether or not to answer. "I am Nathan Trevain."

Trevain. She stiffened. "Relative of the duke of Davenport?"

The right side of his face tipped in a sardonic smile, but then he bowed. "My uncle."

Which made him—

"His heir." He must have read the question in her eyes.

"Congratulations, sir. I hear that that particular dukedom is very profitable. You must be pleased to find yourself the future recipient of the title."

For the first time she thought she might have pricked him with her words. "I hardly give it a thought."

And something was not quite right about his accent. His last words had come out sounding a bit flat. "No? And here I thought all men counted their wealth before inheriting it."

"Not this man."

"Mmm mmm. I'm sure you haven't."

"If you're trying to anger me, it will not work. My offer to dance with you still stands."

"And I refuse, or should I write my response down since you seem to be so hard of hearing?"

"If your penmanship is as pretty as you, you may do whatever you wish."

"Find me pen and paper, then, and I will do as you ask."

His smile returned again. "What? Leave your side so you can run off and hide? I think not, my lady."

Ooo, but he frustrated her.

"Dance with me, Lady D'Archer. I will allow you to impress me with your handwriting later."

She looked up at him in disgruntlement. "Pity about that pen," she growled. "I do believe I could have stabbed you with it."

He drew back, as if he were startled that she dared to spar with him. She saw his eyes spark, a definite improvement over the coldness she'd glimpsed there. "Such bloodthirsty words."

"My hope was that they would make you go away," she huffed in exasperation.

"They will not," he said firmly. He leaned toward her. She resisted the urge to step back. Gracious, but he was handsome. And intimidating. "Within five minutes of your arrival I was being regaled with scandalous tales of your past. You are infamous, my lady."

"Then why, sir, are you standing here conversing with me?"

"Because I rather like to associate with infamous people. So much more interesting. And they do complement my devilish looks, don't you think?"

"And that is why you wish to dance with me?" she said, ignoring his question.

"No, I wish to dance with you because I think it a mistake for you to run away."

"I was not going to run away," she bit out, exasperated.

"Yes, you were."

She stared up at him unblinkingly. "You're not going to leave me alone, are you?"

"No."

She continued to stare. Bothersome man. But he had a point. Society would be scandalized if she deigned to dance at its posh soiree, especially after making its disapproval of her return so well known. And wouldn't that be lovely? For a change she would be behaving exactly in the manner they believed her capable of.

A spurt of rebellion had her tilting her chin. "Very well, Mr. Trevain, I shall dance with you," she surprised herself by saying. The man had the audacity to let triumph shine from his eyes, and while she did not like the look or appreciate it, she didn't care. One dance. That was all. Surely she could handle that.

"A good choice, my lady." He bowed, offering her his arm, the green and red stone catching the light.

"That remains to be seen," she murmured, taking that arm, though she made sure the contact was light. Distant.

He led her toward the dance floor. She tried not to think about how much she'd missed dancing in the recent years. They stopped just shy of the spinning couples, the two of them in plain sight of nearly everyone. She tried to concentrate instead on something other than the fact that he seemed so tall while he stood next to her. They had to wait for the music to stop. Phoebe shot her a look of surprise and then pleasure as she spied her. Ariel wished she could feel as happy, but Phoebe had always been an innocent. Even when the scandal had broken, she'd refused to believe anyone could think ill of her cousin. Ariel, too, had wanted to believe that. It'd taken less than a week to realize how cruel and heartless society could be.

All too quickly the music ended. Ariel took her position with Mr. Trevain, her wide skirts brushing those of the other dancers. Already she could hear the stir of voices, the lifting of one in particular. The word "gypsy" reached her ears. She refused to look at the person, although the mention of her mixed parentage infuriated her more than anything that had come before. Yes, they could think of her what they would, but when they started mentioning her mother's heritage, they maligned a race that cared more for its own than any other culture.

"That's better."

She looked up. Candles in the chandelier above flickered in a small breeze that brought with it the scent of roses and hot house citrus blooms. The light illuminated a face that still looked handsome, despite the scar. It was the eyes. They were so penetrating, so intense, almost as if he tried to see inside her to perhaps read her mind. "What is?"

"You have more color in your cheeks."

She lifted her chin. More color? Indeed she did, for she could feel it. Anger. She was angry. She seized the emotion, pulling it around her like she would an iron cloak.

"You shouldn't let them upset you, you know. By doing so you give them a great deal of power."

The music had begun, Ariel realized gratefully. Hopefully the steps of the dance would keep conversation down to a minimum, but she should have known better. It was a country dance, one that kept him near to her for most of the set. Worse, it allowed him to touch her hand, as he did now, the palm of it flat against her own as he raised it above her head, held it there, his commanding gaze darting to her cleavage as they circled each other. Once again she felt a sense of danger.

"Do you deny you would have fled the room?" he asked.

"I don't know what you're talking about."

They separated momentarily, came back together. "Bull," he said.

She looked up at him, giving him her best I-am-the-daughter-of-an-earl-you-are-the-son-of-a-nobody glare. Only he wasn't the son of a nobody. As she recalled, it was the duke's younger brother who'd sired Nathan Trevain, Nathan's father having renounced his title to live in the colonies. And that explained his odd accent. It wasn't his disfigurement. He was from the colonies.

"I feel perfectly amiable toward the people in this room."

He shook his head. "You, my lady, are a liar."

She lifted a brow. They circled each other like warring hawks. "And you, sir, are a cad."

"Why, thank you. But tell me, what is it about these people that makes you want to befriend them?"

"I do not wish to be friends with them."

"Then why do you care what they think?" Nathan saw her lips tighten. He had no idea why he pushed the matter. He should be flirting with her. Smiling. Laughing. Certainly she was easy enough on the eyes to do so. Instead he found himself wanting to spar with her, enjoying the moment, before he remembered she was nothing to him but a pawn and the daughter of a bitter enemy.

A pretty pawn, he thought, even with her wig on, for he knew beneath it lay thick, black hair, the kind of silky tresses that would surround a man whilst he made love to her. He'd watched her prior to tonight, admired her from a distance. Yea, even wanted her, though she was the type of woman he always sought to avoid: Beautiful. Blue-blooded. No doubt a pampered princess. Beautiful women were not to be trusted, he thought, having to fight to keep his hand from rubbing his scar.

But thoughts of his scar had him remembering the task at hand and the fact that he should not be intrigued by Lady Ariel D'Archer. It was those damn eyes. Cat eyes. They would be something else when aroused, her gypsy heritage plainly evident in the way her cheekbones tilted exotically. Smooth, porcelain-looking skin stretched flawlessly over them. Skin that had never seen more than an hour's sun. Skin that had never been exposed to harsh elements. Skin that he longed to stroke. But this was business, and he would not mix business with pleasure, especially with a woman who was so obviously not for him.

"Not going to answer?" he said, when it seemed she would be silent all night. "Pity, for it's been my observation that most of the people you wish to impress aren't worth the paper their lineage is written upon."

At last she looked at him, those sensual eyes

of hers narrowing. She didn't appear to be repulsed by his scar. That was good, for he'd worried she would be.

"And how have you arrived at that conclusion?" she asked.

"Simple observation."

"And yet you are one of them."

"Am I?" These British, so easy to fool. Even now, not a person in this room knew they had an enemy in their midst, a man more than one British official had sworn to capture. No, he would never be one of them. Bloodlines and titles did not interest him.

"But of course you are. At least, that appears to be what *you* think."

She was trying to insult him again, for her unspoken words were that she considered him anything but a gentleman. Well, bully for her. And against his better judgement he found himself admiring her spirit. She stood in his arms all but thumbing her nose at society, despite the fact that they'd treated her horribly this night. Oh, she might have tried to conceal how much their slander had wounded her, but he could tell. She held herself proud, too proud for someone unaffected by what went on around her. And as someone who'd endured his share of curious and repulsed looks, he knew the feeling well.

"While I cannot deny my bloodlines, I cannot claim to be a true gentleman. I'm too new to England."

"And how new is that?"

"Two months." He saw surprise in her eyes, wondered for a moment what she would think if he told her he would have been here sooner if possible. But with the war so recently over, finding a ship to sail to England had been difficult. "Thus I do not subscribe to the dictum that he or she with the oldest title wins."

"How unusual."

"Indeed. Nor do I particularly like the fashions." He looked around them, then leaned toward her, adopting a look of sincere curiosity. Once again, he was surprised she did not draw away. It gave him hope that his plan might succeed. "Tell me, why must women place the tallest wig upon their head? And wear the widest hooped skirts? Is there some sort of competition going on?"

He saw her lips twitch before a frown of disapproval slipped upon her face. "Indeed not, sir. The women are merely adhering to the fashion of the times."

"Are they?" he asked, pretending to be enlightened. "How interesting. Well, then, perhaps that is where you erred tonight. You should have worn a bigger wig. Your return to society might have been better received then. After all, half the women in this room hide their shocking lack of morals beneath a giant head of false hair. Why should you be any different?"

"You're incorrigible," she muttered, yet he thought he saw a small smile on her exquisite face.

"Indeed I am, but let me make one last observation." He tilted his head a bit, a habit he had
formed to hide his defect, and smiled. " 'Tis obvious you can truly be called a lady while most
of these women behave as anything but." He
spoke rather convincingly, he thought.

"Thank you . . . I think."

He continued to smile down at her. But something in her changed. She all but physically
withdrew. It didn't help that the steps of the
dance separated them. When they came together again, the amusement was gone, replaced
by icy aloofness. In vain he tried to think of
something else to say that would once again
amuse her, but the music ended before he could
do so. She stepped away.

And it was over.

"Thank you, sir." She curtsied.

"You're welcome," he answered. But she was
already gone. He watched her go, her head held
high, a piece of dark hair escaping from the bottom of her wig.

"Damn," he muttered. What had he done
wrong? And just how the hell was he supposed
to befriend a woman who all but ran from his
arms?

2

And Ariel did flee—right to the nearest exit, which happened to be a balcony door that opened to a garden. The source of all the blooms inside instantly revealed itself. A riotous smell assaulted her senses. Roses. Jasmine. Lilies. She inhaled deeply, realized she panted and raced down the steps in search of privacy so that she could better regain her breath. Fortunately, it was all but deserted outside, the evening a bit too chilly for any but the most desperate of partygoers. And she was desperate. Gracious heavens, but the man inside disturbed her. It must be his wicked good looks, for she could think of nothing else that would do it.

She would not think of it. She would compose herself and then go in and find Cousin Phoebe to tell her she wanted to leave. She'd done what she'd set out to do. She'd made an appearance in society. Even danced a set.

A dance that has left you shaken.

No, she corrected herself. It wasn't the dance. It was the man himself. She was honest enough to admit that. There was something about him, something that both frightened and exhilarated her. When he touched his palm to hers, she'd found herself thinking more than once that there was more to him than met the eye. It was that which alerted her to danger and that which piqued her curiosity.

She found a bench at the edge of the lawn far away from the ballroom and prying eyes. Spreading her lavender skirts, she sat down upon the stone seat. Coldness seeped through her dress, but it failed to chill her. Warmth from her dance still permeated her blood. Was it because she sensed within him a kindred spirit? Someone who also endured his share of rude and offensive looks? Is that what it was? Truly, she did not know.

"There you are."

And as if she'd conjured him up, the object of her thoughts stood before her. Light from the ballroom shone on the right side of his face, leaving his left in shadow. And though with the scar he looked roguishly handsome, without it he looked devastatingly handsome. The sight took her breath away. Forceful, silver eyes were like enigmatic pools of mercury, his lips a sensuous invitation that smiled down at her invitingly.

"You raced away so quickly, we didn't have time to say good-bye."

And all she did was stare, and with that

stare came the oddest emotion . . . almost a desire. But that was ridiculous. She'd only just met the man.

Slowly she stood. Her dress rustled as she did so, dew collecting upon the edge of her gown and moistening her slippers.

"You followed me."

Even in the darkness she could see him lift a wry black brow. "How very astute of you to notice."

And still a part of her liked his dry humor. Liked it very well indeed. "Yes, well, I truly wish you hadn't. Just right now I wish to be left alone."

The brow dropped. "Indeed. Off to lick your wounds, my lady?" He invaded her space, not because he moved toward her, but because of the sensual way he looked at her. Even in darkness she could see his eyes flame. "Or are you afraid of me?" And this time he did lean toward her.

"Why should I be afraid of you?"

He shrugged broad, powerful shoulders. "No reason."

The heat increased. Ah, but she was afraid of him, though she refused to let him see it.

"And I repeat, sir, what concern is it of yours if I run away or not?"

"Because I refuse to let you do so."

"I don't need your permission to stay or go."

"No, but it would be a shame to run away before the game has begun," he said mockingly, his expression one of disappointment.

"What game?" she asked, confusion filling her.

He stared down at her, Ariel growing uncomfortable as she waited for his response. He straightened, a gleam in his eyes sparking, or perhaps it was the moonlight. "I've decided to help you."

"With what?"

"Getting even."

She laughed, she couldn't help it. "I see. And what do you propose to do? Help me put snakes in everyone's bedroom? Perhaps cockroaches in their soup?"

"I would certainly like to join you in a bedroom."

Her pulse leaped. And though she told herself he behaved exactly like Archie had, she still felt that surge of excitement that he would say such a thing to her. Gracious, but it'd been a long time since a man flirted with her. She forced herself to relax her stance, to look up at the stars.

"What are you doing?" he asked, when she said nothing further.

"Looking to see if pigs are flying, for that is about when you will ever find me in a bedroom with you."

He laughed. She liked his laugh. Deep. Masculine. Hearty.

"You have quite a tongue on you, my lady."

"Yes, well, I do try."

"And your words sound very much like a challenge."

For some ridiculous reason she found herself

unable to move, even though every nerve screamed *run*! A man flirting with her could only lead to trouble or even worse, hurt. "Only you would think so."

"I suppose time will tell."

"Yes, tell you that you're wasting your time."

He didn't respond. She found herself oddly disappointed by that.

"But are you not the least bit curious about what I propose?" he said instead.

"No. I am wary of men who come bearing gifts."

"I bring you no gifts but myself."

"Thank you, but someone else offered me a bottle of the plague tonight. I think I shall accept that instead."

He laughed again. Ariel was surprised and alarmed to find herself enjoying their banter.

"You know how to cut a man to the quick, my lady."

"Would that it was your wrists instead."

He clutched at his heart as if wounded. "Ouch."

"Ouch? What happened, sir? Did your ego get too big for your chest? Did it hurt?"

He held up his hands. "Truce. I cry a truce. I cannot take any more of your sallies."

"Good, then perhaps you will leave me alone."

"Not before you answer me. Do you or do you not want my help?"

"With what?" she asked, exasperated.

"Setting society upon its ear."

"Indeed?"

"Indeed."

"And why do you have such a burning desire to wreak havoc upon people you yourself said I had no cause to concern myself with?" she asked.

"Because I find the English stuffy bores. Because if I must stay in England, I should like to amuse myself. Because at this moment you're the best chance I have of that happening."

"Or perhaps because you are trying to seduce me." Perversely enough, she found herself holding her breath as she waited for his response. She could see that she'd shocked him. No, not shocked. Something else. She stretched her senses out, trying to get a feel for what this man might want. But it was a sad truth that sometimes her intuition worked and sometimes not. Heaven knows it'd failed where Archie was concerned.

"My lady, no doubt there is a plethora of women more willing to be seduced by me than you."

"Yes, the kind you have to pay."

He laughed, even as she wondered where the words had come from.

"Exactly," he said.

"I would wager that sort of women is not much of a challenge."

"Are you offering to challenge me?"

"Heavens, no, merely stating a fact."

"I see."

"But you must understand why I find it hard to believe you wish to help me, a complete stranger, out of the goodness of your heart. Let us just say that my experience with men has left me more jaded than that." And it had. No matter that she found herself oddly excited by their impromptu meeting. She was wiser than she'd been in youth, more in control of herself.

"Is it so hard to believe that a man would want to help you out of the kindness of his heart?"

"The men I've known have no heart."

"Perhaps I'm not like other men."

She doubted it. All men were alike.

"Perhaps you should take a chance that I'm sincerely trying to befriend you." He took a step toward her. She held her ground, though she felt her body spring alive at his nearness.

Danger.

"Perhaps you should know that I would consider it a mistake for you go scurrying back to the country, content to let society rule your actions for the rest of your days."

She lifted her chin. His silver eyes glittered in the moonlight.

"And perhaps you should know that I consider half the people in that ballroom hypocrites of the first order. That they malign you when they themselves have no honor is the biggest hypocrisy I've seen since coming to London."

He leaned toward her. "Don't let them win,

my lady. If you do, you will be fending off indecent offers from men for the rest of your life."

She felt her breath quicken as she stared up at his handsome face, knowing he was right. Though he hadn't looked at her indecently this night, others had. Those men considered her fair game because of her ruination. She hated them for that.

He waited for her to say something, she realized, grimly holding her tongue. But he could go to the devil for all she cared, he and his silly, ridiculous observations.

"Or is that what you want?" he asked.

Still she held her tongue, though she knew doing so provoked him, perhaps to the point that he'd do something rash.

Like what? asked a voice.

Like kiss me.

"No," she answered.

"No, my lady?" he said, thinking she meant no to his question, not to her ridiculous thought that he might kiss her. "That I wonder." He took another step toward her. And now she could feel the heat radiate off his body like warmth off lantern glass. His smell, too, permeated her senses. A scent that was all maleness and uniquely his. She retreated a step. The back of her legs came in contact with the bench.

"That is a pretty ring," she commented, trying to distract him, grasping at anything that came to mind to do so.

"Is it?" he asked, still advancing.

"Yes . . . ah . . . what kind of stone is it?" she croaked. Gracious, but he still came at her.

"A serpentine."

"Oh." How appropriate. A serpentine for a man who moved like a serpent. "I've never seen one before."

He didn't answer, just closed the distance between them. All thoughts of his ring vanished. "What are you doing?" she asked, and she hated that her voice sounded breathless.

"I'm going to test the waters."

Test the wat—

"Oh, no," she said, instantly gleaning his meaning. She tried to duck around him, but he moved faster. Masculine arms pulled her against him, a gasp of protest turning into a moan of "Nooo" as he lowered his head.

"Yes," she heard him answer, and then she felt the warm pressure of his lips against her own. She stood there, stunned, as myriad sensations flooded her senses: Fear. Shock. And a sweet desire that startled her with its intensity.

And then it was over. He released her. Stepping back almost as if their kiss had jolted him, too.

"Is that what you want, Lady D'Archer— stolen kisses pilfered in a garden? For if that is the life you envision for yourself, then go. But I warn you, if you give in to your cowardly urge to retreat, you will regret it for the rest of your days."

Turning on his heel, he left. She watched his

dark form get swallowed up by the darkness, broad shoulders stiff with disapproval.

Or disappointment?

Or was *she* disappointed? Gracious heavens, she didn't know. Nor did she care to analyze why her shoulders slumped as he walked away. Why her lips felt burned. Or her legs felt as weak as cook's favorite noodle.

She sank to the bench, her hand covering her erratically beating heart. And as his footsteps receded she found herself thinking that he was right. Men would forever treat her as he had. Worse, she wondered if all of them would make her heart race as he had.

He shouldn't have kissed her, Nathan thought, as he rode home in his uncle's elegant ducal carriage. Damn, but he shouldn't have done it.

And just why had he done it? he asked himself, swiping a hand over the left side of his face. He could feel the ridge of the scar tissue there, a memento of why he should never desire or trust a beautiful woman again. Besides, women such as she found his disfigured face interesting for only so long before they went on their way. 'Twas a bitter irony, really, for it was a woman who had shot him and caused the disfigurement. But he would not think of the woman who'd betrayed him. The lying, treacherous whore was no longer his concern. Lady Ariel D'Archer was.

Damn, but he couldn't stop thinking of her. Those lips enticed him. He felt a need such as he'd never known, which made his anger surge to the point that kissing her had seemed reasonable at the time.

Reasonable!

Bloody hell.

The coach swayed upon its springs as he settled back angrily into the plush, red velvet squabs, the luxury that surrounded him completely ignored. Fury at himself had him clenching his fists. He would not make such a mistake again—if she ever let him near her.

Damnation. She must.

Yet as he stared out at the dark London streets, he found himself thinking not of how to rectify his failure but of her. Of those wonderful, seductive lips. And of her eyes—gold and brilliant and fringed with dark lashes. Those eyes dominated her face. She reminded him of an exotic dancer he'd once seen. Stunning. Elusive. Not for him.

No, not for him. Not ever. He meant to use her and then discard her, just as she would no doubt use him if given the chance.

Jerking angrily, he opened the compartment concealed in a panel of the carriage. A crystal decanter sat next to a matching crystal glass. He lifted the brandy out, poured himself a drink, then tossed it down. The liquor burned a path to his stomach. He welcomed it.

Wess, I will not fail again. I promise you I will do whatever it takes to find you.

And that included befriending Lady Ariel D'Archer, daughter of the First Lord, and a man who refused to help him find his brother, Wess Trevain—Wess, who'd been impressed off the deck of his American ship. Wess, who seemed to have disappeared without a trace. But there would be a record of him somewhere. And he knew Lord Bettencourt had that information. Bettencourt merely withheld it because of Nathan's past. Never mind that the war had been over these past six months. His lordship still held a grudge. But what his lordship didn't know was that Nathan Trevain, heir to the duke of Davenport, was also one of the American colonies' most famous spies: Helios. Nor did Bettencourt know that he went by the last name of Mills in the colonies as a safeguard to protect him against exactly that which had happened, being forced to fight with the British against his fellow colonists. No, only few knew of his connection to the duke, and it would stay that way.

Unless Lady D'Archer proved useless for helping him to infiltrate her father's house.

Then all would be revealed. It would be his turn to use a British woman to his advantage, as they had tried to use one to their advantage. Only he didn't plan on killing Lady D'Archer, as that British wench had planned to kill him. He rubbed the scar again. No, he would kidnap her, if need be, but he'd not kill her.

Yet somehow he must recover from today's debacle. He would need to gain Lady D'Archer's trust, then be given access to her house. His overwhelming goal was to find out what lay in the room he'd discovered when he'd broken into the house. The room had no windows; it had a door thicker than any he'd ever seen. What he sought *must* be in there. He knew it. And if he could get close enough to her to enlist her help . . .

The carriage came to a halt. One of his uncle's staff opened the door practically the moment the vehicle stopped. Nathan hardly noticed. Nor did he notice the front door being held open for him, despite the lateness of the hour. Nor the footman who stood waiting for his coat. He shrugged out of it, wanting only to retire to the study and think. He loosened his cravat along the way.

"The duke wishes to see you in the morning, sir."

A lifted hand was all he used to acknowledge the request, the ring her ladyship had commented upon sparking in the light. A serpentine, he'd told her, not the true name of the stone. And really, the gem could pass for a serpentine with its green background. Only a close observer would note the red flecks that made it a bloodstone. But the stone's true name would remain his secret, along with its hidden meaning.

A footman raced forward to open the study door. He walked right by the three-hundred-year-old vase that sat upon a pedestal to his right, nearly tipped over the two-hundred-year-old hunter-green armchair in his haste to pull it out. Next he rested his feet upon an Elizabethan footrest, slipping his buckled shoes off as he did so, putting his feet near the fire.

"Can I get you anything, sir?"

He didn't even look up as he replied, "No."

"If we need anything, we shall ring."

Nathan sat up abruptly, his head turning toward the door.

"Yes, your grace," the servant responded.

He was in time to see the servant bow out of the room. His uncle stood there, a man who looked so much like Nathan's deceased father that he swallowed back a surge of bitterness. Miles Trevain, duke of Davenport, had gray hair even when not capped by a wig. But whereas Nathan's father had been lean and trim, his uncle had a paunch nearing King George's proportions. Still, the shape of the face was the same. Gray eyes, square jaw, high cheekbones that looked prominent despite the layer of fat and the deepness of his wrinkles.

"You're home early, I see."

Nathan nodded.

"No young ladies there to hold your interest?"

Nathan held back a sigh. Since his reunion with his uncle, the man had plagued him incessantly about settling down and producing an heir. He seemed not to notice that most young ladies were either repelled or frightened by his face. Nathan had, but it worked to his advantage, for he had no intention of ever settling down or even staying in England. No, if he needed to dally with a woman, there were those who were intrigued by his scar, those who would suffer his presence for a night, if only out of curiosity. A one-night affair would suit him well, especially if this ridiculous attraction he felt for her ladyship didn't wane.

"None?" the duke asked again, pulling a chair out to sit opposite him.

"Actually," Nathan offered. "I did meet someone tonight."

He saw the hopeful look in his uncle's eyes and for a brief moment felt guilty about his deceit, but then he reminded himself of all the man had put his father through. It was because of the duke that William Trevain had left England, forced to do so by his very own brother. Not a word of communication had ever been exchanged between the two since the break, not a single word, until Nathan had received a letter six months previously asking for a meeting. The duke hadn't even known his brother had died in the war or that his nephew was disfigured. And the reason for his wish to make amends? Two marriages and not a child from either of them. The duke needed an heir, disfigured or no, and Nathan was only too willing to play the part—for now.

"Who is she, then? Someone I know?"

Nathan almost smiled. "Oh, I'll wager you've heard of her."

The hopeful look increased. "Her name?"

"Lady Ariel D'Archer."

The duke's expression turned into one of horror. "The gypsy witch?"

Nathan lifted a brow. "I take it you don't approve of my choice."

An emphatic shake of the head confirmed the duke's next words. "She is unsuitable. Best you settle upon someone else. I assure you, despite your face, there are many women who will have you."

Nathan took a nonchalant sip of his drink to cover his temper. So his uncle had noticed women's reactions. It was a moment before he said, "But I like this woman, uncle. She would make an excellent breeder. Wide hips. Large breasts."

That the man didn't even flinch at his sarcasm disgusted Nathan no end. Were the British so shallow that they actually considered such things when selecting a future bride?

Apparently so. Disgusting lot.

"Nathan, I know you've been in England only a short time, but trust me, my boy, you'll want to pick someone else."

"Why?"

His uncle looked uncomfortable for a moment. "Have you not heard the story?"

"No." And he hadn't. His sources had only told him that she'd been ruined. He hadn't needed to know more than that.

"Then let me tell you." The duke got up, poured himself a drink, then sat down again. He waited a few moments, like a great storyteller about to embark on a favorite tale. "Most people seem to think the girl's problems began with her mother. She was a gypsy, rumored to have seduced the young earl into marriage."

Now that he *had* heard. His contacts had also told him that the usually cold and emotionless earl had been desperately in love with his gypsy wife, so much so that when she'd died in childbirth, he'd refused to wed again. Thus Ariel was an only child.

"The dowager countess was vehemently against the marriage. She told the earl if he married the girl, she would disown him."

His uncle waited for him to comment, and when he didn't, continued with, "Two years after their marriage the new countess produced a daughter, Lady Ariel. Unfortunately, she died three days after giving birth.

"Most speculate 'twas the lack of a mother which made the girl grow up reckless. I suspect it has more to do with the father giving her free run of the estate. Rumor has it he barely gave the girl the time of day once his wife died. Lady D'Archer grew up wild and reckless. No one was surprised when she was found at an inn with Lord Archibald Worth. Rumor has it Archie told the girl he intended to marry her, but everyone knew that he meant to marry someone else. That he didn't come up to scratch surprised no one. What did surprise people was that the earl didn't force the marriage or at the very least arrange for some other man to wed her ladyship. Chances are he tried but failed to marry her off."

"So she's an outcast?"

The duke nodded. "Indeed she is. Truth be told, I'd forgotten about the girl's existence. She's been living in the country."

"Where she should have stayed?"

If his uncle heard the edge to Nathan's voice, he didn't reveal it. "Aye. Society has many freedoms, but it has rules, too. A ruined young lady remains an outcast. Forever. I'm surprised she would dare to venture out again. It just proves that blood tells."

Nathan didn't say a thing. He was too concerned that he might have ruined his chance of befriending her because of their kiss. Damnation, but he was a fool. A fool swayed by a pretty face and enticing eyes.

But it wasn't until the next morning that he realized he needn't have worried. A note was delivered, one so brief as to make no sense to anyone but him.

If the offer is still upon the table, meet me at the Ranelagh rotunda, today, three o'clock.

Nathan felt a smile tug at his face.

So the little bird wanted to disturb the coop? Good. Very good.

With any luck, he would have what he needed by month's end.

3

Ariel felt as nervous as a worm in a hen house when she arrived at the Ranelagh pleasure gardens. Wiping her hands on her peach-colored dress, she then made sure the tan hat she wore sat securely upon her head. She'd worn the wide-brimmed confection more as a way to shield her face from prying eyes than for the sake of fashion, although with its large black bow it did look rather stylish. Then again, why she worried about fashion when she was about to confront a man who'd had the audacity to kiss her was beyond her. As she descended from her hired hack, she wondered what the devil she was doing here.

Confronting a man you thought about all night, answered a voice.

No, no, that was not it, she reassured herself. What drove her to meet him was that despite her vow, she'd found herself near tears after recalling the way people had treated her last eve. That was the reason why she was here. Even though she knew it would be a dangerous undertaking, she wanted to get back some of her own.

Call her petty. Call her immoral. She wanted to reclaim her place in society. That such a thing had never been done before worried her not at all. She refused to let society banish her. Ever again.

And so she'd sent for Mr. Trevain, telling herself that no harm would come of at least listening to the man's plans.

If he had a plan.

And that thought brought another surge of uncertainty, for what if indeed his attentions to her were of the nefarious kind? Would he want to seduce her for her money? Or was she letting Archie's betrayal affect her judgment of other men? Could Mr. Trevain's interest truly be innocent? If so, why did he kiss her? Was it truly to prove a point?

Somehow she doubted it. Her instincts were buzzing like an angry gnat. Something didn't quite fit. And that, too, piqued her curiosity. Who was he really? She sighed, wishing she knew.

The day was warm, despite being partly cloudy, a brisk wind blowing holes in the clouds. Shadows drifted along the ground, easing what little sunshine leaked through. Moisture scented the air, most likely from the canals carved into the parkland around her. Tall trees and low-lying shrubs dotted either side of the pathway. On a day like today, however, it was the smell that caught her attention. She closed her eyes and inhaled. Flowers. Fresh grass. Trees. She opened her eyes. Couples passed her by: ladies twirling their parasols, gentlemen doffing their hats. Ducking her head, she headed off. The only time she looked up was when she rounded a bend in the path and spied the rotunda directly ahead.

And there he stood.

She knew him, though he stood at a distance. The tall wooden structure dwarfed him, yet he still seemed larger than life. From such a distance he looked completely normal. In fact, had she not known who he was, she would have guessed him a lord, although technically he did not hold the title. Still, that he was of noble blood was apparent in his way of dress. He wore a light beige waistcoat topped by a dark gray frock coat whose tails hung near the back of his shiny black boots. Off-white nankeen breeches hugged his masculine legs, and truly, he did have very masculine legs. Firm thigh muscles curved down to firm calves. She blushed, realized she stared at his legs like a beggar would a gold guinea and forced herself to move on.

He straightened as she approached. There was no hat or wig on his head, so his black hair glinted like ravens' wings as he bowed, his long queue swishing over the left shoulder. "Lady Ariel D'Archer."

"Mr. Trevain," she greeted in return, stopping

in front of him. He didn't smile, she suspected because he knew his facial flaw was more visible by daylight. Sympathy prompted a smile of her own. Gracious, but he was still handsome. Even with the scar. She was glad for the fashionable attire she wore. The tight-waisted day gown was decorated with lace near the neckline. She was glad for that, too, for she could see his gaze dip down, narrow appreciatively, then move up again to her lips. Reminding herself that they were in public and that he could hardly force himself upon her again, she stood her ground.

"I see you made it."

"Yes, Mr. Trevain, though a part of me is wondering what the devil I'm doing here."

He seemed surprised by her honesty, then amused, his gray eyes glinting wickedly. "Well, I must say I'm glad the other part of you prevailed."

She wished she had a parasol, something to fidget with as she stood before him or perhaps to beat him with if he made an advance. Instead she told herself to remain still and to quit being foolish. She must look at ease, perhaps try to appear as if she met strange men, alone, every day. Well, perhaps she didn't want him to think *that* of her.

"You've done the sensible thing," he added. "Truly, I'm proud of you."

She lifted a brow at him. "Whether or not meeting you is sensible remains to be seen."

He bowed slightly, the right side of his face

tilting up in a smile. A habit of his, she realized, or perhaps the result of his scar. She wasn't sure. "I assure you it is."

She looked around her, pretending an interest in their surroundings, although the hair prickled at the back of her neck. What had he said that alerted her? Was it just the man himself? His silver eyes looked striking in the sunlight. His physique, too, intimidated her. Large, brawny shoulders, shoulders that looked to have seen a hard day's work. His hands also bore the marks of labor. A white scar crossed one knuckle, another his index finger. She just bet they would feel wonderful against her smooth skin—

Ariel! she immediately chastised herself. *You should not have such thoughts.* Especially about a man who might have ulterior motives in befriending her.

"Shall we walk?" he asked.

She forced her attention up, chastising herself for getting lost in his splendid form. Gracious, but she found him handsome.

"If you wish." And she did wish, for they would attract less attention if they kept on the move. Plus there was the fact that it gave her an excuse to look at their surroundings instead of him.

He offered her his arm. She eyed it for a second.

Now, Ariel, don't be a ninny. Do take the man's arm.

And yet. And yet. She was almost afraid to.

She swallowed, placing her hand upon his forearm, prepared, yet still starting at the way it felt to touch him: forbidden yet exciting. Her blood pounded.

He gave her the full brightness of his lopsided smile. Her swallow turned into a gulp. Heavens, she'd never seen teeth so white. And so perfect. Truly, he must have not had a single sweet in his entire life.

"See, nothing to fear."

The realization that he'd noticed her hesitation sent color through her cheeks. She tilted her chin up. "I don't know what you're talking about."

His grin seemed to say, "Liar."

She ignored it. "Mr. Trevain, we came here to discuss your offer of help. Therefore I would like to begin discussing the subject, if you do not mind."

Apparently he didn't mind for he said, "Very well, what did you want to know?"

"For one, I would like to know why you want to help me." She chanced a glance up at him. He had bent to see beneath her hat, his eyes roving over her face in a fashion that made her distinctly nervous. She looked away, tilting the brim to shield her face.

"I told you last night why it is I wish to help."

She stopped, turned to face him, placing her hands on her hips for added effect. "And I say poppycock."

He lifted his black brow.

"There is another reason. I wish to know that reason now."

For a second, just a second, she wondered at the expression she saw flit through his eyes. Surprise? But it fled so fast it looked like it was never there. The dark lids narrowed, his pupils fixing upon her own eyes.

"Very well. I see you have found me out."

Her pulse leaped. She waited, breath held, for him to be truthful with her.

"My uncle is pushing me into marriage." He waved his free hand, the one with the ring on it. "Produce an heir and all that rot. I don't wish to disappoint him, but I need to make it clear I shall not be bullied about. By claiming to be besotted with you, I shall kill two birds with one stone. One, my uncle will realize that he cannot control me, for he's already warned me away from you. And, two, hopefully, my scandalous association with you will scare away some of the matrons so diligently forcing their daughters upon me. Quite tedious, you know."

So he would use her to scare away the matchmaking mamas. Why the realization should hurt her so she had no idea. She should have suspected something like this. Far be it from Mr. Trevain to think her any less scandalous than the rest of society.

"Do you not think it will work?"

Ariel didn't answer. She couldn't answer.

Sadness caught her in its grip so suddenly she had to inhale to keep herself in control. Obviously her secret hope of coming to London to find a man who could love her for herself had been a foolish one. If a man like Mr. Trevain saw her as scandalous what must the rest of the *ton* think of her?

She looked away, turning to stare blindly at the canal that flowed by their path. A duck floated upon the surface, the ring around its neck catching the sunlight and turning a vibrant white. But the image blurred. She realized then that she had a tear in her eye.

But, no, she would not cry. She'd shed enough tears over society's treatment of her.

Taking a deep breath, she turned to face Mr. Trevain. "Very well. I see your point. Truth be told, 'tis a good plan." She felt more tears burn, quickly turning away again lest he see them. "I can see how my sullied reputation would scare away matchmaking mamas. Why, you might even want to reconsider, for you chance doing your reputation irreparable harm if you come too near me. I am, after all, soiled goods. Or didn't you know that just the sight of me can turn virginal daughters into frightful hussies?"

A hand upon her shoulder startled her. He turned her. The hand lifted her chin. Her breath caught. People strolled by, but she didn't care. Obviously there was nothing left for her to do that would shock people.

His face was kind, intent, the look in his eyes earnest. "Don't let them do this to you, Ariel."

She didn't move. Truly, she felt as still as a

lamb in a wolf's mouth. "Don't let them do what?" she said huskily, ignoring his use of her Christian name.

"Don't let them wound you. I assure you, your countrymen aren't worth crying over."

He held her gaze, Ariel realizing that another tear wobbled on her lashes. He wiped it away. The contact of his work-roughened finger against her soft skin made her tremble, made her wish for . . .

What?

More of his touch? Yes. That was it.

The thought panicked her. She drew away.

A look of consternation entered his eyes, almost as if he, too, were startled by result of their touch and their words. For endless seconds neither of them spoke.

Finally Ariel could stand it no more. "What do you propose to have me do?"

He kept staring at her, though Ariel noted now his eyes had grown cold. "I want you to pose as my fiancée."

The words jolted her so much she immediately cried, "Your *what?*"

He smiled, though the smile didn't reach his eyes. "My fiancée. That way my uncle will be less vocal in his attempts to get me away from you, for as I understand it, once a British gentleman asks a woman to wed, only the woman can cry off. That puts you in the seat of power. Also it will keep away those matchmaking mamas, as you call them."

"I see," she murmured. Again silence dropped around them like a cold blanket. Ariel considered his suggestion. It was a sound idea. Not only would it rub society's nose in her presence, it let society know that she cared not a whit for its disdain.

"Well?" he asked. "What do you think?"

She looked up at him, telling herself what she was about to say might be the biggest mistake of her life. But she didn't care. Suddenly she just didn't care. Truly, she had absolutely nothing to lose by agreeing to such a scheme.

"Very well," she said at last. "I agree."

She wondered at the sudden flare of emotion in his eyes. There was triumph there, certainly, but also something else, something that made her shiver and feel suddenly ill at ease, especially when his lips tilted up crookedly. For the first time since meeting him, she found herself thinking he looked devilish. Truly devilish.

Pray God, she found herself thinking, 'twas merely an illusion.

4

"Ariel, you cannot be serious!"

Ariel stared at the disapproving face of her cousin Phoebe, wondering if she should have told her dear friend of her plan. Then again, it was hardly as if she had any choice.

"To pretend to be someone's fiancée is beyond ridiculous. Why, it's positively scandalous."

Ariel rolled her eyes then shook her head. "As if I need worry about scandalizing anyone."

Phoebe, the skirts of the pretty green dress she wore scrunched in clenched hands, gave her a look one would associate with a woman who watched another woman set her hair alight. "Yes, but this is beyond the pale, Ariel. Why, if word gets out that your engagement is nothing but a fraud, you'll be . . ." Pale pink lips opened and closed as Phoebe searched for a word to use.

"Ruined?" Ariel supplied.

Her shoulders hunched as she settled back in her chair. Late afternoon light from the window to her left highlighted her black hair as she shook her upswept curls. They wore day dresses, neither of them having any plans to go out that evening, much to Ariel's disappointment. Ariel looked forward to the expressions on people's faces when she returned to society again. She withheld her grin with effort.

"Well, yes, more so than you already are."

"Phoebe, I doubt a person can be ruined to different levels. It's like being with child—either you are or you aren't—there's no in between. Ruined is ruined. Frankly, I have nothing to lose."

"It is madness," Phoebe argued. "Utter madness. Yes, your reputation is somewhat tarnished—"

"Somewhat?" Ariel scoffed, snorting. "That is an understatement."

"Very well, you're quite horribly ruined," and here her cousin's eyes dimmed in the light. "After last eve I suppose there's no sense in thinking otherwise."

No, indeed, Ariel silently agreed.

"Still, doing as this man suggests is ridiculous, far too risky. Why, the very thought of it fair bogs my mind. I cannot imagine what you are thinking. Why, your father will string me from a gallow should he hear of it."

"But that's the beauty of it," Ariel said, collecting her light pink skirts before settling in a chair next to her. She leaned forward, reaching out to clasp Phoebe's hand. "My father will hear nothing of this until after he returns. By then the engagement will already have been called off."

"But will not people think it odd that you've become engaged whilst your father is out of the country?"

Ariel released Phoebe's cold hand then settled back in her seat. "No, for we shall put it about that we were engaged prior to his leaving."

"But your father will know that to be a lie."

"Yes, he will, but I will deal with that later." Frankly, she doubted her father would even care. After her ruination their relationship had deteriorated. Granted, they'd never been close, but her scandalous behavior had destroyed what little affection there had been.

"You have it all planned out, I see," Phoebe said with a concerned frown.

"I do."

Still her cousin shook her head, her lower lip captured between her teeth. "I do not like it, Ariel. How can you trust this Nathan Trevain? Why, he is a stranger to this land. We know nothing of him other than the fact that he is Davenport's heir. Why, he could be anybody."

Ariel rolled her eyes at such a fanciful notion. "Do not be ridiculous, Phoebe."

But Phoebe didn't look convinced.

"When do you plan on announcing your news?" she asked.

"At the Fitzherberts tomorrow."

"Tomorrow? But isn't that rather soon?"

Ariel shrugged. "Tomorrow or the next day, it

makes no never mind. You shall see. 'Twill all work out." She leaned forward again and patted her cousin's hand.

But Cousin Phoebe held firm in her disapproval. She made it quite known, too. Oh, not to her husband. No, what they discussed would forever remain between the two women. But in private Phoebe made it abundantly clear that she thought Ariel a nodcock.

"But you make a beautiful nodcock, though," she said the next evening, adjusting the cameo that hung from a black satin ribbon tied around Ariel's neck. "Still, I'm half tempted to strangle you with this ribbon. Truly, Arie, I wish you had not agreed to this."

Ariel didn't comment. Why, when they'd discussed it a hundred times already? Instead she studied her appearance. Her cousin did have excellent taste, despite being two years her junior. But Phoebe had always had excellent taste, except, perhaps, in her friends: Ariel in particular. She knew her cousin took a great risk in bringing her to London, yet the kind-hearted Phoebe hadn't cared. For that Ariel would forever be grateful and if possible love her cousin even more.

"You were correct, Phoebe. The maroon is not as garish as I supposed it would be. You have an excellent eye."

The compliment didn't soften the frown on Phoebe's brow. Ariel suspected nothing short of finding a pot of gold could do that.

"Yes, well, you are fortunate to be of age to

wear the color. It looks wonderful on you. The modiste did an excellent job fitting the gown to your figure."

And she had, though Ariel could wish it didn't fit *quite* so well. The tight-waisted garment had panniers atop the skirt. The two large loops of fabric made her waist appear even smaller. Ariel tugged at the neckline. A bit low, perhaps, but she'd been assured its dip was all the rage. So were the large, black bows that dotted the middle of her skirt. A large bow rested just below the neckline, too, something Ariel suspected was done on purpose to draw men's attention to her bosom. She almost shrugged. Phoebe's own dress was similar in style, only the color was more sedate: pale blue to match her cousin's beautiful eyes. Ariel reasoned that if she looked half as stylish as her cousin, she should be pleased, although it made no difference, for there was no one she wanted to impress.

Oh? asked a voice. *Not even Mr. Trevain?*

Certainly not, she answered.

Still, when the time came to go downstairs and then to get in the carriage, she felt so nervous she could barely stop her hands from shaking like old Lady Alberly's. It didn't help that Phoebe kept shooting her dark looks meant to remind her of the childhood governess they'd shared. She did a remarkable job of glowering in exactly the same manner as that good lady. The

one blessing was that Reggie had elected to go
to his club instead of accompanying them to the
ball. The wise Reggie would have known something was up. Why Phoebe had decided not to
tell him of their plan Ariel couldn't fathom, but
the end result was that Reggie was blissfully un-
aware of the stir his wife and cousin by marriage
would cause that evening. Ariel rather wished
she could join him at White's. What she wouldn't
give to be able to smoke away her troubles.

It took them a short amount of time to reach
the Fitzherberts'. Ironically, the wait to descend
from the carriage was longer than the drive.
Ariel hadn't specifically been invited to the
soiree. Phoebe had been the recipient of the cov-
eted invitation. Ariel rather doubted their host-
ess had her in mind when she'd scribbled "and
guest" upon the card.

The dancing had already begun, obviously,
when they arrived, for she could hear the sound
of violins playing inside, something energetic
what with feet tapping the floor rhythmically. It
was crowded inside but warm compared to outside. Those gentlemen not escorting ladies were
off to one side of the door, smoking. The air was
filled with the scent of burning tobacco. The
younger ones made no secret of gawking at
ladies who arrived. Ariel tried not to feel self-
conscious as they eyed her up and down. One of
them dipped his head toward his friend, the rest
of them bursting into laughter. She blushed,

knowing they spoke of her, and not in kind terms, judging by the snickers.

"Perhaps I should have insisted Reggie accompany us," Phoebe muttered, as they passed.

"No," Ariel answered quickly, lifting her chin and pretending to ignore them. " 'Tis better he is not here. Once word spreads of my engagement, he will be furious at you for not telling him."

"Hmph. I suppose you are correct. I only hope word does not reach him at his club."

Ariel looked at her cousin's frowning face. "Why didn't you tell him?"

"I was too lily-livered."

Despite her nervousness, Ariel found herself smiling. "I believe Reggie will not disapprove as strongly as you believe. In fact, it might be well to have him in on the plan. He could play the role of my protector in the event Mr. Trevain has ulterior motives."

"Do you think he might?" Phoebe said quickly, her face instantly filling with concern.

Ariel cursed her tongue for a moment. "No, no, no. I was just jesting."

Liar, murmured that annoying little voice in her head.

And Ariel knew she was. She couldn't trust him or any man, not ever again. She'd learned that lesson the hard way. No, it was best to be on her guard and keep her fears to herself. She clutched her skirts as she made her way toward the line of people waiting to be announced, tilting her chin up for good measure. No man would ever get the better of her. Not again.

But her concern over her fears was forgotten as they stopped at the back of the line. Obviously word of her return to society had spread, for if she'd thought her reception the evening before had been cool, it was nothing compared to tonight's. Ladies actually turned their back on her, their lords raising quizzing glasses, brows arched beneath sausage-roll wigs. She felt like a condemned felon. And though she tried hard not to let their actions hurt her, standing there waiting to be announced was one of the hardest things she'd had to do in a long time. Things were made worse in that Phoebe shared in her humiliation. Poor, innocent Phoebe, who's face had paled, two bright spots of color burning near her ears. Her small hands were clenched in the folds of her gown, the sapphire necklace she wore sparkling nearly as brightly as her eyes.

"They should all be shot," she murmured furiously.

And instantly Ariel felt her humiliation fade. How could it not when she had such a champion by her side?

She reached for her cousin's hand, squeezed it, blue eyes meeting gold in a moment of commiseration. Though they were two years apart, Phoebe felt closer to her in age at the moment than ever before. Odd that Phoebe was younger and yet still considered to be Ariel's chaperone because of her marriage.

"You are the best of cousins, Phoebe."

"I am your only cousin."

"And a better one I could not ask for."

Blue eyes instantly softened, filled with sympathy. "If they knew you as I do, Ariel, they would not look at you thus."

No need to ask who they were, and best to look away from Phoebe before she did something embarrassing, like cry. She turned. And froze.

There he stood.

By the entrance to the ballroom he leaned nonchalantly against the wall. Lords and ladies eyed him, some in curiosity, for his scar was noticeable inside the ballroom. Others eyed him no doubt because of who he was, or more specifically, who he would one day be. She eyed him back, feeling pinned in his stare, like one of Reggie's butterfly experiments. For a moment she felt just as immobile, too. The line advanced. People still snickered and stared, but she just stood there.

"Ariel, move forward."

It was Phoebe's voice reaching her as if from a distance. Ariel blinked, forced herself to look away, turning to her cousin to smile—and she had no idea where she pulled that smile from— and to do as asked. What was it about the man that tugged at her so? Was it that she felt sorry for him? Or was it something more?

"Forgive me, Phoebe. Seeing Mr. Trevain there startled me."

Phoebe's eyes widened. "He is here?" she asked in a low voice.

"Aye. By the entrance to the ballroom." They both looked in that direction, Ariel stiffening when she realized he was no longer there. Instead he was making his way toward them. And as she watched him advance, Ariel was reminded of a panther. Once again that inner voice spoke. It fairly screamed *danger*. Heat fired through her body so instantly her heart pounded in her ears. She felt flushed of a sudden, and frightened.

"Lady Ariel D'Archer," he said, when he gained their side.

The couple in front of them turned, the gentleman eyeing Mr. Trevain up and down. When he got to the face, Ariel watched as his expression turned to one of revulsion before he quickly turned away. The sight angered her, for Mr. Trevain's face was not at all unpleasant. Certainly it was not perfect, but nobody was perfect.

Ah, but society adores perfection. 'Tis why you are banned, Ariel, for you are not perfect anymore. They think your innocence has been taken, even though it has not.

She clenched her hands, staring at the man before her in sudden sympathy. Mr. Trevain either hadn't seen the look or else he ignored it. Either way Ariel was still miffed. "Mr. Trevain," she said, trying to distract him in the event he had seen the look. "May I present my cousin, Lady Sarrington?

Nathan bowed. Ariel felt further troubled by the look upon her cousin's face. Though she'd warned her friend, she'd hoped Phoebe would be better able to conceal her absorption with the defect.

"Lady Sarrington," he said, bowing, and though he hadn't been raised in British society, though he hadn't been immersed in its customs and culture, his manners were as impeccable as any of the men she'd seen here tonight. He dressed more elegantly, too. He wore a dark gray coat, a light yellow waistcoat and elegant beige silk breeches. Once again he wore no wig, but the lack of false hair only made him stand out more. She felt dowdy by comparison, like a vicar's daughter, and suddenly as naively tongue-tied as well. She resisted the urge to fiddle with the single gray curl that dangled from the back of her wig, especially when he turned to her.

"You look beautiful tonight, Ariel."

Once again, the couple turned, Ariel knowing they were probably scandalized by his use of her Christian name. But she didn't care. Suddenly she didn't care about anything. The way he looked at her with those wonderful eyes—gracious, it took her breath away. And the sound of her name rolling off his tongue . . . wicked.

Careful, Ariel, 'tis but an act.

Oh, but what an actor he was. And from nowhere came the wish that it wasn't an act, that a man could look at her as he looked at her and actually mean it. She bowed her head, so confused by the feelings coursing through her that she could barely think, much less converse. Thankfully, her cousin took matters into her own hands.

"I confess myself relieved to see you here tonight, sir." Ariel realized her cousin had gotten herself under control. Her face was filled with friendly interest as she said, "We could use some male company, I fear."

"Can you?" he asked, but it was to Ariel that he addressed the question. When once again she stared up at him, she saw a twinkle come into his eyes. "But of course, where else would I be but by my fiancée's side?"

Someone gasped; Ariel didn't know who. And with those simple words it was done. Word would now spread throughout the ballroom like fire. It would begin with a murmur here, a word there, the result being everyone would know she'd become engaged to Mr. Nathan Trevain, heir to the dukedom of Davenport, by night's end.

She could hardly wait.

"Take my arm," Trevain ordered. They stepped forward, Ariel realizing they were about to be announced. The ballroom spread out before them like a sea of moving color. People stood around the edge of the dance floor, eyeing them. She saw eyes widen. What an odd couple they must look, she thought. A misfit and a rake. Yet she held herself proudly and when their names were announced, stepped gracefully into the room, lifting her skirts elegantly as she moved. And as people stared her up and down, never was she more grateful for a man's presence. He may not have had a perfect face, but at that moment he was the most beautiful man she knew. His arm felt solid, his presence so commanding that for the first time since rejoining society she felt more in control.

"Shall we dance?" he asked her, just as he had the night before, his look a polite question.

"We should probably wait for Phoebe."

"Your cousin will not mind our dancing one dance."

Yes, Phoebe would, but he gave her no time to argue. Shooting Phoebe an apologetic glance, she allowed him to lead her toward the dance floor. He'd placed her hand on his arm, his ring catching the light. A serpentine, he'd called it, but she knew that was wrong. A serpentine was all green, like a snake, hence the name, whereas this stone had those spots of red in it. Like the skin of a poisonous snake or blood.

She stiffened. That was it! A bloodstone. That was what the gem was called. She felt sure of it, even thought about telling him, but he spun her around to face him, making her momentarily breathless. The dance was already in progress, but he didn't seem to care. He led her into position, the feel of his hand holding hers more pleasurable than she would have liked. With his body so near she could feel the heat radiate off it, her thoughts scattering like leaves in the wind. She looked up at him. 'Twas no country dance. This was a French dance, one that kept them close together, at times circling like birds in a mating ritual. Mating ritual. What an odd thought.

Gracious, but she had a lot of odd thoughts about him. Was it his wickedly handsome looks? Or was it the way he seemed only to have eyes for her? Though they were occasionally separated, his gaze never left her own. She told herself to concentrate, told herself that appearing moonstruck with the man did her reputation no good. Then again, what harm in letting society think theirs was a love match?

A love match?

She stiffened. What a silly notion. As if they acted in love. She forced herself to look away, just to prove to herself that she could, forced herself to think of something to say, something mundane.

"Did you have a pleasant ride over?" She nearly cursed. What a ninny. There was mundane, and there was mundane.

He appeared amused by her question. "Indeed I did, thank you for asking."

What was it her governess had often said? When conversing with a man, one should stick to his health and the weather. Well, he looked perfectly healthy. She shivered: too much so. And the weather seemed like a silly topic.

"Your ring is a bloodstone," she blurted, at a loss as to what else to say.

His gaze suddenly intensified. Ariel felt sweat bead upon her lip.

"Is it?" he asked, black brows raised.

"Indeed."

"And how do you know that?"

She had to wait for them to come together again, the time that it took for him to return to her side only reinforcing Ariel's nervousness. "I've studied such things."

"Have you?" he asked. "While in the country?"

She nodded, feeling rather proud of her education, and suddenly anxious to show it off. "Yes. A bloodstone is a chalcedony, also known by another name, though what that name is escapes me at the moment. It is said that the stone has the power to turn the sun blood-red, to cause thunder, lightning and rain to hail down. Is that not amusing?"

He didn't look amused. He looked rather perturbed. They moved apart again, Ariel wondering if he was the sort of man who didn't like women to be educated. Well, fie on him if he didn't. Women were every bit as smart as men, although men much preferred to think the opposite, but that only showed their ignorance.

When they came back together, she expected him to say something derogatory. Instead he merely smiled down at her. "Your knowledge amazes me," he surprised her by saying. "Tell me, what other things have you learned?"

She shrugged, unaccountably wanting to impress him. "Human anatomy. Greek mythology. Principals of general carriage mechanics. Things of that nature. " Not to mention following the war closely, but she didn't think it wise to mention the recent hostilities between their two countries.

"Human anatomy?" he queried with an amused smile.

Something nagged at the back of her mind, something about what she'd just said. She put the thought away for later. "Indeed. A most interesting subject, human anatomy." Especially the part about human reproduction. Her father's library was most complete.

"And what sorts of things did you learn?" He moved closer to her, far closer than the steps of the dance dictated. Ariel wanted to move away, knew she should for the sake of her reputation, but in an instant the steps sent them apart. She almost sagged to the ground in relief, the dancers around them a blur as she waited for them to come together again.

"Well?" he prompted, when next they met. He took her hand, stepped close to her, his silver gaze intense.

She swallowed. Gracious heavens, what this man could do to her with only a look. She forced herself to concentrate, to remember their conversation. "I learned about the parts of the body. Liver. Kidney. Heart."

Hearts that can be broken, Ariel told herself. But her heart didn't want to listen. She felt her legs begin to tremble, felt herself stumble.

He caught her. "Careful, my lady. It wouldn't do for you to come to any harm."

She pulled back, mortified to realize the dance had ended and she hadn't even noticed it.

"Ariel?" he asked when she didn't say anything in response.

"I need a moment to catch my breath," she gasped, lurching away from him.

His expression actually turned concerned. "Would you like something to drink?"

She nodded, not really wanting anything, just feeling the need to be alone.

He stared down at her a moment longer before turning away from her, reluctantly, it seemed. She watched him go, feeling the stares of people as he did so. They stared at Nathan, too, though for a different reason. Like a Greek god he moved through the crowd, his face chiseled, his bearing that of a warrior. Purposeful. Commanding. Intimidating.

She looked down at the ground, wondering what it was that drew her to him. And would she ever have the courage to trust a man again?

Somehow she feared she wouldn't. The ring he wore had caught her attention. She had stared at it. A bloodstone. There was a Greek name for the stone, too. Something that had to do with the sun, so named for the red color.

She stiffened.

Helio. Meaning sun. The stone was also called a heliotrope. Nathan Trevain, recently from the American colonies, wore a heliotrope.

The spy Helios was suspected of being in England.

"There you are," Phoebe gushed, gaining her side after shooting her a look of triumph. "Goodness, Ariel, I had to skirt the entire dance floor to reach you."

"I need to be alone, Phoebe."

"I—you what?" she asked, surprise etching her features.

"I need to be alone for a second. To think. Some fresh air." She spun toward one set of three double doors allowing air to circulate through the ballroom.

"Ariel, wait," Phoebe called, stopping her with a hand on her arm. "What is it?" A look of concern clouded her cousin's pretty eyes.

She shook her head. How could she tell Phoebe about the horrible presentiment she'd just had? "Just give me a moment alone."

Phoebe nodded. "Very well."

Ariel walked away, knowing Phoebe felt hurt at being excluded. But how could she express her fear to a cousin who already disapproved of the man in question? And how farfetched was that fear? She plunged into the evening's darkness. Fresh air. Cold fresh air. She inhaled sharply, her mind clearing.

Helios.

Nathan Trevain wore a heliotrope.

It seemed too much of a coincidence to ignore.

The stone was not that rare, yet it was an uncommon stone to choose for a setting. And why had he lied to her about the kind of stone it was? For as certain as she knew he wore a bloodstone, she also knew he'd lied.

She stopped by a fountain, which glowed a muted gray in the moonlight. Cherubs were clustered in the middle of it, water spewing from their mouths and noses. Frogs and crickets chirped nearby. She looked down at the dark water, the vague shadows of fish floating beneath the surface a focal point for her eyes.

Was she being ridiculous? Had her mistrust of men clouded her judgment? And really, out here in the fresh air of the garden, the idea seemed far less plausible.

"My lady," a deep voice said.

Ariel spun, not surprised to see him standing there, suddenly not surprised at all. She looked up at him. His dark hair glistened with silver streaks, his eyes were bright even in the darkness. And as she stared up at him, her suspicion returned. He looked like a spy. Darkness and danger. Shadows and lies.

She took a step away from him. "Mr. Trevain, there was no need to follow me."

He looked at her as if he sensed her withdrawal. "I thought you wanted your refreshment."

Could she tell him that she suddenly feared him? That she suspected he might be a spy? She couldn't very well ask him outright and arouse his suspicions. But there might be another way to gauge his reaction. She held out her hand to take the glass he offered her. He used the hand with the ring on it. Perfect.

"Where did you get your bloodstone?" she asked, taking a nonchalant swallow of the drink while watching his face carefully. Punch.

" 'Tis a serpentine," he corrected.

She shook her head. "No, for it has flecks of red. 'Tis the iron deposits. That makes it a bloodstone."

He was quiet for a second, his gaze in the darkness hard to gauge.

"Where did you get it?" she repeated.

But not by word or deed did he give himself away. "I can't remember, truth be told."

Her hand tightened around the glass, knowing she must ask her next question, yet suddenly afraid to. "Did you know 'tis also called a heliotrope?"

He drew back a bit, and even in the darkness she could see the expression of surprise cross his face. *Well, and why wouldn't he look surprised?* a voice of logic asked. Most women could barely read the Bible, and yet she could recite facts about gems.

"No. I did not."

"An interesting name, do you not think?" she asked nonchalantly, watching him closely. "It derives from the Greek Helios, god of the sun."

She didn't want to believe he could be a spy. It would mean things she didn't want to face. But she couldn't mistake the way his hand twitched at the name. Couldn't mistake the way he drew back a tiny bit. Had she not been watching for such signs, she might have missed them, but not now.

"And how do you know all this?"

"I studied much in the country. The names of various stones and their rumored powers was one of many subjects I entertained myself with."

Whatever he would have said to that was cut off by Phoebe's voice saying, "There you are, Ariel. Gracious, I feared I would never find you."

And Ariel was glad, so very glad to hear her familiar trill.

"You should not be outside," Phoebe chastised her. " 'Tis far too chilly."

It wasn't that cold, but as an excuse to leave Mr. Trevain, the weather would work perfectly. Suddenly she wanted to leave. Desperately. "Yes, it is a bit cold." She turned to Nathan, not meeting his gaze for fear he would see the accusation in her eyes. "If you will excuse us, Mr.

Trevain, I should do as my cousin advises." She handed the glass back to him, trying not to stare at that ring. "Thank you for the refreshment."

"My lady," he called as she turned away. Reluctantly she faced him again. He stared down at her with a look of concern. "Will you allow me to escort you in?"

"I hardly think that would be appropriate, sir," Phoebe answered for her, her cousin's chin tilted in a disapproving way. "It is bad enough that you were alone for a short amount of time. If you return together, 'twill look even more incriminating. I thought your goal was to help restore Ariel's reputation, not harm it."

And to that Nathan could say little, Ariel supposed. She held her breath as she waited for his response. But he must have realized that to anger Phoebe would not be in his best interest. "I see your point, Lady Sarrington. However, I will insist upon a dance later."

"Perhaps," Phoebe said. "In the interim, if you will wait a moment to follow us inside."

Nathan nodded, then met Ariel's gaze, but Ariel remained silent. As her chaperone—as ludicrous as it seemed, given Phoebe's age—her cousin was well within her rights to dictate her dancing schedule. Mr. Trevain knew it, though he obviously didn't like it. Nor did he like that Ariel didn't contradict her cousin's dictum.

"I will see you inside," he said, looking directly into her eyes.

Ariel only nodded, shifting her gaze away. She couldn't look at him. Not now. Not with all she suspected.

"Come, Ariel."

She followed her cousin in without a backward glance, feeling Nathan's gaze upon her. She knew he was displeased. But she didn't care. Truth be told, she didn't care about anything but escaping.

"You should not be alone in a garden with the man," Phoebe chastized her.

"I know," Ariel admitted distractedly.

"Then why did you agree to meet with him privately?"

When Ariel looked at her cousin, Phoebe's blue eyes stared into hers earnestly, her cousin's expression more concerned than chastising. "I didn't, Phoebe. He followed me."

She looked surprised, then displeased. "You should stay away from him, Ariel. Obviously he cannot be trusted."

"I know."

Phoebe looked surprised by her admission. "So you agree that your plan to appear his fiancée was ill advised?"

Ariel didn't know what to think, she only knew that with each step, the urge to run grew more and more pronounced. "I want to leave."

Phoebe drew back, but once she realized Ariel was serious, she turned all business. Her cousin didn't suggest they say their good-byes, she didn't offer to have a servant deliver a note of explanation. She seemed to realize that Ariel was beyond making decisions and just ushered her from the ballroom under the scathing gaze of society.

Ariel ignored the looks, ignored the comments she could overhear, one thing on her mind. If Nathan Trevain was Helios, what did he want with her? And how would she prove it?

5

But the only plan she could come up with later that night had holes in it at best. Still, she thought it might work, and that alone made her consider it. Truly, it was a simple idea. She would send Nathan a note, a loosely worded note, one that would read like it'd been sent to the wrong person if he was not Helios, but one he would have to act upon if he were.

Still, as she wrote the words late that evening, she wondered if her imagination hadn't gotten the better of her. Yet her suspicions plagued her so that she decided to have the note delivered that night. She would not sleep until she had proved he was a spy.

Or not.

How she hoped not. It frightened her how much she hoped.

Why? she asked herself? Why did it matter if he was a spy or not? She didn't care for the man.

No, she'd just begun to trust him, and trust

was not something she gave easily. If he was indeed using her, she would be devastated by the discovery.

Sanding the letter with a shaking hand, then sealing it, she rang for a servant. A maid appeared only moments later. It was still early. Ariel half wondered if Nathan might not stop by their home once he realized she and Phoebe had fled the ballroom. But it might be a while yet before he realized they had fled.

"Give this to one of the grooms to deliver to Mr. Trevain." The maid reached for the letter. Ariel held it back. "It is important that the groom not tell the Fitzherberts' servants who he is or whom the letter is from."

The maid looked at Ariel in a speculative way. Obviously she thought the letter contained a request for a secret tryst. If only it were that simple.

"Aye, my lady. I'll have me brother John deliver it personally."

Ariel nodded, handing the letter over. "And if he is not at the Fitzherberts', deliver it to him at home." Another nod. Ariel's heart pounded as the maid took the letter. If her suspicions were correct, Nathan would leave the ball quickly. Then again, he may already have left. Either way she would know by midnight.

"I will need the carriage later tonight, too."

The maid's expression turned to that of a fellow conspirator. "As you wish, my lady."

She didn't wish. She would rather do just

about anything than venture out alone at night, but there was no escaping the fact that she needed to do this alone. She just hoped she was wrong about the whole thing.

Sir,

I have the information you seek. I know, too, that you prefer not to be identified. So I ask that you meet me at the Black Swan, midnight, so that we may discuss this without fear of being recognized.

Nathan read, then reread the note. Surprise and shock made his blood quicken as he studied the words one more time.

That the note was meant for him there could be no doubt. And that the writer knew his true identity there could also be no doubt. In an upper corner, in letters so small as to be noticeable by only the most careful of observers, was the name Helios.

No other name graced the parchment.

Helios. His true identity. His jaw tightened as he thought of her ladyship. Why she'd fled he had no idea, but he meant to find out. But tonight, tonight he needed to get to the bottom of this letter.

He studied the paper more closely. Obviously the author knew who he was. Equally obvious was that he didn't wish it to be revealed to the eyes of probing servants. Unfortunately, the note gave no indication as to whether this person was friend or foe.

But it must be a friend, he decided a moment later, for a foe would have simply had him arrested.

"Do you know who delivered it?" he asked the still waiting servant.

"No, sir," the man responded, staring somewhere above his head, the servant's green livery spotless despite the lateness of the hour.

"And it was delivered when?"

"Sometime this evening, sir. We're not sure when."

Nathan glanced at the clock on the mantel. For the first time since realizing Ariel had left the ballroom, he felt a modicum of calm. Perhaps this night would not be a loss after all.

"Have the carriage brought around again."

If the servant thought it an odd request, he concealed it well. Of course, his uncle paid them to conceal their emotions well.

It took time to harness the vehicle, then more time to reach his destination. By the time he reached the Black Swan, it was a few minutes before midnight.

Surprisingly enough, the inn was not at all in a bad part of town, an indication that his benefactor must not be of the lower orders. In his experience, like socialized with like. The structure was large, with paned windows that spilled light onto the street. The sign that hung above the door was shaped like a swan, the words

"The Black Swan" carved into the surface painted in white. And though it was late, voices still rose and fell inside.

Could one of those voices belong to the person who would help him find his brother? His hands clenched in anticipation. Pray God it did.

The door was heavy, the iron handle cold. A blast of warm air hit him in the face. He blinked, his eyes adjusting to the light. The voices dipped in volume as they assessed the newcomer, then swelled again. Not a lot of occupants, he realized, his nerves stretched taut as he waited to be recognized.

No one came forward.

He moved into the room. Waiting. Took a seat at a table with a well-polished sheen to its surface. Another indication of the establishment's ability to cater to the wealthy. A glance around the room confirmed his supposition. The men inside were well dressed, their appearance neat. Nathan met the eye of every one of them, yet no one nodded, no one stood up, no one spared him a second glance.

His frustration mounted. Damn. What nonsense was this? Had the man decided not to show?

But Ariel D'Archer had shown. She stared through Phoebe's carriage window to her left, her eyes still burning with the image of Nathan descending from the ducal carriage, anger, humiliation and unexpected hurt making it difficult to breathe.

Fiend. Miscreant. Cad.

Tears clouded her vision as she leaned against the black carriage squabs. "Drive on," she ordered the coachman. She'd seen all she needed to see.

Nathan Trevain, her "friend," was none other than Helios, master spy from the colonies.

And on the heels of that thought came the realization that her father would have her hide.

Used. Again. By another man.

She wiped her eyes, forcing the tears away. She would not cry when it was her own stupidity that had landed her in such a situation. But she hadn't been ignorant, she reassured herself. Her internal warnings had gone off enough times to know something was odd about Mr. Trevain's sudden offer of help. But what made it so awful, what made it nearly unbearable to take, was that she'd started to like him. Truly, truly like him. That he wasn't the man he wanted her to think he was made Ariel's hands clench in the dark gray cloak she wore. A sickness crept into her throat. The urge to vomit on Phoebe's carriage floor was nearly overwhelming.

Buck up, my girl. At least you've found out now.

Found out what? she asked herself. *That a man you've actually liked has turned out to be just like Archie, only worse?*

She closed her eyes and exhaled a breath. Gracious, what a fool she was. Twice. Twice she'd trusted a man only to have that trust whipped away like a dirty blanket.

Her nails dug into the fabric of her cloak. The motion of the carriage made her upper body sway as they rounded a corner. 'Twas bad enough to have to find out Nathan Trevain was also Helios, a spy, but to know that he'd intended to use her was further humiliation. For as surely as she knew her name, she knew that it was no coincidence he had sought out the First Lord's daughter. She took a deep breath, composing herself.

Very well, he intended to use her.

For what? she wondered. Her father would know, she realized. Or perhaps not. Obviously he had no idea who Nathan Trevain really was. If so, she was sure he'd be apprehended . . . or imprisoned. Very well, so what should she do about it? Confront Nathan with what she'd learned? Should she unmask him? The idea filled her with a fair amount of anticipation. How she'd like to accuse him, then slap his face. No. She would stab him in the heart. No, she would shoot him.

Outside, a coach rumbled by. She watched it pass blindly. But to unmask him might put her own life in jeopardy. No. She should report his presence to the Admiralty. That seemed to be the most expedient thing to do. But what if they required proof? She had only her word that Nathan was Helios. Would they believe her? She nibbled her lip, picturing Lord Howell patting her head and telling her to go home with her silly ideas.

He would do it, she was sure. As would the other admirals. No. She must have proof. Perhaps she could catch Helios in the act of pilfering whatever documents he sought.

Yes, she liked that idea. She'd been used. And she would be damned if she let Nathan get away with it. No, indeed. This time she would make a man pay the price for his betrayal. Nathan Trevain would pay. That she vowed.

PART
TWO

Sigh no more, ladies, sigh no more,
Men were deceivers ever;
One foot in sea and one on shore,
To one thing constant never.

SHAKESPEARE

6

The prospect of facing Nathan after what she'd discovered left Ariel feeling rather like a cat with a hair ball stuck in its throat. It didn't help that she'd spent a sleepless night, tossing and turning. Time and again she replayed her meetings with the cad. Staged. All of them. Her coming to London he no doubt considered a boon. But with each memory of their conversations, each recollection of how cynically he'd intended to use her, she grew more and more angry.

And an angry D'Archer was a frightening thing. Between her gypsy blood and her father's love of battle, she'd inherited a terrific propensity for war.

And she declared war on Nathan Trevain.

So when she received a note from him asking to see her, she declined. If he wanted to play cat and mouse, she would play cat and mouse.

In fact, it was two days before she agreed to

see him, and then only because they would meet in public.

"Will you go?" Phoebe asked.

"Yes," Ariel said, reading his note again. "There will be several guests at his uncle's, too. 'Twill be the perfect place to break the news to him that I no longer wish to see him."

"I still do not understand why you do not simply send him a note."

No, Phoebe couldn't understand, and Ariel wouldn't tell her. It was bad enough to bear this humiliation alone. She didn't think she could cope with Phoebe's pity over the situation, too.

So it was that later that evening she chose a gold satin that exactly matched the color of her eyes. The hoops were subtle rather than large, a dark-brown, wide bow above the waist that accentuated her figure. The neckline was modest. Her hair was swept away from her face. She hated wigs, and the thought of wearing one through tonight's battle was more than she could stand, so she elected to go against fashion. She had to look her best. To be brave. To remember that she had much to gain by proving Nathan Trevain a spy. Revenge. Satisfaction. Perhaps even redemption with society.

Be brave she repeated to herself as she went down to meet him before they departed for the duke's. Her palms were sweaty. And her hands shook. And she wasn't at all sure she could face the man without going at him with her nails.

She curled her fingers into her palms just to safe-guard herself against the urge.

"Mr. Trevain, good evening," she said, her tone even although her jaw felt all but locked shut.

He stood by the window in the drawing room, his scar in shadows cast by the candles. She could do this, she told herself, heart pound-ing, but gracious, this evening he looked every inch the spy. Or was that her own cynical assess-ment? She narrowed her eyes as she studied him. He wore dark clothes. The better to skulk around the city at night, she surmised. His breeches were black, a severe fashion faux pas, not that he appeared to care. Perhaps he had an appointment tonight to break into somebody's home. Perhaps her and her father's home.

"Lady D'Archer," he said, his expression one of concern and . . . pique? Yes, he was piqued. Well, good. She would pique him until he turned blue in the face.

"I confess myself relieved that you agreed to see me tonight."

She would wager he was.

"Yes, I do beg your pardon for being less than social. However, I was rather ill, or didn't Phoebe explain that to you?"

"Oh, she explained it," he murmured, but his eyes told her he plainly didn't believe it.

She felt her eyes narrow. "Well, that is all be-hind us, for we are here now, and I am set to go to your uncle's with you."

He stared, his eyes probing her eyes intently. What he saw she had no idea. Truth be told, she feared he could read every angry thought she had about him on her face.

"You look lovely," he offered.

"Do I?" she found herself snapping. Lovely enough to seduce?

His eyes traveled down the length of her, and was it her imagination, or did they warm? "That color suits you well."

Yes, no doubt he enjoyed the modest neckline. And no doubt he hoped the stays would release easily in the event he wished to kiss her in that most tender of spots.

She colored, clenched her hands. Never. Never would she allow him such a liberty.

"Yes, well, thank you." She gave him what she hoped was a smile, though she knew it was tight at best. "Shall we be on our way?"

She thought she saw his eyes narrow, realized she needed to be more careful. It wouldn't do to anger him now, not when she most needed to get close to him.

Still, it was hard. She attempted conversation a few times on their way to his uncle's, but her answers came out short, terse, even to her ears. She wasn't sure if Nathan noticed. Honestly, the evening had already begun to blur.

A line of carriages had already formed outside the duke's home, suggesting that this would be much more than just a small dinner party. She wore gloves tonight; her hands were sweaty beneath the white material. She tried to calm her shaking limbs, wondered if she'd bitten off more than she could chew with her plan, then glanced over at Nathan Trevain.

Helios.

She straightened. No. She could do this. Taking a deep breath, she allowed him to help her down a few minutes later, reluctantly placing her hand upon his forearm as he led her up the steps to the duke's home.

The sudden brightness of candles nearly blinded her as she stepped through the open door. They were everywhere, lighting the place as brightly as the sun. A gray and white marble floor, so polished that it reflected the image of those candles, echoed the sound of their footsteps. Cherry wood furniture, rare for its red wood, decorated the hall.

Couples were gathered in an elegant tan and white room to her right. Gilt frames surrounding mirrors and portraits conveyed an instant sense of elegance and extreme wealth. Her attention, however, was pulled away from the room's decor by the instant drop in the level of conversation. She eyed the fashionably dressed ensemble before her proudly.

It was worse than any ball she'd been to thus far. Much worse. Ariel knew it in an instant. Obviously the duke meant to humiliate her. His dislike for her was evident in that he didn't even come forward to greet her. She studied him. He wore a long wig, curls rolling down the sides of it. His face was powdered, yet it could not conceal the striking resemblance to Nathan. But for the large girth and aged, wrinkled face, the man was the spitting image of Nathan Trevain.

She pulled her gaze away. Ladies eyed her up and down rudely. The men, too, stared at her. Ariel forced herself to take a deep breath.

"Uncle, may I present Lady Ariel D'Archer."

"You may," the duke drawled. Ariel's lips tightened. His pompous wig and equally pompous air made her want to poke him in his overlarge, corseted girth.

"Your grace," she said, giving him an elegant curtsy. Not for nothing was she an earl's daughter. She could behave with as much refinement as the rest of them. "You have a very elegant home."

"Yes, I do. Too bad some of its more recent additions are not to my liking."

She stiffened, for 'twas obvious he meant her. She almost turned and left the room then, but Trevain must have sensed what she was about to do, for he covered her hand with his own, patting it.

"If everyone is present, uncle, shall we go in to dinner?"

It was usually the host's duty to say such a thing, but obviously Nathan did not care about such formalities. His voice sounded clipped, his anger at his uncle obvious. He turned Ariel away, not even waiting for the duke to answer. Instead he propelled her from the room as if balls of fire scalded their heels.

"Ariel, I am sorry," he said, dipping his head

and hurriedly whispering. "I had no idea—"

"Do not say a word," she interrupted. "If they hear you apologize, it will only make it worse."

She chanced a glance up at him, surprised to see that he appeared genuinely chagrined by the happenings. It made him appear as if he had a heart, but she knew better. No man could plan to use a woman as he did and have anything approaching a conscience. Yet he did look remarkably contrite, seeming to take extra care in seating her. There were place cards on the table. Ariel realized that Nathan was to sit nowhere near her. For a brief instant panic assailed her; then she chastised herself. Gracious, what did she need the lying cad for? She could do this. Not for nothing had she been taught the finest of manners.

She kept her rear firmly planted upon the seat. If it was a show they came for, then it was a show they would get.

The duke took his seat at the head of the table three chairs away. Other people followed the duke's example. It became apparent immediately that her presence was not welcome to many.

"My dear Lady D'Archer," said the woman to her left. "How good it is to see you back in society. I confess, I never thought to see the day."

Ariel turned. "I confess myself surprised, too, my lady."

Her ladyship stared at her for a moment longer than necessary, then turned her attention away, most likely for the entire night. Ariel resigned herself to her fate. She would behave as she was born, the daughter of an earl. And though these people might not like her presence, she was determined to give them no reason to gossip about her further. So when she heard someone say something about tainted bloodlines, she ignored him. Yes, she was half gypsy and proud of it. And when she heard a lady near the end of the table mention what an affront her presence was, she ignored that, too. Still, as she sat there, one course after another served, it grew harder and harder to ignore the barbs. Oh, not everyone was so openly hostile. Nathan watched her with a look of concern from his end of the table. But only one or two rude people were needed to make her feel miserable. Her hand tightened around her fork. Her body shook with the effort it took to hold herself erect. But she sat through it all, and when the meal was over, she felt as if her face would crack as the ladies rose. Heaven help her, she didn't think she could take much more.

"Are you well?" a deep voice asked.

Ariel started, surprised to realize Nathan had come to help her from her chair. She sat there for a second, wondering how to answer, or even if she dared to open her mouth. If she did, she feared what might come out would not be at all pleasant.

"Ariel?" he repeated, his voice not unkind.

She rose slowly, took a deep breath as she prepared to face him. "I enjoyed the meal immensely, Mr. Trevain."

His expression clearly told her he knew the words were a lie. That he had overheard many of the barbs there could be no doubt. Most of the table had no doubt heard.

"You are a courageous woman," he said in a low voice, and heavens, but his words sounded sincere. Too bad she knew them for what they were: a sad attempt at making her feel charitable toward him.

She would make him pay.

"Lady D'Archer, I wonder if I might have a word with you." Both she and Nathan turned. His uncle stood there, his expression all politeness, his eyes anything but.

"Uncle, her ladyship is not feeling well. I thought I might take her home—"

"No," Ariel interrupted, squaring her shoulders. Whatever this man had to say, it could be no worse than the snippets of conversation she'd overheard that night. "I am well enough to converse with your uncle, Nathan. Truly, I'm sure what he has to say will not take long."

Nathan's lips tightened. He looked at his uncle. "Then I shall join you."

His uncle's own lips tightened, then he said, "I'd rather speak to her alone, if you do not mind."

"I do mind," Nathan said, his voice low so as

not to be overheard by the guests leaving the room. "I warn you, Uncle—"

"Nathan," Ariel cut him off by touching his arm, surprised by the way she wanted to hold onto that arm, which just went to show her how much the evening's activities had upset her. "I'm sure your uncle will be a gracious host."

Nathan's expression said he was sure he would not. Ariel understood his concerns. She was sure, too, but she would bear it. After all, she would need to make peace with the uncle if she wanted to maintain her relationship with Nathan. And maintain it she would, at least until she could expose him.

The vow gave her courage. She mustered up the willpower to smile, then turned to follow his uncle to a private room. The sound of the other guests faded as he closed he door behind him. Ariel realized in an instant that he'd chosen this room as a way of intimidating her. The library.

Masculine artifacts surrounded her. High bookshelves with voluminous tomes meant to remind her that she was only a woman and as such would never have the intelligence to glean the information between the covers on the pages. She wondered what his grace would do if he knew she'd read many of the books surrounding them. No doubt he wouldn't believe her.

"Won't your guests mind your leaving them?" she offered by way of opening the conversation, since he seemed content to let her wallow in the discomfort of silence. Only the sound of the fire crackled through the room. The smell of burning candles was barely masked by the smell of books. She watched him settle himself in an overlarge armchair, the leather squeaking as he sat.

"My guests will understand where I have gone and what I hope to do."

"Scare me away?" she offered, taking a seat opposite him, though he hadn't offered it to her. "Remind me of what a disgrace I am in the hope that I will tuck my tail and run?"

The duke's eyes narrowed. "So you prefer plain speaking, do you?" he asked.

She nodded. "As I'm sure you would prefer, too."

He didn't say anything, just stared at her as if assessing her worthiness as an opponent. "Very well," he said at last, "plain speaking it will be."

She tensed, waiting for the barrage. Not for nothing was she an admiral's daughter. She could be patient as she waited for the attack.

It wasn't long in coming.

"I do not approve of my nephew's involvement with you."

She lifted a brow. "I did not expect you would."

"Then you must know why."

She gave him a chilly smile. "You believe me soiled goods."

He looked surprised by her frankness, murmuring, "Indeed," his wrinkled face filled with disapproval.

"And so you will ask me to do the honorable thing by bowing out of this engagement?" she offered.

He was better at concealing his surprise this time. "Will you?"

"No," she answered bluntly.

If she'd thought him angry before, it was nothing to the expression on his face now. "No." He repeated the word as if never having heard it before. And perhaps he hadn't. As a duke she would wager there weren't many who said the word to him.

"No," she repeated, resting her hands on the arms of her chair nonchalantly.

"And if I tell you I will leave the Davenport fortune to someone else if you persist in this marriage?"

"I would remind you that I have a fortune of my own, despite my sad lack of morals."

His face turned as red as the book binding to her left. "You scheming seductress."

She laughed, actually laughed. It felt good to do so, truth be told. It'd been far too long since she'd felt she had the upper hand. "Is that what you think I am?"

His face tightened. "What else am I to think? You charm my nephew into proposing marriage within days of meeting you. Obviously you lured him with your body into doing so."

She laughed again. If only he knew the truth.

"Really, your grace, do you think anyone could force your nephew into doing something he didn't want to do?"

"I find it harder to believe that he would align himself with someone like you."

Someone like her. The words pricked at the bubble of her composure, though she refused to let him see it. "And what bothers you more? That I refuse to be cowed by your orders? Or that I would dare to deem myself worthy to become a duchess of Davenport after being so thoroughly ruined?"

His jaw began to tic.

"Or is it neither of those things," she continued, knowing she pushed him, but helpless to stop herself. "Perhaps it is my bloodlines. Perhaps you are bothered by my gypsy heritage."

His hands tightened on the arms of his chair.

"Are you worried, your grace, that I might teach the Davenport children black magic?"

"Get out," he roared, shooting up from the chair. "Get out now. I will tolerate no more of your insolence."

"As I will tolerate no more of yours."

"You are worse than a trollop," he yelled. "You are the most common of women, a whore—"

"I am an earl's daughter," she interjected.

"With a gypsy's morals," he shot right back.

"Enough!" roared a voice.

Ariel jumped. They both turned. Nathan stood by the door, his face livid, his hands clenching and unclenching as if he didn't trust himself not to hit his uncle.

"Ariel, come with me. I should like to take you home."

Out of the frying pan and into the fire? she wanted to ask. Still, an enemy ally was better than no ally at all.

"Stay," the uncle bellowed.

They turned toward the enraged man.

"You will remain behind, Nathan."

"Not if you plan to continue humiliating my fiancée."

Shock held Ariel immobile for a moment. He was defending her.

Well, of course he is, Ariel. He wants to gain your trust.

A deep bitterness filled her. Would that he was the sort of man who would defend her for honor's sake. But she should have known better than to wish for such a thing. Men were ever deceitful creatures.

"Your guest will be treated as she deserves."

"That is not good enough, uncle." Nathan turned to her, his silver eyes blazing. "Come, Ariel," he repeated.

"If you leave, I will disown you."

Nathan turned back once again. "If you do that, you will be doing me a favor."

Ariel wondered if he really meant the words. He was a remarkably good actor if he didn't. They moved toward the door. Nathan held the door open. He didn't look back as he placed her hand on his arm or as he crossed the threshold. Not until he'd handed her into the ducal carriage, then settled himself opposite, did he say something, and then it was to absolve himself from guilt.

"You know I had nothing to do with what just transpired."

The carriage lantern outside the coach lit the interior of the plush vehicle, showing off its red velvet squabs, brass door handles and mahogany walls. It smelled like lemons inside, as if someone had just cleaned it. Rich. Decadent. One day to belong to the traitorous wretch in front of her.

"You do, don't you?"

At last she looked at his face. He appeared concerned. She gave a silent, ironic laugh. Concerned. She would wager he was. And, yes, she knew he spoke the truth. He would never have risked angering her by arranging such a performance.

"His words were beyond deplorable. They were despicable."

As despicable as his own? she wanted to ask. Instead she remained silent, her hands curled into her elegant skirts. All dressed up with nowhere to go.

She felt her eyes burn with unwanted tears.

"I am sorry, Ariel."

"Are you?" She used a clipped voice. He

would say something sweet, she would wager, something geared to softening her pique.

He surprised her when he said nothing at all, merely leaned across the space between them to grab her hand. She was surprised by how much she wanted the contact, nay, needed the contact, despite her loathing for the man.

She tried to pull her hand away. He wouldn't let her, despite the fact that she grew more and more disturbed by the way her traitorous body reacted to his touch. He looked out of the carriage, his expression troubled. Aye, he probably worried she would refuse to see him again. He had a right to be concerned.

She studied his profile. His scar was evident, even though he sat across from her. And out of nowhere came the thought: Why, oh, why did he have to be such a lying cad? And why, oh, why did she care? She turned away lest he see the disappointment that surely shone from her eyes.

"They have not been very kind to you, have they?"

She glanced back at him, surprised to note he was back to staring at her. Yet for the first time his look seemed almost sad. Her eyes narrowed, wondering if this, too, was part of the act.

"If by 'they' you mean the *ton*, then, yes, it has been less than kind to me."

"Has it always been this way?"

"What do you mean?"

He looked uncomfortable for a second, almost as if he did battle with himself over something.

"Is it always this way when a young lady is ruined?"

"Yes. Always. I have overstepped the mark by coming back to London."

"So you are expected to retire to the country for the rest of your life . . . never to marry, never to have children?"

"I am."

"Even if you were duped into being ruined?"

"Ah, but they do not think I was duped. They think I had as much to do with Archie's behavior as he did. Blood tells, and all that rot." And despite her resolve not to cry, she felt more tears come. She turned her head away, staring out of the carriage. The night was so black she could see nothing but her own reflection, a pale face with shocking dark eyes.

"You refer to your mother?"

She tilted her chin before looking back at him. "You know about her, do you?"

"My uncle," he explained.

"Hmm. And what did your uncle say?"

They bounced over a bump. It was a second before he answered. "He said that your father had fallen in love with a woman unsuitable to his station. A gypsy."

"She was that." Ariel looked away, and much to her surprise, she found herself saying, "But my father was said to have loved her very much." *More than he's ever loved me*, she privately added.

"And do you miss not having a mother?"

Another bump. She reached up for the hand-strap with her free hand. "I miss not knowing what she was like. She died while giving birth to me, you see. And though my father tried his best to raise me, we do not get on." She frowned at herself for revealing too much. "It has not helped that I ruined myself at the tender age of eighteen."

"You are not on good terms with your father, then?"

Ah, was he concerned? He should be. "That would be an understatement," she found herself answering, yet at the same time wondering why she bothered to share so much. She should be directing the conversation elsewhere, perhaps to his life in the colonies. Perhaps she could glean a clue as to what it was he wanted in England.

"Tell me why he has not forgiven you for your mistake," he said, when she dropped into silence.

"Surely you don't want to hear my opinion on that?"

"I do." He squeezed her hand from across the carriage. Ariel found herself momentarily taken in by his look of sincerity before she remembered who he was. A spy. A master spy. Someone so good at playing games, the Admiralty considered him one of the best spies in the American colony. No doubt she was merely his latest victim.

"Can you not figure it out on your own?"

If he seemed taken aback by her surly tone, he didn't reveal it. Instead he said, "He blames you for ruining the family name."

"Indeed. My father does not suffer fools lightly, and I was the queen of fools." And never had she felt the truth of those words more.

The lantern flickered as they turned a sharp corner. He hadn't released her hand, she noticed. She tried to tug it away. He wouldn't let her. They rounded another corner, and suddenly she found herself leaning toward him. She leaned the other way.

"Did you believe yourself in love with him?"

The pain of his question took her by surprise. Long ago she'd thought herself recovered from Archibald Worth.

"Ariel?"

"Yes," she snapped. "I did believe myself in love with him. I trusted him. He told me he loved me, but all he wanted to do was bed me. I was a challenge to him. An earl's daughter who happened to be half gypsy. And I had a dowry. Not as much as Lady Mary Carew, as it turned out, but I was a nice second in case Lady Mary did not come up to scratch. So you can see why my father is right to loathe me. I loathe myself for being such a fool. Never again will a man use me in such a way. Never."

Nathan stared at her in mute surprise. He had the oddest sensation that she spoke directly to him. And perhaps she did. Perhaps she thought him after something, as this Lord Archibald had been.

How right she was.

And from nowhere a mass of guilt reared its ugly head.

For the first time he found himself doubting the wisdom of his plan. Perhaps his doubts came from his hope that whoever had sent him the note last eve would come forward. Perhaps it was seeing the way she'd been treated by society over the past few days. When those same people found out she'd been used yet again, how much more hateful would their spite be?

He didn't want to think about it. Instead for the first time since meeting her, he felt a genuine rush of sympathy for her plight. She might be of noble blood, but he suspected she was as different from most of England's ladies as light was from darkness.

"Have I made you speechless, Mr. Trevain?"

"Nathan. You should call me Nathan."

Did he imagine it, or did her eyes narrow. Oh, yes, they narrowed. Obviously she mistrusted him. Damnation.

"Very well, Nathan. Have I shocked you?"

"No," he answered honestly. "I admire your candor."

"Candor? Is that what you call it?"

"Yes. Or honesty. Take your pick. Either way I appreciate your straightforward answers."

Her nostrils were pinched. What was it that he'd said that had irritated her so?

"I'm sure you do," she murmured. "Would that you were as honest with me."

Once again he had the feeling that she suspected his duplicity. Her lids were narrowed in suspicion. Her sensuous lips were pressed into a firm line. Her right hand clenched in her lap even though she tried to shield it from his eyes.

"Ariel, I am not trying to deceive you."

He heard her release a huff of disbelief. "No?"

And for the first time the lie stuck in his throat. Bloody hell, what had happened to him?

He'd been taken in by a pair of lovely eyes. Eyes that reflected a deep-seated disappointment he'd never noticed before.

"Damnation," he muttered, releasing her hand to wipe his own over his face. He looked away from her, out of the carriage, suddenly, unaccountably, feeling a scoundrel. "You don't believe me."

"No, I do not."

He looked back at her. There was such a look in her eyes . . . so much anger, so much hurt and so much bitterness that he found himself thinking something had changed in their relationship, something that had started last night.

He straightened in his seat. She couldn't know of his scheme, could she?

From nowhere came the notion that she had mentioned his code name yesterday, albeit in an offhand way. But had the mention been coincidence? Was it more than a coincidence that he received a note the very same day? Yet if she knew, why had he not been apprehended? Surely she would tell the War Department what she knew? Yet here he was. No, she couldn't know. She must merely be reacting to her treatment tonight. Obviously she thought he'd been in on it.

"You look blue-deviled, Mr. Trevain."

"Nathan," he corrected her automatically.

"Nathan," she conceded.

"I am."

"And why is that?"

"Because you do not trust me, and I am stymied as to how to prove I can be trusted."

She stared at him intently, her eyes narrowed. Then she leaned toward him a bit. Her dress dipped down. He found his gaze dipping down with it. Her scent enveloped him. Elusive. Provocative. Enticing.

"Have dinner with me tomorrow night," she shocked him by saying. "Alone. At my father's home. He is not in residence, and we shall be private there. You can prove you are trustworthy by sharing a simple meal with me and keeping your distance."

What was this? He could hardly dare believe his ears. She invited him to her father's home? Dare he trust his good fortune? Excitement had his blood pumping. It was too good an opportunity to pass up.

"Very well, I accept your challenge."

She nodded. The carriage slowed. Much to his surprise he realized they were near her cousin's home. Seconds later he handed her down.

"I shall see you tomorrow?" she asked.

Lifting her hand to his lips, he smiled. "That you shall."

She didn't smile at him in return, didn't even glance back at him as she turned away. He watched her go, wondering if she truly desired to test him or if there was another reason, a nefarious reason for her invitation.

Could she know who he was? Once again, he found himself wondering, and he'd learned to trust when his instincts sent him a warning.

Either way, by tomorrow night, he would have found out.

7

If Ariel had thought herself nervous the first time she'd confronted Nathan, knowing who he truly was, that was nothing compared to this night's excursion. She paced her father's salon. The musty smell of a house long closed up filtered into her nose. She hadn't wanted Trevain to bring her here, had needed the time alone to compose herself. But now she wished she had her cousin with her, even though she would have hated to involve Phoebe. No, this would be the last night to confront him. That she was settled upon.

"My lady, he is here."

One of the few members of the staff left behind to keep up the house stood by the salon door. "Very good. Show him in."

The man nodded, turned.

"Is everything ready?" she asked in a rush.

The man turned back. "It is, my lady."

"Very good. We shall eat at half-past the hour."

Once again the servant turned, once again Ariel wanted to call him back with a question, but delaying the confrontation would serve no purpose.

One last night, Ariel. 'Tis all you must endure.

And she would do this. She could. Whatever Nathan wanted, it must involve this house and her father somehow. Why else would he befriend her? And if he was after documents, they must be documents he could not find on his own. She had no doubt that he was professional enough to have looked in the obvious places before selecting her to unwittingly help, though what he could be looking for she had no idea.

"My lady."

And there he was by the doorway, his broad shoulders covered by yet another black coat, his scar more pronounced tonight for some reason. The same black diamond winked from his stock, his leather shoes catching the glitter of the fire. His white stockings were stark against his black breeches.

"Mr. Trevain. I'm glad you've come."

He walked forward. Ariel felt her heart speed up with every step. "Are you?"

He was flirting with her. Or was he? His silver eyes were intent, his look seeming to pierce her soul. What was it he sought in her eyes, she wondered.

"I thought you might change your mind," he said, stopping before her.

She stared up at him, at his tan, masculine face. Up into eyes that glittered as they stared down at her. "As you can see, I did not."

He reached for her hand. Her breath caught. He lifted it, kissed it softly, then released it. She felt almost disappointed by the loss of contact.

He stepped back from her, placing his hands behind his back, his gaze focusing on the room around them. "This is a very lovely home."

"Thank you."

"Perhaps you could give me a tour later?"

She looked at him sharply. Her senses went on alert. "Of course." She gestured to the sideboard. "Would you like something to drink?"

He seemed pleased by the suggestion. "Yes, I would, although I insist on pouring." He crossed to the sideboard, which held three bottles and four glasses. "Would you like some wine?"

"Yes," she answered, knowing she shouldn't. Wine was something she drank rarely, but tonight she found herself wanting something stronger. Truly, she should have had a glass of brandy to steady her nerves before he'd arrived. She should have had ten drinks of brandy.

"What is the view out of that window, by the way?" he asked over his shoulder as he poured.

Ariel watched the glass fill with liquid. "The house sits next to one of His Majesty's parks."

"It must be beautiful."

She glanced at the window as if she could see out of it. "It is."

He turned back to her, a glass held out. "To trusting me," he murmured, lifting it and taking a sip.

She did the same, the wine tart on her tongue, the taste foreign. He watched her intently, so much so that she felt her face heat like warming stones. She took another sip to cover her nervousness.

"Did you have a pleasant ride over?" Mundane, silly question, she knew, but she needed to say something to cover her nervousness, a nervousness that increased with each passing moment.

"Very pleasant. Thank you."

Hmph. Now what? She elected to sit down on the sofa, relieved when he sat on the sofa that stood across from her. "And your uncle. Are you on speaking terms with him after last eve?"

His expression turned rather wry. "I am, more's the pity."

She took another sip, the liquid burning a path down her throat.

"I am sorry for what happened."

She would wager he was. " 'Tis of no import. I know you had nothing to do with it."

Already she could feel the effects of the wine, one of the benefits of drinking nothing but lemonade for the past few years. "I assume you didn't tell him our engagement was a sham?"

"No, I did not."

She nodded, wondering what to say next.

"You seem nervous," he said, his voice low.

"Me?" She feigned innocence. "What have I to be nervous about?"

"You are alone with me."

She settled back on her sofa, suddenly feeling rather languid. "Yes, there is that, I suppose. I don't make a habit of seeing strange men alone." She frowned. "At least I didn't until I met you."

He leaned forward, his elbow resting upon his knee. "And has meeting me been such a bad thing?"

She found herself nodding before she realized what she was doing. "I rank my meeting with you right up there with the day my horse lost a shoe on Archibald Worth's estate."

"How flattering."

"Yes, well, at least the horse wasn't injured."

"But you were."

She waved her glass around in a gesture of dismissal. Some of the liquid sloshed. She hardly noticed. "Only later, and just my heart. But really, what matters a broken heart when one has lost one's reputation?"

"And that bothers you?"

"No," she answered, her tongue feeling thick. "It doesn't bother me. It annoys me, and sometimes when I see the way people look at me, it hurts. Only 'tis worse when they direct that animosity at my cousin, too. I tell myself to pay it no heed. After all, most of them are a bunch of no account snobs."

"And what do you think of me?"

She peered at her glass. She hadn't drunk much wine, but it certainly felt like it. Yet she was more than lightheaded. She felt odd, her body heavy, her thoughts sluggish. "What kind of wine was this?" she asked, staring into the glass.

"The kind made from grapes," he answered.

She flushed again. "Why, thank you for that edifying bit of information."

"You didn't answer my question."

She looked up at him, having to blink a bit to focus. "Mayhap because I do not want to answer it."

He smiled. She became entranced with that smile for a moment. Heavens, but the man had a heavenly smile.

"Why don't you want to answer it?"

"Because I do not wish to insult you."

The smile spread. "Go ahead. Answer me. What do you think of me. Honestly."

"Very well. I think you're a lying, cheating, traitorous bastard."

His amusement abruptly faded. Not surprisingly. Her words would have had a dampening effect on most people's mood.

"Why do you call me that?"

She almost told him the truth. She almost opened her mouth and let fly the words, "Because you are a spy." But something stopped her at the last moment, some last drop of sanity that floated through her brain. "Because all men are that."

He seemed to buy the words, though his eyes had narrowed. "Not all men."

"No? Name me one man in my life who deserves my admiration."

"Your father."

She snorted. Actually snorted. Gracious, but she felt odd. "My father is the coldest man I've ever met. How he ended up with my mother I shall never know."

"Why do you say that?"

She shrugged, liking how relaxed her shoulders felt. She wiggled them again, almost closing her eyes. "Everyone knows how cold he is. At the Admiralty they call him Block of Ice Bettencourt."

"So he does not speak much? He does not share with you any of the county's secrets?"

Something nagged at the back of her brain, something insistent. "Oh, no. I'm lucky if I hear two words out of him when he deigns to see me. Pity, really. The secret of how he ties his cravat will go with him to the grave." When she focused on him again, she noticed he was smiling. How odd, for she couldn't remember him ever smiling so, so . . . sincerely.

"Has he ever told you what is in that hidden room of his?"

She found herself nodding before she realized what it was she did. A buzzing had begun in her head.

"What is it?"

She shrugged. *Something is most odd, Ariel.* The

voice rang out so clearly in her head, she found herself looking around for the speaker.

"Ariel?"

She had a hard time focusing. An even harder time remembering his question.

"What is in that room?"

She blinked, her eyes narrowing sluggishly. "You drugged me."

"I did," he admitted.

"Why?" she slurred.

"I need information from you. This seemed the most expedient way of getting it."

She sat up, knowing her upper body swayed but helpless to stop it. "Hmph. What a sterling idea. I'm surprised you did not try that earlier. Would that I had thought of it."

"And why would you want to drug me?"

"Because you," she pointed at one of the two Nathan Trevains, "are a spy."

She thought she saw him stiffen, thought he might have risen half out of his chair, but she couldn't be sure. Things had grown rather fuzzy of late.

"How do you know who I am?"

She began to lean to one side. He shot out of his seat before she fell.

"Ariel, answer me. How do you know?"

"Your ring." She smiled triumphantly. "And the way you responded to the note I sent you— Helios."

He released her. She immediately fell over, her upper body landing on the arm of the couch.

She wanted to close her eyes. Just for a second. But he wouldn't let her.

"Damnation," she thought she heard him murmur. But then he came to her again, grabbing her arms. "Tell me how to get into your father's private room."

So that was what he wanted. Access to the hidden room off her father's office. How . . . funny.

"Ariel."

"Just a little bit of sleep," she murmured. "That is all I need. Then I will deal with you and your devious, tasty drugs later."

"Ariel!"

She closed her eyes and was firmly, blessedly, asleep.

8

"What have you done to me?" Lady Ariel D'Archer asked nearly two hours later. Her hands were tied to the headboard of her bed in her father's town home.

Nathan stared down at her. He sat in an armchair next to her bed, a comfortable fire snapping to his left, darkened window with frilly rose-colored drapes to his right. He'd rather liked the sight of her lying there earlier, though he knew he should not have. He'd had ample opportunity to study her while she slept, ample time to admire her perfection as he reclined next to her bed. Her hair had lain beneath her like black, satin ribbons. Dark lashes inky smudges against alabaster skin. Her face relaxed such as he'd never seen before. Now her eyes glowed with inner fire as they stared up at him. Cheeks that had looked pale moments before were filled with color. His manhood stirred. That she was his enemy and a woman as deceitful as the woman who'd given him his scar deterred his lust not a whit. He'd begun to realize that he would always want Ariel D'Archer, even as he would firmly never allow himself to have such a conniving woman.

"Well?" she demanded again.

"Why, nothing but bring you up to this room, my dear." She tried to sit up, but the ropes he'd used wouldn't let her. "Do not try to struggle, for it will do you no good."

"Then I'll scream."

"No one will hear you. I've given your servants an unexpected night off. No doubt they think we mean to have a secret tryst. A good number of them watched me carry you up here, you see."

"You bastard."

"Aye."

"I feel like a fool for not realizing sooner what depths you would sink to."

"That is a bit heavy-handed coming from a woman equally capable of deceit."

"It was nothing less than you deserved."

"And just why did you continue to see me, knowing who I am?"

"I was trying to find out what you were after. Plus, after learning that your offer of friendship was nothing but a sham, I was only too willing to turn the table on you."

She stared up at him, her eyes filled with accusation and hurt. He looked away, telling himself he should not feel guilty. After all, she was only too willing to play a game of deception, too. It only served to confirm what he'd always known. She might have been beautiful, but she had a traitorous heart, like the rest of her sex.

"Well. Do you deny that you were going to use me?"

He looked back at her. "No," he said firmly.

She lifted her chin. " 'Tis as I thought," he heard her murmur as if there was a part of her that had hoped he'd befriended her out of kindness.

He almost told her that he had not time for kindness. But he held his tongue, his eyes firmly fixed on the emotions crossing her face. Sadness. Anger. Disappointment.

"So, now that we know where we both stand, would you mind untying me?"

"I would mind very much, especially since I have no doubt you will try to escape."

"Bastard," she repeated.

He smiled. "No, just cautious."

She tested the strength of the ropes, clearly uncomfortable with his stare and the bonds. "What do you plan to do with me?"

He forced himself to concentrate. It was the eyes. Those damn, mysterious gypsy eyes. With her staring up at him while lying supine the bed, he suddenly felt rather sordid. "That depends on you."

Her gold eyes narrowed. "How so?"

"If you cooperate, I shall be out of your life within the hour. If, however, you prove to be uncooperative, I shall be forced to use more drastic measures."

"And what is it you want?"

"Information."

She gave him a look of frustration. "As I recall, but I do not see how what is in that room could be of help."

"Let me decide that."

"And if I do not tell you?"

"I will not go easy on you."

"What will you do, hold me hostage?"

"Oh, I don't know if I need go that far, but it is a fascinating possibility."

She compressed her lips. "Cad. Scoundrel. Blackguard."

"Thank you."

"In case you are too much of a nodcock to understand, that was not a compliment."

He shrugged, watching with fascination as her face filled with even more angry color.

"You should be shot."

"Indeed? Then pray God you shoot me soon, for I do not think I can take much more of your prattle."

"Why, you—"

"Silence," he ordered.

To his surprise, her mouth clamped closed.

"Tell me how to get into your father's room."

She tilted her chin up. "No."

He lifted black brows. "You would deny me?"

"I will do whatever it takes to thwart you."

"Then you will pay the price."

He saw her eyes widen as he slowly stood up. Good, perhaps he wouldn't need to proceed any further. But she remained stubbornly, obstinately silent as he leaned over the bed. He stood so close he could smell her sensuous, feminine scent.

"Stay back," she ordered.

"No."

She warned him away with a glare. "I will not let you do whatever it is you think to do."

"Do you think yourself strong enough to stop me?" he asked with a mocking smile.

"I shall certainly try."

"Then try."

Her eyes widened as he reached for her shoulders. He made quick work of the rope, holding it in his hands when he was finished.

She must have thought he was going to strangle her with it, for she said, "No," trying to twist away.

He wouldn't let her, his hands going to either side of her body. She'd begun to pant, the motion making her breasts rise and fall enticingly. He tried to ignore the sight, but it proved to be impossible.

"Tell me how to get into the room," he ordered again, glancing down before looking up again. God, but it took an effort to do so. He wanted to lean closer to her. To kiss those plump lips. To stroke her silky flesh.

"I will not."

"Then pay the price." He saw her eyes widen,

heard her yelp just before he reached his hands around her waist and slung her over his shoulder.

"What are you doing?" she screeched, as her chest hit his shoulder. She beat his back with her fists.

"I am kidnapping you."

Oddly enough, he felt her relax into his shoulder before stiffening again, "*Kidnapping!*"

He turned to the door. Obviously she'd thought him about to rape her. But he would never do something so deplorable. Still, touching her as he did now, her breasts snug against his shoulder, her rear high in the air, did things to him that he truly wished not to think about.

"Yes, kidnapping, for if you will not allow me access to the room, or at the very least tell me what is in there, I am left with little choice but to blackmail your father for the information I need."

"Blackmail?" she cried.

"Do you have trouble with your ears?" he asked, shifting her on his shoulder as he exited the room. "Or do you always repeat words back to your captors?"

"Put me down," she ordered, beginning to struggle again. "I do not want you to be my captor."

"That is too bad, my lady." He wasn't sure which way to turn once he left the room. Right or left? Right, he decided.

"Let me down, I said. I can walk."

"I will put you down if you tell me what I wish to know."

"Fine, then I'll tell you."

Immediately he swung her off his shoulder. Her breath *omphed* out of her as she hit her feet. Truth be told, he was relieved to do so. Bloody hell but she enticed him, especially when she looked like she did now, her hair tumbling about her in wild, gypsylike disarray. Her eyes flashed fire; her stance was both proud and challenging.

He loved a good challenge. Frankly, he was glad the charade was over. The idea of pretending to befriend her had grown distasteful over the past few days. Now he could do battle as he preferred. Head to head.

"I will tell you how to get into the room, but I will do no more than that."

"Very well."

"And you must promise to let me go afterward."

He narrowed his eyes before saying, "I promise."

She didn't look like she believed him—not surprising, given the events of the past few days.

"Follow me," she said, heading toward the door.

He did as ordered, for some reason amused by her demeanor. She didn't act like a captive. Then again, had he really expected her to?

He followed her down a flight of stairs. The servants had left candles glowing in silver wall sconces. No doubt her staff expected the two of them to take their pleasure and leave. He frowned upon realizing Lady D'Archer's clandestine meeting would be all over town by the morning, not that he should care.

He took the last step, following her toward her father's office.

But he did care.

Ridiculous. After tonight he would leave her, and with any luck, England, with his brother in hand. For the first time in months he felt himself grow optimistic. His excitement only increased when she lifted a candle from a sconce and entered her father's study.

"Turn around."

"Whatever for?"

"I do not want you to see."

"See what?"

"How I do this."

He crossed his arms, his excitement waning in the face of her ridiculous request. "My lady, perhaps you do not realize this, but you are hardly in a position to order me about. Now, open the door."

"Turn around, I said," she stubbornly repeated.

"Open the door!" he roared.

She jumped, actually jumped, the candle flickering with the motion. He saw her lips tighten, saw her eyes narrow before she crossed to the far wall, opened the glass cover of a grandfather clock, then moved the hands to twelve o'clock.

And just like that it was done.

He heard a click, a snick, and then realized she pushed against the wall as though it was no more than a door. Elation filled him as her candle illuminated a room beyond.

"Move aside," he ordered.

She did as asked.

Nathan moved to take her place. But he felt an instant surge of shock that turned into a bellow of rage at what he saw.

Wine.

Hundreds of bottles of wine.

"Now, you didn't really think my father would keep important papers in his home, did you?"

He turned back to her, for the first time understanding what it meant to see red.

That was, of course, exactly what he'd thought.

A half-hour later, Ariel had grown impatient with his search.

"I tell you, 'tis just wine."

It wouldn't be so bad, waiting for him to realize the truth, but he'd tied her hands behind her back, and her upper body was wrapped to the back of her father's chair like a sacrificial offering. It wouldn't have been so bad except that the chair was a great, big leather monstrosity that engulfed her and smelled of tallow and lemons. A most unfortunate combination. Truly, if she'd hated Nathan Trevain before, she absolutely despised him now. The cad was worse than Archie. At least Archie hadn't treated her like a Bastille prisoner.

"They must be in here," she heard him mumble.

She wished the bloody chair would move, but she'd tried rocking it away from her father's oak desk at least twenty times.

"If you tell me what it is you're looking for, perhaps I can help." She tried to loosen her bonds again, but to no avail. Her hands were snug between her back and the chair. "I do, after all, live here when my father is in town."

His head poked out of the cellar. There was a cobweb in his black hair. She let it stay there out of spite.

"I doubt you can help," he answered.

"Then why did you involve me in the first place?" she asked with a huff.

He shrugged. "I conjectured the best way to discover what was in this room was to seduce the information out of you."

"Seduce?" She blasted him with a glare. "And what did you hope to do? Kiss me senseless before asking how to get in there?" She motioned to the room with her head.

"Something like that."

She snorted. "Men. They think women's heads can be turned by pretty words and passionate kisses."

"I haven't heard you object to any of my kisses yet."

"No, but then I was acting for a good portion of the time we were together."

It wasn't true, but he must not have realized how much his touch affected her. He shot her a black look before turning back to the cellar.

"They are not in there."

"So you say."

She sighed with impatience, her hands beginning to go numb. The bloody chair was uncomfortable when one was tied in such a position. "Why don't you tell me what it is you are looking for," she repeated plaintively. "Gracious, we could be here all night at this rate."

He stuck his head out again. Another cobweb had joined the first one. Good. His body emerged, too, his hands dusty with cellar dust. She caught a whiff of it and fought the urge to sneeze. He shook the filth off his fingers, some of it alighting on his clothes. He still wore his coat, only now she knew why he'd dressed in black. Obviously he skulked about houses quite a bit.

The realization had her narrowing her eyes. Fiend. Miscreant. She would see him captured for his crimes. Somehow. Some way.

"I am looking for my brother," he finally said.

She lifted a brow. "I assure you, sir, your brother is not inside my father's cellar."

This time it was his turn to give her a sarcastic look. "Obviously. I am searching for papers that might tell me where he is."

"In there?" she asked, lifting her brows in disbelief. "What makes you think my father would keep those sorts of documents in a room at his private residence?"

"Because they are not at his office at the Admiralty."

"How do you know?"

"Because I have searched."

"You broke into the Admiralty?"

"Indeed."

Heavens, that took courage. *Silly ninny, Ariel. Only a traitor would do such a thing. You should not think a traitor's actions courageous.*

"And what sort of documents would these be?" she asked.

He stepped further out of the cellar, the spiderwebs fluttering about him like Medusa's snakes. "Anything that might tell me what ship my brother is captive on."

"He was taken aboard a ship?"

"Yes, my lady, by your British navy."

She felt a stab of surprise followed by dismay. His brother had been pressed into service. Aye, she knew it happened. Often times she'd wondered what fate those men suffered. She'd wondered about their families, their friends, wondering if captives were allowed any contact with their loved ones back home. The thoughts had made her miserable, especially since it was her father who headed the Admiralty.

"When did it happen?" she asked.

"Four years ago."

"And you have been searching ever since?"

"I have."

"And no one will tell you where he is? Not even now that the war is over?"

He snorted. "Tell the infamous Nathan Trevain where his only brother is? They would rather shoot one of their own in the head."

Most likely true. Truly, the man had a way of getting under one's skin, and she'd only known him a few days. She could only imagine how the Admiralty felt about him.

"How old is he?" she asked.

His lip curled. "What difference does that make?"

"None, but I want to know."

His scowl turned into a frown. "He is twenty-one."

She felt her eyes widen. Why, just a year younger than herself. That meant he'd been—

"Abducted when he was seventeen," Nathan provided, obviously reading the direction of her thoughts.

Seventeen and taken off a ship by complete strangers, forced to serve under men who no doubt despised him, never allowed to see his family and to go home.

"Could he be dead?" she found herself asking.

She'd been looking at his face intently, so she saw the way it changed, how his jaw tightened, his eyes dimmed.

"He could be, but they will not tell me even that."

"Perhaps they do not know. From what my father tells me, naval records are not the best. You would be lucky to find a list of crew members."

He didn't look like he wanted to hear that. "Then I will find sailing plans. Perhaps a map showing which ships were off the coast of Virginia in 1779."

"That you might find, but not here."

"How are you so certain?"

She shrugged, though it was difficult to do so, what with her arms tied the way they were. "My father does not spend a lot of time here. When he is not aboard a ship, he prefers to be in the country. I believe he likes the smell of earth after months at sea."

"You're certain?"

"Of course I am. He is, after all, my father, for all that we don't see eye to eye."

He didn't say anything.

"So you see, sir, you've set yourself a fruitless task. The papers you seek are no doubt at the Admiralty or perhaps in someone else's possession. It would take forever for you to find them."

"Ah, but you forget something, my dear."

He advanced upon her. And Ariel didn't like the look upon his face. Not one bit. She would have moved away, but she couldn't. She consoled herself with leaning her head as far back as she could.

"And what is that, sir."

"I have something your father wants."

She didn't want to ask the question, truly she didn't. "And that would be?"

"You."

Her heart stopped, restarted again at twice the rate. "And what do I have to do with anything?"

"Why, nothing, my dear, but I am certain your fellow countrymen will do whatever it takes to insure that one First Lord's daughter does not come to harm."

And that, Ariel realized, was exactly what she'd been afraid of.

PART THREE

Weep not for little Leonie,
Abducted by a French Marquis!
Though loss of honor was a wrench,
Just think how it's improved her French

HARRY GRAHAM

9

And so he'd kidnapped her. He'd disappeared for an hour to return with a hired hack. The fiend deposited her inside like a bag of corn. That coach rattled around them now, a rackety affair with a piece of stuffing hanging out where Nathan sat.

Nathan the spy.

Nathan the abductor.

She wanted to poke his eyes out, except she couldn't, because her hands were tied behind her back. Still.

"Where are you taking me?"

He didn't answer. His face was turned to the left, so she had a view of his good side. If the man could have a good side. Truly, he seemed enamored with the view out of the carriage window. She supposed a view of absolute and utter darkness would intrigue a man with an absolute and utterly black soul.

"Well?" she repeated when he didn't answer.

Finally he looked at her, his silver eyes having turned a dark, dark gray. Or perhaps it was the lighting. The inside of the coach had a carriage lantern with such dirty glass the flame looked dim at best.

"Where I am taking you is no concern of yours."

"Oh, but I beg to differ. Since I am the latest victim of your machinations, I feel I have a distinct right to know."

He looked like he couldn't believe her audacity in insisting. Well, then, they were even, for she couldn't believe his audacity in abducting her from her own home.

"You will know soon enough where I am taking you. In the interim, I suggest you sit still and be quiet.

"It would be easier to sit still if my rear was not deposited on a broken spring."

He lifted the right side of his mouth, his scar more noticeable when he did that.

"And I really do wish you'd untie my hands. Frankly, I fear I shall fall over every time we round a turn."

"If I untie you, you will undoubtedly try to escape."

"From a moving carriage? Do not be absurd. I would break every bone in my body."

"As long as one of the bones was your mouth, I would count that a blessing."

She pursed her lips before saying, "Mouths do not have bones, they have muscle."

His eyes narrowed at her pointing out what he obviously knew. "Then pray God your muscles seize up."

"Well, Mr. Trevain, I shall make you a deal. I will keep myself quiet if you untie my hands."

They rounded a corner. She made an exaggerated lurch.

"Oh, very well," he snapped, reaching for her hands. From nowhere he pulled a knife. Her eyes widened at the sight. Where had that come from?

With one sure stroke he cut the knot, but she noticed he kept the rope on the seat next to him. Heavens, what if he intended to tie her up again? But she wouldn't let him. She would escape. And despite what she'd told him, she found herself contemplating the wisdom of jumping from the coach.

Smashed, bruised body?

Or wait until a better moment?

Wait until a better moment. Yes, indeed.

But it was a long ride into the country. At least that was where she assumed he was taking her. The roads grew progressively worse, the ruts so deep she would wager a person couldn't see out of them. And then, finally, blessedly, the vehicle began to slow.

"We're here."

Yes, but where exactly was here?

She deduced the answer herself a moment later as the carriage door opened. He stepped down first. Ariel was mortally disappointed when he retied her hands before allowing her down. Gracious, but this night had begun to frustrate her no end. Imagine. Being kidnapped. Why, it defied belief. And by a man who was heir to a dukedom. Gracious, it felt positively medieval.

"Follow me," he ordered, stepping away from the coach.

Ariel wanted to decline. Truly she did, but he didn't look to be in the mood for resistance. He glared down at her, and even with nothing but moonlight illuminating his mammoth form, she could see the glower he gave her, a glower made more ominous by his scar. Gracious, but he was a forbidding-looking man.

"Now," he added.

She rolled her eyes, then did as instructed, though it near killed her to do so. She hated having her hands tied, especially when she wanted to wrap them around his throat. And the cad didn't help her keep her balance. Her feet met the sodden ground.

Just where was she anyway? she wondered, turning.

She asked the question aloud, surprised when he said, "Somewhere where it will be safe to hold you until I hear from your father."

"Oh," she answered, studying the place.

Moonlight illuminated the dark gray stones of a manor with a flat, crumbling roof and windows so black they resembled rotted teeth. Tall, gnarled trees shot up from the overgrown grounds. Her eyes widened. The pungent stench of waterlogged vegetation assailed her nose. This was no secret love nest he used, she realized, this was a shamble. A stagnant-looking pond butted up against the right side of the structure. The driveway was so overgrown with waist-high weeds the carriage had had to drop them where they stood. It looked exactly the sort of place a mother would warn her children against visiting, like the home of a villain in a children's bedtime story.

She looked back at her captor, frowning, then beyond him as a small man with an odd gait approached, his knee-high boots and carriage jacket announcing him the coachman. Trevain stopped. The coachman held out a lantern. Golden light slipped over ruts and tufts of grass. He stopped near them, looking her up and down.

"Were we followed?" Trevain asked, stepping in front of her and blocking his view.

"Not as far as I ken tell."

"Good."

Ariel peeked around Mr. Trevain in time to see him take the lantern from the fellow's outstretched hand. The driver shot her a last look of curiosity before turning around and hobbling away. Nathan turned around, too, almost smashing her in the process. His silver gaze swept down. The look on his face was so grim, so cold, she grew, if possible, even more nervous.

"Come," Nathan said.

Ariel held her ground, suddenly afraid of being alone with him, despite what she told herself. Truth be told, she hadn't had much luck with men when she was alone with them. A backward glance revealed the driver climbing aboard the coach.

"He's leaving?" she squeaked, dread stabbing her stomach.

"He is."

"Are there any other servants inside?"

A glance revealed a frown. "No, my lady. I'm sorry to report there will be no one to wait on you hand and foot."

That wasn't what she'd been concerned about. Gracious. It was being alone with him that worried her.

"Come," he said again.

Ariel held her ground, wanting to turn, run after the coach, screaming, "Wait, come back. I beg you!"

"My lady, we can do this the hard way or the easy way."

Her gaze shot up again, Ariel wondering what he'd do if she said, "The hard way." Perhaps toss her over his shoulder as he'd done earlier. She didn't relish the notion. When he'd picked her up, she'd felt deuced odd.

"My lady?"

"I . . ." she gulped, her hands clenching behind her back. "I, er, would prefer the easy way, Trevain."

"Don't call me that," he snapped.

"Don't call you what?"

He grabbed her arm. She yelped.

"Do not use my last name as if I am part of your British society."

Well, there was no questioning his bloodlines, even if his manners did proclaim him less than a gentleman. "But you *are* British."

"I am Mr. Trevain, as people address me in America."

Oh. She leaned away from him. His grip tightened. "Let me go," she gasped. "*Mr.* Trevain."

He did. Ariel took a step back, breathing heavily. The distance made her feel better, not wonderful, but better.

"Enough of this. We are going inside even if I have to toss you over my shoulder."

Oh, heavens. Pray God, no. Not again. He grabbed her by the forearm and all but dragged her on a zigzag course through weeds to the front of the house. He hardly paused when he reached the front door. His hand pushed on it with more force than necessary. When he lifted the lantern, the door swung wide to reveal an inside as gloomy as the outside. Spiderwebs hung like arachnid draperies. Pieces of broken furniture dotted the dusty floor.

"Damn," he muttered.

"I believe someone needs to hire a new decorator."

He ignored her sally, pulling her forward.

"No," Ariel gasped, planting her heels. The floor was so covered with filth and grime that the soles of her slippers left twin clean streaks on its surface.

"No," she repeated, trying to twist way.

"What the devil is the matter with you?"

"I'm being kidnapped. What do you think is the matter?"

"I'm not going to harm you."

"So you say, but you've been less than honest with me in the past."

"I am being honest with you about this. Now, come."

"But I don't want to go in there."

"My lady, as you mentioned, you're being kidnapped. As such, you've no choice but to go exactly where I want you to go."

"And where exactly would we be going?"

"Inside this wreck of a home."

"Yes, but to what room?"

Never had she seen such an expression of impatience on a man's face. "What the devil does it matter?"

Gracious, he almost blew her hair out of her face with the volume of his voice. "It matters to me."

He didn't speak. Ariel could see his hands clench and then unclench as he struggled for patience. Well, good, the cad deserved whatever discomfort she could give him. He turned to her, appeared to come to some sort of internal compromise and said, "Very well. I'm taking you to the master bedroom."

"The bedroom?" she squeaked. Another bed. More rope. Him leaning over her. Oh, no.

"The bedroom," he repeated, turning toward the staircase.

She dug in her heels.

"No, wait. I would prefer to stay down here, if you please."

"No, I do not please."

"You don't?"

He seemed to realize she was stalling—which she was—for he flicked her a look of disgust mixed with impatience before tugging her toward the staircase again. Ariel had no choice but to follow, feeling rather like Lady Chalmer's poodle. Mr. Trevain appeared unhappy, too, for he slammed his foot down on the first step.

It broke in two.

Ariel heard his teeth clack together. She stared, wide-eyed, at the rotted wood, then up at Mr. Trevain, who, undaunted, dragged her over the splintered wood and took the second step.

It broke, too.

This time he was better prepared. His hand let go of her arm to clutch the balustrade for balance.

The handrail broke, too, inch-thick dust puffing up around them as the wood clattered to the floor.

Ariel stared from the railing to where the railing used to be, to Mr. Trevain, back to the railing again—much less ominous-looking—then back to the floor, wondering what he would do.

"Bloody hell," he cursed. "Bloody, bloody hell," he repeated. "Will nothing go right this night?"

Since he didn't seem to be asking her the question, she ventured to say, "Does this mean I can go home now?" in a small, hope-filled voice.

He turned. Ariel shrank back. Silver eyes narrowed. His scar made a vivid slash across his face.

She realized in that instant that the man before her was an entirely different man from the one she'd come to know in the past few days. This man seemed colder, more cruel. He looked horrid now, his expression so dire the urge to escape grew in direct proportion to the fire in his eyes.

"Come," he snapped. "If I remember correctly, the servants' quarters are back this way."

Servants' quarters? Any relief Ariel felt at having escaped the bedroom suddenly returned. "Mr. Trevain," she wheezed out breathlessly, for he was back to making her totter along behind him. "If it's all the same to you, I'd prefer to stay in the hall."

But he ignored her. Ariel almost tripped as he pulled her over the broken rails. The lantern illuminated a door directly ahead, spiderwebs hanging down the door frame. Lots and lots of spiderwebs. Ariel shivered. Trevain pushed against the door.

It fell over, too.

At that moment Ariel was struck by the sudden, inexplicable urge to laugh. She couldn't help it. The night had been such a disaster, the realization that she wasn't the only one to have a streak of bad luck was almost more than her strained emotions could bear.

"If I huff and puff, do you suppose I could blow the whole house down?"

He turned again. Ariel wondered where the words had come from, except that she felt a secret, vindictive urge to bait him. Most likely because she was miffed that he would dare try to use her and failing that, kidnap her. She tensed, and for an instant, just a brief moment, she thought the lid might blow off the barrel of his temper. Somehow he managed to hold on to it, though. Ariel wished her father could exercise such control.

A yelp escaped her as he grabbed her at the crook of her elbow.

"You," he gritted out through teeth that were surely clenched—quite an amazing feat, actually, "are coming with me."

Nathan watched her eyes grow round. She darted a look at the door, her face seeming to pale, her heels digging in again. Her hair had grown more wild, more riotous, he noted, not that he cared, his frustration with the night and his reluctant captive coming to a head. Gods, he couldn't believe the place was in such disrepair. Leave it to his uncle to do such a thing. Long ago his father had told him about his British family's hatred for anything connected to his father's name—this estate for example, the one and only piece of property Nathan could rightfully claim as his own—but until tonight he'd never fully realized the truth of those words. At least they could have hired a caretaker. Lord knows the duke of Davenport had enough coin to pay the wage.

He tugged her forward. She didn't budge. His patience snapped again as he whirled back to face her. "My lady," he gritted, feeling the right side of his mouth lift in a snarl. "Once again, we can do this the hard way or the easy way."

"I don't suppose if I say the easy way you'll tie me to the kitchen table, instead."

Kitchen table? Why in God's name would she want him to do that.

"Or any piece of furniture." He saw her swallow. "Anything but a bed."

Understanding dawned. He straightened. The chit thought he was going to rape her. Again. Frankly, he didn't know if he should be offended or amused by her obsessive fear of his touching her. While she was certainly beautiful, he would sooner bed a viper than another British woman, especially one as untrustworthy as her.

"My lady, let me assure you, I have no intention of bedding you. Ever."

"Do you promise?" She swallowed.

He wanted to yell at her that of course he promised, only to realize how ridiculous this whole conversation was. When did he lose such complete control of his captive?

When he saw the fear in her eyes.

He clamped down on the thought. He didn't care if she thought him the Devil of Dralock. Didn't she realize any desire he might have felt for her had faded upon learning of her duplicity?

And yet, even with his pulse pounding in anger, he found himself saying, "I promise."

She looked a bit reassured.

He grabbed her arm again, ignoring her small gasp as he turned back to the fallen door, raised the lantern and stopped dead.

If the main hall looked neglected and decayed, then the narrow hall leading to the servants' quarters looked positively tomblike. Spiderwebs stretched from floor to ceiling, a rat scurried across the hall.

"I'm not going down there."

He didn't blame her. Not even the militia would want to go down there. Damnation, but why hadn't he examined the interior of this place prior to bringing her here?

Because he was in a hurry. Because he was angry with her. Because he didn't think, only reacted. And an angry man is an ineffective man, one who doesn't plan as thoroughly as he should. He should have known better than to ignore one of his primary rules.

He would have to hold her in the main part of the house, he realized, although that presented more of an opportunity for her to escape, since they would be on the ground floor. He shrugged. It would have to do, even if it meant tying her to him all night. He tugged her back toward the front door.

"Are we leaving?"

"No," he gritted out.

There were four doors off the main hall, and it was toward the one nearest them that he went. The evening air caused the webs above them to ripple. Nathan ignored them. A quick inspection of the door hinges revealed bronze patina and rotted metal, which had been responsible for the other door's downfall. The next one proved no better, although the one nearest the front of the house looked reasonably sound. He frowned, left with little choice but to give it a try, but when the door wouldn't open, he turned back to his captive to order her to stay.

She was gone.

He stared at the spot where she'd been standing. "What the—" Where had she gone?

She's escaped, you fool.

It shouldn't have surprised him, but it did.

"Ariel!" he roared.

But he knew she'd left. The evidence of her perfidy lay before him: ten tiny footprints led back to the front door.

Little hellion.

Ariel knew trying to escape with her hands still tied behind her back was the height of foolishness, but goodness, she'd had to try. He'd abducted her, for goodness sake. She still couldn't believe it.

So she pressed on. Her feet hurt from the uneven ground beneath her, and branches slapped her in the face. Worse, she knew she made a horrible racket. Trevain would have to be deaf as Lord Sinclair not to hear her. But she had no choice but to keep going. She had to escape. The word was like a drumbeat in her ears. *Escape. Escape. Escape*.

"Ariel!"

She froze.

Bullocks, bullocks, bullocks. He sounded right behind her.

"Ariel!"

She plunged on, not even looking where she went, just heeding the urge to run. Which was probably why she didn't realize the pond was so near. And why she didn't see it until it was too late. Frankly, she couldn't have planned her plunge into the icy water better if she'd tried. Like a child taking a summer dip, she tumbled in, the shoreline dropping away so abruptly, it felt like her head sank before her feet.

Gracious heavens. Her head did sink before her feet.

She gasped, bubbles rising up around her. Too late she realized she should have held her breath while she could. With no hands to paddle toward the surface, and her skirts tangling in her legs, the thought penetrated that she might drown.

What a disappointment.

Oddly enough, however, the thought didn't panic her, although a part of her realized that it should scare the life out of her. She'd heard tell that people sometimes saw their life flash before them at such moments. Ariel waited patiently for that to happen, but it didn't. Instead she thought about odd things, things like why was a butterfly called a butter fly? It didn't look like butter. And butter certainly didn't fly. And where exactly did all the flies go when it rained? They all just disappeared when drops started falling.

And then to her great relief she heard another splash followed by a rush of bubbles as a body landed near her own.

Nathan.

Oh, ho, that annoying voice sang inside her head. *When did he become Nathan again?*

When he became her last chance of rescue, that's when, she firmly answered.

Arms clasped her waist, then propelled her to the surface. Their heads emerged at the same time, Ariel inhaling a deep, stagnant breath of air. Nathan held her that way for a long moment as she gasped in an out. Gracious. This must be what a fish felt like when it was taken out of water.

Somehow he managed to pull them to safety, then up on the bank. Ariel shimmied further from the edge. Two arms clasped her from behind, tugging her to him.

Well. As far as escapes go, this one was a rather dismal attempt. Of course, it was her first attempt ever, and so she supposed she shouldn't expect great things.

She tried to move away from him, trying not to blush as she realized their positions. His legs straddled either side of her, his arms encircling her from behind. She wished he'd quit panting in her ear. Oddly enough, the feel of that breath as it caressed the shell of her flesh made her begin to tingle. She shot into a sitting position. No, no, no. She did not still desire him. She couldn't possibly. The man was a liar and a scoundrel.

He'd kidnapped her!

She tried to move away, but his arm tightened around her again. Masculine legs lay on either side of her, his warmth shielding her.

It was then that she realized where her tied hands lay, or rather, what they rested against.

They were, heavens, they were snug against his manhood.

She blushed. Wiggled a bit to try and get away from him again, only to be pulled closer still.

"Stop moving," he said.

"Unhand me."

A poor choice of words, given the location of her limbs. She looked at him over her shoulder.

His silver eyes glittered with anger and something else, something she refused to identify. Besides, it couldn't really be lust, not after all they'd been through.

"I think not, Lady Ariel," and his voice raked her with its anger. "You'll be fortunate if I ever let you out of my sight again." He moved away from her, keeping his hand on the crook of her arm.

Ariel wheezed with relief at the loss of contact. That was better. "And just how long are you planning on holding me?"

"As long as it takes to find the location of my brother."

"And if my father can't help you?"

He didn't answer, but she could feel the tension that resonated from his body. At that moment she forgot about male body parts, forgot about the cold chill that had begun to rack her body. For the first time she wondered what it would be like to lose one's brother. Would she not do whatever it took to save Phoebe? Granted, Phoebe was a cousin, but she felt like a sister nonetheless.

She ducked to the side, tilting her head to stare back at him again. Their gazes met, his as cold as the lake he'd just retrieved her from, a lingering something floating in the depths of his eyes.

Was it desperation? She thought perhaps it might be. And with the customary sympathy that always filled her when she saw someone or something in need, she found herself saying, "I'm sorry," before she admitted how ridiculous it was to apologize to one's captor, especially one who'd tried to use her in such a way.

His gaze narrowed.

"I'm sorry that captain stole your brother," she forged on, despite her mental castigation. "It must be awful not knowing where he is or even if he's alive."

If she'd known the effect her words would have, she might have considered saying them earlier, for he pulled away from her, then jerked her to her feet.

Without a word he pointed her toward the brush, then propelled her toward the house.

10

A few minutes later they neared the house, but not as quickly as she would have liked. Gracious, but she was as wet as the bottom of a canoe. Worse, she had no change of clothing. She might well have frozen to death by night's end.

"I don't supposed you thought to bring me a change of clothes?" and her teeth chattered with every word.

He didn't say anything.

"An extra coat for yourself?" One she could borrow?

Silence again.

"Perhaps some blankets?"

"When we get inside."

Well, at least there was that. And a fire. A nice, warm fire.

They entered the house, Trevain pausing by the front door as he retrieved something. A bag of supplies, she noticed. One she hadn't seen before. He didn't even glance at her as he clutched the burlap bag in one hand, then grabbed her by the arm again, leading her through the front door and to the right. The discarded lantern sat near a doorway, the sudden light making her squint and blink away spots. Trevain let her go, stepping behind her to nudge her in the back toward a nearby room.

It was a disaster, not that Ariel had expected it to look different from the rest of the house. Gloomy, dust-covered windows allowed muted moonlight to filter through one side. Bare walls that bore the outline of long-gone portraits surrounded the other three sides. No furniture looked to be in sight. Spiderwebs hung from a wood and iron chandelier with curved arms reaching up. Ariel wondered if it was a good or a bad thing that she couldn't see the webs' inhabitants creeping about. Probably a bad thing.

"Here."

She turned toward him, just in time to be hit full in the face by something, a something she couldn't catch with her hands as they were tied behind her back.

"Thank you," she murmured, feeling sorely vexed by his oversight.

He grumbled something under his breath, bent down to retrieve the blanket he'd tossed at her and said, "Turn."

She turned. And all he did was touch her with his fingers. Jolts leaped up and down her arms, the same kind of static that danced through her veins during a particularly wild storm. She inhaled sharply. Gracious heaven above, she did still feel desire for him. What a nodcock. Obviously she enjoyed the company of men who threw her over. She sighed in impatience with herself.

Nathan must have thought her sigh a gasp of pain, for he gentled his touch, then murmured soothingly, the words wafting across her ear and then her cheek. His breath was sweet, she realized. As if he'd just nibbled a piece of fruit.

A final jerk on the ropes, and first one hand sprang free, then the other. He turned her toward him, rubbing her wrists.

She really wished he wouldn't do that.

She really, really wished it.

But God had obviously decided she'd sinned one too many times, because Nathan kept touching her. Short of jerking her arms away, she was helpless to move. She'd be damned if she'd let him see how much his touch still affected her.

"Might we start a fire?" she asked on a wheeze, hoping and praying he would take the hint and let her go.

Silver eyes met her own, his face less ominous-looking of a sudden. "If I start a fire, it might alert the locals to our presence."

"And that would be bad?"

He didn't say anything, not that she'd expected him to. Nathan Trevain had grown good at conveying his thoughts with a single look in

the past few hours. There was his you-are-noth-
ing-but-a-bloody-blueblood look. And his be-
quiet-or-I-shall-gag-you look. Right now he gave
her a I-don't-care-if-your-arse-freezes-to-the-castle-
walls look. She sighed, her breath a stream of
white vapor. To think, she'd actually thought
him her friend once upon a time, but she should
have known once upon a times only existed in
fairy tales.

Just then a giant shiver racked her body.

"Why are you shaking?"

"Because I'm bloody cold," she answered.

He frowned.

"Truly, Mr. Trevain, I do believe I shall need a
fire."

"No fire."

"Then I will need to remove this gown."

"Fine," he snapped.

She stiffened, another chill sending her muscles into spasms. "What do you mean, fine?"

"Remove your dress."

Her eyes must have bulged. "I beg your pardon?"

He gave her a look of impatience. "You were
the one who suggested it. Since you seem to be
so thin-blooded, it looks to be a fine suggestion."

Hoist with her own petar. But truly, she
thought, as another chill racked her body, if she
didn't do something fast, she would indeed
freeze to death.

"Very well, turn around, and I will disrobe."

He gave her a look, one meant to question her integrity. "You will not try to escape if I turn my back?"

"If I try and escape, you will find my dead blue body on the road in the morning."

For an instant, such a brief instant that she thought she might have imagined it, a flash of amusement shone in his eyes. But of course, that couldn't be. Besides, he had turned around before she could be sure.

"I'll need your help with the lacings beforehand."

He turned back, and now his eyes had a very definite glimmer of impatience in them. "Give me your back."

She did as asked, approaching such a state of discomfort that she would have shown him her legs if it meant getting out of the sodden dress. The chills came with more frequency now, so severe she clenched her jaw to keep her teeth from chattering.

"Please hu-hurry," she stuttered.

His hands felt hot against her neck, and how that could be when he was just as wet as she was she had no idea, but just then she was tempted to press those hands all over her freezing-cold body.

"You're trembling all over."

"I kn-know," she answered.

She felt his hands move lower, felt the dress begin to part.

"Here," he said, turning.

It was a sign of how cold she felt that she didn't even flinch when she felt his heated hands at the neck of her gown. Nor did she move when he pulled it off her shoulders. She closed her eyes. She was cold. So cold.

He jerked the dress down.

Her eyes sprang open. "What are you doing?"

"Taking your dress off."

"I can do it."

"Can you?"

She nodded, but Nathan noted her body shook so much, he doubted she even realized how cold she'd become. But he'd not lived with winter snows for most of his life not to know the signs of someone who had become too cold for her own good. How she had done it so quickly he had no idea.

"Remove your petticoat. And your hoops," he ordered.

"B-but—"

"Do it."

He turned his back again, hearing the rustle of the sodden fabric. Damnation, but women wore a lot of clothes.

"Are you done?"

"Y-yes," she said in a small voice.

He turned back to her. She stood there shivering in nothing but her chemise and corset, her arms crossed in front of her as if he had magic vision that could see through fabric. Frankly, she shouldn't have been concerned about his seeing through the fabric; she should have worried that he could see every delectable contour of her body—which he could.

He gritted his teeth, telling himself he didn't care that he could see the outline of her flesh. She was nothing to him. Nothing.

But he still looked away as he removed his coat.

"Wh-what are you d-doing?"

"I'm going to warm you."

She tried to move back, but she was so cold her legs buckled. Nathan caught her just before she fell, tugging her up against him. Her body felt like a wall of snow. Demme, but her temperature had dropped quickly.

"Here," he said, pulling her to a wall. If they leaned up against it, they could use it to keep their backs from getting chilled by the musty breeze that blew through the room. She could hardly move now, so he scooped her up in his arms. She didn't even protest. Her wet hair slapped against his arm, and even the silky strands felt cold.

Setting her down gently, he then went for the blankets. She'd closed her eyes again, her alabaster skin pale as parchment. Bending down, he placed one blanket around her, then used the other to dry her hair. Her eyes didn't open. That concerned him.

"Ariel."

They still didn't open.

"Ariel," he repeated, shaking her.

"What?" she cried, eyes opening, those golden orbs glowing with irritation.

He told himself he felt relief because she hadn't fallen into a cold sleep, not because of any concern. He wouldn't feel concern for a woman who'd deceived him as she had.

Ah, but you deceived her too.

And what did that matter? he argued. He, at least, did so for his brother. She had no reason other than that she had a treacherous heart, like the rest of her sex. Bloody hell, that he'd begun to like her still rankled like a sore thumb.

"I merely wanted to insure that you had not expired," he said, when she continued to glare up at him.

"I assure you, s-sir, had I expired, I w-would be haunting your from the g-grave by now."

He ignored the threat. The chit was too cold for her own good. "Here," he said, jerking the blanket off her.

She looked about to protest, but then her eyes widened when he plopped down next to her, covering them both with the blanket, but not before he pulled her into his arms. Damnation, but the wall behind them was cold, too. He shoved his arm between her back and the wood paneling.

Foolish woman. She could die and ruin his whole kidnapping.

Ah, but she feels good.

So would opium, if you took too much of it, and it could kill you, too.

But Ariel wouldn't kill him. She didn't have a killer's heart. Just a treacherous one, and a damn delectable body, one he found hard not to think about as he snuggled her next to his own.

"You're so w-warm," she murmured.

"Yes, and you are so cold," he answered.

She nodded, but a few minutes later she wasn't shivering so violently. He pulled her closer still, the better to warm her, he told himself. She didn't protest, even slipped a hand between his arm and his side. Hell's bells. Any ardor he might have felt—and he told himself he didn't feel any—would have died an icy death at the feel of that cold, cold limb squeezed between his flesh.

Slowly, too slowly for Nathan's peace of mind, she stopped shivering. The trouble was he'd begun to feel things, too. Like her thigh pressed against his own. Or her breath as it warmed the skin of his neck. Against his better judgment, against all damnable reason, he felt his body begin to stir. He closed his eyes, on the verge of muttering a frustrated oath. How the hell could he desire her after all she'd done?

He was on the verge of getting up angrily when she said, "Nathan?"

"Yes," he answered, having to grit out the word.

"How did your face get that way?"

He jerked away from her as if her body had turned to ice. Her eyes snapped open. The look on her face was one of surprise.

"I didn't mean to offend you, I just wanted—"

He stood, tossing the blanket over her. "The question is not a good one, my lady."

He saw her swallow. Saw her nod. "And while we're in a chatty mood, let us get a few things straight. You are now my captive. Any kindness I may have shown you in the past was purely to lure you into thinking I was your friend. I am not your friend. Nor will I ever be."

He expected her reaction to be anger, he truly did; instead all he saw was hurt.

"I see," she murmured. She tilted her chin up, just as he'd seen her do when confronted by society's maltreatment of her. "Thank you for clarifying the matter. I confess myself relieved, for I was about to suggest you and I become blood brother and sister, and I do so hate the sight of blood."

Her sarcasm wasn't lost on him. Damn, but he liked the way she snapped back at him.

"See that you remember my words," he warned.

"Oh, I will, Nathan Trevain. I will."

Minutes later he'd retied her wrists, wound the blanket around her and sternly warned her not to move as he lay down next to her.

Ariel would have been glad to comply, except she was bloody well uncomfortable wrapped up like yesterday's meal.

Wiggling a bit, she tried to loosen the bonds. But with her hands tied behind her back, her struggles were as effective as trying to untie stays with teeth. It rained outside. Despite the doors he'd wedged back into place, the smell of wet leaves and sodden ground permeated the room. She was cold again in her still damp chemise and growing colder by the minute. She tried to shift in the blanket, but only ended up sinking deeper into the roll, her vision partly blocked by the gray edges of the fabric.

Bullocks. Now what?

"Stop wiggling," he growled.

She stilled, blowing a hank of dank hair out of her face before peeking over at him. He hadn't moved. The hateful man looked blissfully comfortable. His shirt was already dry, she noted, having no wet layers beneath it, unlike her chemise and corset.

When she noticed him still staring at her, she lifted a brow, shooting him a scathing look of impatience. "I would love to stop wiggling, sir. But it's a bit uncomfortable with every limb save my ears tied."

"Then don't think about them being tied."

"Are you mad?"

He still hadn't moved. Impossible man.

"I had no idea English women were so delicate," he drawled.

The words got her back up, as she supposed they were meant to do. Delicate, indeed. Why, she'd once spent a whole evening out of doors. Of course, she'd accidentally locked herself out of her cousin's home, but that was beside the point. She wiggled some more.

"Can you not sit still for a minute?"

"Can you not keep quiet for a minute?"

He opened his eyes, tilted his head a bit to peer at her. "Go to sleep, Lady D'Archer. We've a long day ahead of us tomorrow."

"If you think it easy to sleep this way, sir, than I encourage you to do it."

"I have done it."

"Really?" she asked, not believing it for a minute.

His eyes narrowed. "I was a prisoner of war for several months, my lady," and the way he said "my lady" was akin to the way most people said pig saliva. "A guest of His Majesty the King's army in Charleston. It's where I learned to love your fellow countrymen so much, for they were quite generous hosts."

Her mouth dropped open, a part of her thinking he'd made the story up just to suit the moment. Then again it was entirely possible he'd been taken prisoner. Such things happened in war. "Is that where you learned your manners?"

"No, it's where I learned to hate anything British." And with that, he lay down again, ending their conversation.

Ariel started at him with narrowed eyes. Cad. Blackguard.

But when she closed her eyes, she only heard his words again:

It's where I learned to hate anything British.

Is that how his face had been wounded? Had something happened while he'd been a prisoner? She settled herself beneath the blanket, telling herself it didn't matter how it happened. A pox on him. He deserved to be taken prisoner. What was more, it was not possible to sleep this way.

But despite the anger she felt, she was human enough to admit that he was also a man whose brother had disappeared. He'd crossed an ocean to find that brother, and though she told herself that this should not make her feel sympathetic or even a wee bit sorry for him after all he'd done, a small, tiny smidgen of her did feel sympathetic.

Bloody stupid man.

She turned her head, studying him, her eyes somehow drawn to his face. The good side of his face was turned to her, his lids still shut, the man feigning sleep. He had a rather strong jaw, she thought, not at all like Archie's. Phoebe had said Archie had a jaw like a catfish and the lips and whiskers to match. But Phoebe always said such things about Archie. She hated the man for what he'd done to her.

Ariel shifted even more, facing him fully now, knowing she should stop looking, but unable to stop herself. For a moment she became intrigued by the fact that no frown lines marred his face, no scowl curled his lips, no sneer lifted the corner of his mouth. With his face so relaxed, his cheekbones seemed less prominent, softer, younger.

It struck her then that Nathan Trevain, heir apparent to the duke of Davenport, really was a handsome man. Oh, not beautiful like the sculpture of Apollo she seen in a book. No. Nathan was handsome in a wild, untamed sort of way.

He shifted. Ariel caught her breath. He turned to his side, facing her. Gracious, his lips almost brushed hers, he was so close. She prayed he wouldn't open his eyes, but as always happened when she truly wanted something, the opposite happened.

He opened them.

"Bloody hell," he roared, sitting up. "What do you think you're doing so near to me?"

"I . . . ah . . ." She'd been caught staring. "My, ah, arms have become numb, so I moved to my side."

It was a lie. She knew it was a lie. He knew it was a lie. Queen Charlotte would have known it was a lie.

"Get comfortable facing the other direction," he growled.

She blinked. Nathan sitting above her was a sight. Suddenly, she felt as if the blanket was wrapped around her too tight.

"Go back to sleep, my lady."

Yes, indeed, she should.

She watched as without another glance he lay down again, turned his back to her and closed his eyes.

Ariel felt like a broom whose handle had been cut. Gracious, how was she to get through this night? She could hear him breathing, and though she told herself to ignore him, that the man was a liar and a bounder, she discovered it was nearly impossible to do as she ordered. Moisture from outside stirred lazy air currents, currents that brought the smell of him to her nose. His scent was unlike any she'd smelled before. Unique. Wholly Nathan Trevain. It reminded her of their time together in the garden.

She groaned. She was certainly in trouble if she found the smell of Nathan Trevain attractive. She should hate the smell of him. Truth be told, she should hate everything about him. Yet no matter what she told herself, she only became more and more aware of him . . . of the way he sounded as he breathed, of the way his warm body felt lying next to her. That he slept was patently obvious by the way he inhaled deep breaths of air. The sound was rhythmic, foreign and so utterly masculine she found herself wanting to listen.

Escape, screamed her mind.

Yes, escape. A most excellent notion. Without another thought she rolled away.

She wiggled the blanket loose, then pushed herself to her feet gently, so as not to startle him or worse, lose her balance and fall atop him.

Heaven knows what he'd do if he found her trying to escape.

The blanket slid down to the floor. Ariel side-hopped over it, peeking glances at her captor the whole time. When that was done, she used a shuffling motion to move away from him, feeling rather like an octopus with its legs tied. She had to move at the pace of a snail. At this rate the sun would rise and birds chirp before she made it to the door.

She glanced at her captor again, only to pause. Gracious, he'd begun to sweat. She could see big beads of it on his brow. Curiosity made her stare, light illuminating features gone suddenly gaunt. That gave her pause, too. He jerked. She started, then chastised herself for being such a ninny. He was asleep. A troubled sleep, for his head thrashed back and forth, but a sleep nonetheless. Her own head tilted as she stared down at him. What demons haunted his soul? she wondered, for it was obvious that some did. Well, that was as it should be. He deserved whatever horrible dreams his past brought him.

She turned away—well, shuffled around, really.

A hand reached out to stop her.

It spun her back to face him. Ariel gulped, for the man must have bounded to his feet.

He looked livid. Absolutely put-her-over-his-knees livid.

"Minx," he spat.

"Unhand me."

"You were trying to escape," he accused.

"Of course I was. You kidnapped me. I'm supposed to try and escape."

He looked like he didn't know what to say to that outstanding piece of logic. They stared, Ariel wondering what he would do next. Apparently stare some more.

"Lie back down," he ordered.

"If it's all the same to you, I should prefer to sleep standing up."

"Lie back down," he shouted.

She jumped. "But I—"

"Now," he shot. "Or do I have to put you on the floor myself?"

She gulped. "No." Please no. She didn't want him touching her. Moving back, she carefully lowered herself to the filthy floor, feeling rather like a sacrificial lamb. But that feeling faded when he lifted the hem of her chemise. She shot away, horrified. "What are you doing?"

"Tying you to me."

"You're what?"

He held up a rope. "Tying this end of the rope around your ankle and this end around my waist, so you cannot try and escape again."

Bullocks. If he did that, then she would not be able to try and escape.

Well, yes, Ariel, that would be his point.

"Very well, sir," she said, knowing that to protest would do her little good. "I give you leave to lift my chemise."

He stared at her a moment longer, seemed to

grit his teeth, then lifted her skirt, tying the rope around her left ankle, then the other end around his waist.

When he was finished, he straightened, saying, "Get some rest."

Not bloody likely, Ariel thought, closing her eyes. How could she sleep next to such a cad? Likely she'd lie awake all night.

She rolled to her side. Instantly she fell asleep.

II

He was going to die.

Wess Trevain supposed the realization ought to bring him pain, but he was in so much pain now, he didn't care.

"Flog 'im again," cried a man.

Wess tensed, waiting for the pain to pierce his flesh again, that momentary instant of agony as acute as the sting of a jellyfish.

And then it hit. Through sheer force of will, he didn't cry out. He'd never give these British the pleasure of hearing him cry out. They'd kidnapped him from the deck of his ship, forced him to serve in their damnable navy, taken him from his family, his home, his homeland. They would not hear him scream. Still, a small moan escaped.

The crowd murmured at the sound, though some of the men remained quiet. Those he'd made tentative peace with in the past months.

Those he could count on as friends, despite his forced tenure aboard the HMS *Destiny*.

The lash fell again.

Once again he couldn't stop the gasp that escaped, though God, how he tried. Heat seared its way down the back of his bare legs. Someone cheered, instantly silenced by one of the officers standing to his left.

Again the lash fell.

Twenty more to go.

Then fifteen.

By now he was crying out in pain, tears escaping from his eyes. Then suddenly he found himself cut down, his body falling to the deck.

"Run him the gauntlet," intoned a well-modulated voice.

The crowd broke out into murmurs. Wess well knew why. Running the gauntlet was a punishment usually reserved for thieves; so was flogging. But he wasn't a thief, he was a deserter, and by the Articles of War should be subject to a court-martial, not a flogging at the hands of the crew. But apparently Captain Pike cared not for maritime law.

If he doubted his death before, he knew it now. Ten, perhaps fifteen days hence he would succumb to an infection. Or perhaps malnutrition when they sent him to the hold to "contemplate his crimes."

Two men came forward, lifted him, causing another unwanted cry to escape his lips. They strapped him to a wheeled seat, then dragged him toward the crew. Wess knew what came next. He watched as the bosun handed the cat-o'-nine-tails to the nearest crew member. It was a brutish seaman Wess knew well. The man had never liked him. None of them did, with the exception of his five fellow countrymen.

"Bloody patriot," the brute muttered, raising the lash.

It fell with more force than any of the bosun's blows. The pain never went away. He never entered that plane some men talked about, that state where no pain existed. He felt each blow, felt each piece of leather lick at his flesh, tear into it, only to crack through the air to land again. He tried, dear God he tried, to let his spirit float free. Tried to think of things familiar and dear. His father. His brother.

Nathan. I hope they didn't kill you, too.

"Bastard," cried another man. "Your friends killed me da'." The cords fell.

"I lost half me family to one of yur troops." It fell again.

And on and on it went. Wess lost track of how many men he passed. The strands were raised, brought down, then lifted again.

Suddenly it stopped. Pray God it was over.

"I can't," said a familiar old voice.

Wess lifted his head. A wizened face stared down at him, two front teeth missing. Samuel.

"Don't make me do it," begged the man who'd taught him how to tie his first knot.

"You must," Wess rasped.

"I can't, Captain," he near sobbed. "Lord, when I looks at what they done to you—"

"Do it," snapped the man holding his chair.

Do it, echoed Wess's eyes. For if he didn't, they both knew what would happen. Samuel would suffer a similar fate, only worse, for the British crew members didn't take kindly to men holding back.

Samuel raised the tails. The nine ends shook in his grasp. "I'm so sorry," he murmured, tears gathering in his eyes.

The whip came down. It wasn't a hard blow, but it was enough. Wess gasped, his body beyond him now, his reactions automatic.

He lapsed into unconsciousness.

Water brought him back, salt water that trickled down his back and brought fresh waves of agony. He waited for more blows to fall, but apparently the captain was through with him. Through blurry eyes, Wess saw the bastard raise his hand and turn toward the crew.

"Let this be a lesson to those of you not anxious to serve aboard my ship." He clasped his hands behind his back. "I will brook no deserters aboard this ship. The next man who tries to leave will suffer the same punishment." He let his words sink in, then turned to Wess. "Take him below."

12

Ariel decided the next morning that sleeping on a dusty floor wrapped up like a sausage did not, as a rule, put a person in a good mood. It didn't help that she'd only managed to doze as she'd fought to get comfortable. It also didn't help that Mr. Trevain had awoken looking as refreshed and as relaxed as a man with eight hours of sleep. It irked her no end, the only thought to console her that she would take pleasure in seeing him bound and gagged one day. Soon. Thank goodness he'd untied her limbs. They still buzzed as if asleep, but she had some sensation in them. Jolly wonderful.

She studied him. He'd donned his coat again, not black, she suddenly realized, but dark, dark gray. It hung to just above his knees. His dusty-from-the-floor fawn breeches pouring into black boots. And yet despite the rather plain look of his attire, there was a brief instant, half a heartbeat, really, when she thought him quite handsome, but then he turned to her. His eyes glared. He turned ugly again. Or so she told herself.

"How long are we going to stay here?" she asked.

"We're not."

She felt her brows lift. "We're not."

He shook his head.

"Well, then, where are we going?"

"To Bettenshire."

"Bettenshire! Why, that's the town where I live."

"I know," he answered, pinning her with a stare.

Understanding dawned. "You want to search the house there, too."

"I do."

"I'm surprised you haven't already. You are, after all, a master spy."

"And how do you know that?"

"I asked someone at the Admiralty."

"How thorough of you."

She nodded.

"Then it may interest you to know that I already have searched the house, though not as thoroughly as I would have liked. It was difficult with your staff in residence. Now, however, I have you. You will dismiss the staff then aid me in my search."

"I will not," she huffed.

He took a step toward her. His face and the scar, something she'd hardly noticed this morning, suddenly looked ominous. "You will aid me, my lady, for if you do not, I shall send word to have your cousin taken from her home and disposed of."

"And how do you propose to do that?"

"Simple," he snapped. "I arranged for some-one to do exactly that, should I send word."

Her mouth dropped open again.

"One of the benefits of having been in battle, my lady. Think of every possibility. I reasoned last eve that you might be less than cooperative, therefore before we left, I arranged a bit of insur-ance. 'Twas simple enough, for there are any number of miscreants willing to do a job, should there be enough blunt at stake."

He wouldn't dare.

But mightn't he?

He hadn't thought twice about using her. Or kidnapping her. The realization left her reeling, but she raised her chin nonetheless, determined to endure her time with him with dignity.

"Very well, sir. I shall do as you order."

They engaged in a staring war. Ariel was pleased to note she was not the first to look away. He turned, bending down to pick up his bag of supplies.

"When do we leave?" she asked.

"As soon as you're ready."

"I'm ready."

"We'll eat first."

"I'm not hungry."

His patience looked to have snapped. He strode forward. Ariel tensed. When he stood before her, the long, tall length of him looming over her, she swallowed.

"You will eat when I tell you to eat."

Yes, she rather thought she would. "As you wish," she croaked. "But what is for breakfast?"

"This," he answered, holding out dried sticks.

"Bark?" she asked.

"No. Dried beef. Here." He held a stick out to her.

Ariel tried to hold out her hand, she truly did, but the bloody thing wouldn't do as she commanded.

"Open you hand," he ordered impatiently.

"I'm trying," Ariel shouted back, her temper snapping. "If you hadn't tied my wrists so tightly, I might be able to use them."

"Use what?"

"My hands, sir. They are numb. You tied them too tight last eve."

Instantly guilt rose in his eyes. Ariel thought she imagined it.

"Let me see," he said, shoving the beef back in his pocket. Ariel decided then and there she wasn't eating the stuff. His pocket, indeed. Goodness knows what'd been in it. Then she gasped as he grabbed her wrists.

"They're bruised," he observed.

"Very observant of you, sir."

His touch was surprisingly gentle. Then again, a club could have been pounding on her hands and she doubted she'd have felt it.

"Why did you not say something?"

"Because I didn't notice it until you untied them."

He nodded, and Ariel became transfixed by the look on his face. His whole expression had gentled, his face relaxed on both sides, a look of genuine concern came into his eyes. Hmph. He began to rub her hands with his fingers. Ariel almost groaned, not because she enjoyed it— heavens, no—because her bloody wrists hurt.

"Why did you stop?" she asked, watching as he knelt before her.

"I'm checking your ankles."

"Oh." Her ankles. She almost jumped back as he lifted her chemise, but then the touch of his fingers sent a jolt through her. Heavens, she'd never had a man touch her ankles before. She stared down at his bent head, telling herself now was the perfect opportunity to escape. He was on his knees before her, a position every man should aspire to, or so Phoebe told her. If she could find a piece of furniture—She turned her head, searching.

Almost as if reading her mind, he looked up.

She looked back. It felt as if she'd been caught with an uplifted club in her hands.

"I wouldn't advise it, my lady."

"Advise what?" she asked, feigning innocence. Goodness, how had he read her mind so easily?

"Whatever it is you're planning."

"Whatever could I possibly be planning?"

She wondered if she could get her hands

around his thick neck, perhaps choke him. Yes. She could throttle the life out of him. That would be deeply satisfying after all he'd done to her.

But he stood up again before she could gain the courage to do something so bold. Her ankles tingled where he'd touched them. She wiggled her toes experimentally, thoughts of throttling him fading as she realized that her hands did, indeed, feel better. Besides, she wasn't exactly certain she had the strength to choke him.

"Your hands will feel better if you start using them."

"They will?"

"Aye, but I warn you, one wrong move, and I shall bind them again."

Pray God, no. She swallowed. Still plotting, but agreeing nonetheless. She was a captive, and captives had a God-given right to plot their escape. Certainly she had no idea how to accomplish such a feat, but the day was young. She had merely to wait, certain that the opportunity would present itself. He was, after all, a man and prone to mistakes.

So she waited, biding her time as she dressed in her damp clothes.

"Come," he ordered, when she was done, scooping up his bag of supplies without even a backward glance.

Hmph.

She followed him, her body aching after sleeping on the floor all night. But moving felt good. It warmed her a bit. The air inside the room was chilly. The house looked even more run-down in the light of day. In fact, she felt a bit frightened that they'd dared to spend the night between its rotted beams. Gracious, they could have fallen through the floor, or worse, had the ceiling fall upon them.

God should be so kind to her.

Sunlight did not improve the outside, either. It was a half-hour past dawn, judging by the gray light surrounding them. Clouds covered the sky. The morning air was rather chilly and smelled of vegetation. She rubbed her shoulders, following Nathan on his trek around overgrown weeds, but she couldn't resist a peek back, stopping in her tracks at what she saw. Oh, the shape of the house was pretty enough—square turrets on one side, round ones on the other—but that was all that was pleasant. Crumbling chimneys tumbled upon the roof. A neighboring outbuilding had completely caved in on one side, the granite stones that had once been its walls tossed on the ground like discarded teeth. Overgrown trees obscured the front of the house.

"It looks like someone unburied Pompeii."

"Welcome to my home, my lady."

"*Your* home?" she asked, hurrying to catch up to him.

He nodded, his eyes clearly disgusted by the disrepair. And, really, it was quite unfair that his eyes were so beautiful in the morning light. Grays and blues and black all mixed in like liquid mercury. Her eyes were probably military-coat red.

"It belonged to my father," he said.

She lifted a brow. "Did your father have a penchant for children's horror stories?"

He turned to look at her. "No, my father had no interest in this place or in anything to do with the Davenport name. And when he left England, my uncle vowed to let the place go to rot."

"I take it your father and your uncle did not see eye to eye?"

He looked down at her. "You would take it correctly."

She felt curiosity overcome her before she could stop her tongue from saying, "Why not?"

"Because 'tis none of your business."

"No, but I am curious to know, and since we're walking, you may as well share it."

She made her way around another overgrown weed. Only they were not really weeds at all. No. They were overgrown topiaries. Her brows lifted. At one point the estate must have been quite beautiful. How sad that someone would let it fall into such disrepair. The topiaries had become so huge, he was forced to zigzag around them in an odd pattern.

"Mr. Trevain?"

He stopped. She almost slammed into his back. "If I tell you, will you promise to be quiet for the rest of the trip?"

She drew back a bit. "Well, I suppose—"

"Good." He faced forward. But it was a while before he began, a while during which Ariel wondered if he'd changed his mind. But then he said, "When rumors began to surface of a possible war between the colonies and England, my uncle was very verbal in his disapproval of our family's participation."

She felt her spirits lift, glad for some odd, ridiculous reason that he would share the tale.

"The duke sent my father a letter telling him that if the report were true that we intended to fight for the patriots, he hoped that our legs would be shot off during the first volley."

"That was rather rude," Ariel said.

"Indeed. The man had a great deal of nerve. My uncle had all but disowned my father when he came to the colonies. He treated his younger brother, my father, as a pauper, refusing to give him the stipend that was his right by birth, although he could not withhold the courtesy title."

Ariel felt her eyes widen. "So being a villain runs in your family?"

He frowned, ignoring her insult. "Needless to say, there was no love lost between the two sides. Thus my father was surprised to receive such a letter from his brother, a man who'd communicated with him exactly twice. Once to inform my father he'd been cut off, and the other this missive."

"He sounds perfectly dreadful."

"He is, which is why I was so incensed." She saw his lips tighten before he continued, "I decided to show the man how little we cared for his directive. Upon first occasion I asked our cook for the leg bone of a cow—"

"Oh, Mr. Trevain, you didn't?" she said, instantly surmising what he'd done.

"I did. I had that leg bone mounted with a plaque beneath it." He turned to her. "Would you like to know what it said?"

She nodded, feeling a smile begin to build. How odd to be smiling with one's captor, especially one who'd used her so ill. The smile faded.

"It said that we would rather be patriots with one leg than royalists with two."

She stared at him a full two seconds before the words sank in. Then she threw back her head and laughed. She couldn't help it. She just laughed. "Oh, Mr. Trevain, how perfectly dreadful."

"It was, but I laughed for weeks afterward as I envisioned his reaction to my little package. Unfortunately, I hadn't told my father what I'd done. Several months later he received a missive back, a missive that had obviously been written in the midst of a rage."

"What did it say?"

"According to my father, it was most unpleasant, although I never did learn exactly what the contents were, more's the pity. I expected my father to be angry, but much to my surprise, he clapped me on the back, told me 'Well done,' then sent me on my way."

Ariel stared at him, wide-eyed, before erupting into laughter again. "I should have liked your father, I think."

It was as if ice had been thrown on his mood. "He was killed at the battle of Trenton."

"Oh, sir, I'm so sorry."

They had reached the main road. Ariel wondered where the horses were. She had assumed they were tied somewhere, but they weren't.

Trevain stopped and looked at her. "If you attempt to stop any passersby, it will go ill for you."

Gone went her smile. Really, the man knew how to spoil a lady's mood.

"I hardly think I shall have time to flag someone down if we are riding fast enough."

"We aren't riding."

She shrugged. "Well, then, you may rest assured I promise not to fling my body out of any carriages, either."

"We won't be in a carriage."

"Then how will we get to Bettenshire?"

"We walk."

She stopped. He stopped, too.

"Walk?"

He lifted his right brow. "Aye."

"Are you mad?"

He lifted the right side of his mouth in a damnable smirk that made Ariel want to poke his eyes out.

"I shall walk, my lady, to the local village where I will secure a horse for us to ride."

She felt her spirits lift. "You will walk?"

"Aye, me."

"But what about me?"

"You will stay here."

She stiffened. Oh, no.

No, no, no.

"Mr. Trevain, really, I think there must be a much better way—"

He grabbed her by the arm. She yelped.

He tied her to a tree.

Bloody bastard. Bloody scoundrel. Tied her to a bloody tree far enough away from the road so that no one could see her. At least she'd been able to loosen the gag somewhat in the past half-hour. Now she could make some noise. With any luck at all someone might hear her, for she had every intention of trying to gain someone's attention, despite his threat that it would go ill for her if she did. How ill could ill be after all she'd been through? She inhaled a lungful of air, but what emerged past the filthy-tasting gag was nothing more than a muffled gurgle. That irritated her so much she began to struggle against her bonds in earnest.

"Well, well, well. Don't you look a sight."

She stilled, long strands of hair covering her face. She flicked her head, banging it against the tree trunk in the process. He'd chosen a giant oak with a huge canopy of leaves to hold her hostage, its base so wide that with her arms pulled back behind her, Ariel felt rather like a figurehead on the prow of a ship. Worse, she just knew little bugs with lots of legs were crawling down the neck of her dress. They swarmed through the air, buzzing by her face once or twice before landing. She could feel their horrid little legs now, the things no doubt calling to their cronies to come feast on the silly human stuck to a tree.

"Bloothy brute. Bloothy beast," she screeched. "Geth off thath horsth an unthy me this inthance."

"Do what, my lady?" He cupped a hand to his ear. "I'm sorry, I can't understand you."

She narrowed her eyes. Rogue. She would get even with him one day.

"What's the matter, my lady. Cat got your tongue?"

And now he baited her with his words. The bounder. "I thaid unthy me this instant."

"Un-thigh you? I don't believe I know how to un-thigh a lady. Now stroke a thigh, that is something I'm most good at."

Ooo. She stamped a foot. He knew well and bloody good what she meant. "Un-thie me," she spat out slowly and succinctly.

He rested his arm against the pommel, the expression in his eyes so filled with mock confusion that she stamped her foot once more.

"Un-thigh me," he muttered. "Un-thigh me," he repeated again before suddenly stiffening as if enlightened. "Oh, I see. You would like me to untie you."

She glared, feeling her facial muscles flex beneath the gag, knowing well he'd understood her the first time she'd said it.

"Of course, my lady. As you wish."

He threw a leg over the horse, hardly making a sound as he landed in the ankle-deep grass, but he took his bloody time getting to her, running the stirrup irons up the leathers, first on one side, then on the other. When he finished, he led the horse toward her, stopping a few feet away.

"Hmm. I must say, you do look a sight. Frankly, I'm tempted to leave you here just so I won't have to listen to your chatter all day."

At that moment, at that very precise moment, she wanted to kill him. At the very least she wanted to fling cow dung upon him. There was a pile of it nearby, for she smelled it.

Instead she forced herself to stand there as he appeared to contemplate his options. His eyes traveled up the length of her from her muddy hem and torn skirt, pausing for an instant at the curve of her hips, then moving on to her breasts, where they lingered for a good long while. A blush filled Ariel's cheeks, a blush that burned nearly as hot as her anger and something else bubbling inside.

Desire.

But she was too bloody angry to care about her ridiculous, unwanted, unacceptable attraction to him, and too bloody furious to care about the way he shook his head in mock concern.

He crossed his arms. "I shall untie you if you promise to behave."

Ha. As if she'd promise him anything.

"No more trying to escape," he ordered, tossing the reins over his arm to tick off items.

She'd try to escape until her legs gave out on her.

"No more complaining about being uncomfortable."

She'd complain until her voice gave out.

"And if you violate any of these rules, I will tie you to the nearest roadside tree and leave you there to await my return."

Jolly well try, she dared him with her eyes. As if he could do a thing without her help. He needed her to search her house. The realization was power.

"Do you give me your word?"

She wanted to give him something, alright. The pox. The ague. At the very least cankerous sores. "Thake your bloothy offer an stick it—"

"Ah, ah, ah, my lady," he interrupted. "You'd best watch your unladylike tongue."

"I'll watcth thomeone thoot you," she growled, her mouth dry from the gag. "In th'arsth."

He turned and walked away.

Ariel let him go. The fool. Didn't he realize he needed her? He would stop before he cleared the trees that shielded her from the road.

But he didn't stop.

"Where you goingth?" she called.

He stopped, turned to face her.

"There was an inn in town, one with food. I thought I'd eat some breakfast before I leave for Bettenshire."

"You can'th leave withouth me."

"This is quite true, but I can leave you here until I feel like coming to fetch you."

Ooo, he wouldn't dare.

She looked into his eyes.

He would.

She clenched her hands behind her, wanting to scream, to yell, at the very least to kick something. "I'll bethave," she promised, and oh, how it near killed her to say the words.

He gave her that grin males used when they felt vastly superior to the female sex. She was tempted to scar the other side of his face.

He came forward once again, the horse following along behind him like an obedient lamb, shaking its black mane as if upbraiding her for daring to challenge him. She wanted to make a charge for the beast when he untied her hands, then leave Trevain in a trail of dust. But she knew that wouldn't be possible. For one, she would never be able to mount in skirts. And two, she doubted she would get two steps before he'd catch up to her. Bloody man. Bloody dress.

Bloody kidnapping.

She felt the rope give way—thankfully, without him touching her—and felt her arms fall to her side. In a flash she had the gag off her face, some of her hair entangling in the knot and pinching as she pulled the material away. She didn't care, she felt too bloody glad to have the thing off of her. A part of her was half tempted to stomp upon it when she tossed it to the ground. She worked her jaw instead, then opened her mouth, not caring that she no doubt looked like a fish gasping for air. It simply felt too splendid to move her lips.

"At last. You have learned how to open your mouth and not say a word."

She whirled on him, half tempted to clout him over the head. "Would that you knew the same trick."

"I know a trick worth two of that."

"Then I pr'thee, lend me thine."

His brows lifted. "A woman who knows Shakespeare. How remarkable."

"Indeed. About as remarkable as a man with charm, a trait I fear you lack exceedingly."

He lifted black brows. "Indeed, just as you lack a lady's morals."

Ooo, that wasn't very nice. "A man who hardly exhibits gentlemanly behavior should not cast stones."

"Ah, but I never asked to be born an English gentleman."

"Have no fear, sir, no one would mistake you for one."

"I see you are piqued by my daring to leave you behind while I fetched the horse."

She glared her answer. Smart man.

"Did you think I was foolish enough to take you into the village with me?"

"I thought you gentleman enough to treat me like a lady."

"You'll need to act like one first before that happens."

If she had had a brick, she would have thrown it at his head. Truly.

They stared at each other for a time, Ariel refusing to look away. During their battle of I-can-stare-the-longest she was overcome by the silliest urge to cross her eyes and stick her tongue out. She didn't. And when he looked away, she felt a small measure better. He'd glanced up at the thick canopy of leaves above them, and as always happened when someone looked up, Ariel found herself doing the same thing. Nothing but leaves. Hmph. She looked back at him in time to see him frown, then turn his back to her—conversation apparently at an end. It was then that Ariel noticed something she should have noticed before.

There was only one horse.

One horse. *Oh, no,* she thought. No, no, no. She would not ride with him. Would not.

With quick snaps he lowered the stirrups, led the horse out from under the tree and mounted.

"Come," he said, holding out his hand.

"No," she said right back, crossing her arms.

He gave her that jutting-jaw look males assumed. The horse shifted beneath him, apparently sensing his agitation. But she did not want to ride with him. Impossible man. She'd rather ride upon the devil's pitchfork. While it was afire.

"I shall walk," she pronounced, uncrossing her arms to wag a finger.

"Do not be ridiculous. Give me your hand."

"No," she repeated, crossing her arms again on the off chance that he would take it into his dense head to lift her before him.

The horse once again shifted, Nathan expertly calming the beast. He looked to have stepped from a canvas entitled *Tally ho, the mighty lord rideth astride.* Not a hair escaped from his queue, not a wrinkle creased his gray jacket. He'd cleaned up in town, she realized. Really, it was quite bothersome, especially since her own appearance was in such disarray.

"My lady, I lack the patience to sit here and argue with you. You will ride with me. At once."

"No."

"And why not?"

"Because."

"Because," he mimicked, "A sterling reason."

She crossed her arms, daring him to make her.

He took up the silent challenge.

She barely had time to react, so quick were his movements as he dismounted, grabbed her arms then tied them behind her back.

"Why, you—"

"Ah, ah, ah," he drawled by her ear. "Not another word, my lady."

Oddly enough, the feel of his breath against

her ear silenced her. The realization flummoxed her. She stiffened, her back upright, as she waited for him to put the gag in place. But instead of the material binding her mouth, it fell over her eyes. She didn't say anything, expecting him to turn her around, realize his mistake, then he would tie the material correctly. Instead she felt the black fabric pulled tight, heard the whistle of the material as it was knotted, heard him step alongside, then turn her around.

"Now, my lady. One word out of your mouth, and I shall gag you, too."

Only then did Ariel realize what he planned. He didn't want her to see where they were going, no doubt his way of hindering her should she attempt to escape. Bloody clever man.

When he was done, she heard a rustle. The blanket, she realized, feeling him cover her head and shoulders, then secure it somehow in front of her neck. Obviously he meant to conceal her blindfold by covering her head. Wonderful. No doubt she looked like Sister Mary Cazignotti.

He clasped her arm again. She stumbled as he dragged her forward.

"What are you doing?" she moaned.

"Putting you atop the horse." He lifted. She gasped, then swayed back and forth as she landed sideways in the saddle. She felt off kilter somehow. Was it from the touch of his hands? Or was it the result of having to sit upon the horse with nothing to brace her legs. Truly, she did not want to know.

"Give me your foot."

Give him her what? Then she gasped as she felt his fingers close around her ankle. The touch seemed to reach clear into her heart. But how that could be when she hated his bloody guts, she had no idea. And was it her imagination, or did he still for an instant, too? She blushed. Truly, it was a very odd feeling being blind. Did he gaze at her exposed flesh? Leer? Perhaps he stood mesmerized by the sight of her pearly white flesh?

At that moment Ariel was overcome by a feeling of desperation such as she'd never felt since finding out Nathan truly intended to kidnap her. Perhaps it was her fear of him. Perhaps it was her fear of herself, but she dug her heels into his horse's side like they were battering rams.

It was a sign of how flummoxed she was that she didn't think to brace herself before doing so or at the very least grab onto some mane. The horse, as expected, charged forward. She felt her legs lift, felt her seat slide, felt her body tilt back. What happened next was a foregone conclusion.

She landed with an *oomph*, one that turned into a gasp when she heard the horse snort, then buck, its hooves seeming to whoosh past her ears.

Silence descended—well, silence but for the horse galloping away.

Nathan didn't say a word. For half a heartbeat she wondered if he'd been kicked by the horse.

Perhaps he'd been knocked unconscious. The thought filled her with hope, then immediately remorse. She sat up, her shoulders aching from the force of her landing. The blindfold had shifted more. She turned her head to scan the ground for Nathan.

Boots stood a few feet away from her. She told herself she should be disappointed, but all she felt was a heady sense of relief.

"Are you quite satisfied?" he growled, and Ariel wanted to sink back down to the ground. If his voice had sounded awful before, it sounded positively more than awful now. She swallowed.

"We no longer have a horse," he growled.

She kept quiet. Truthfully, she didn't think speaking would be wise just yet.

"You have just wasted the time it took for me to fetch the horse."

"Well, your time was wasted in any event, sir, for the horse you hired bucked me off."

"He bucked because you kicked him."

"I did not."

"You are a liar."

"I am not," she wanted to say, but she couldn't. Lying was something she'd never done easily. Witness how quickly she'd given up on being a female spy. "I am lying. And I am sorry for it."

Her admitting this must have taken him by surprise, for he said nothing in response. Then she saw his feet move her way, heard them crush the leaves beneath them. Truly, they were big feet. He paused next to her. Ariel wondered if he held out a hand she couldn't see. But he gave no indication that he did so, only said, "Congratulations, madam, you are now going to walk all the way to Bettenshire."

"Surely the horse has not run that far?" *Drat this blind.* How she wished she could see.

"To the next county."

He lied. She tilted her head back, but she could see nothing but leaves and his feet from her current position. Bother.

"Get up."

No, he wasn't holding out a hand, she could tell by his tone of voice. In fact, she was almost glad for the blindfold, for she had a feeling she didn't want to see his face. The boots moved out of her field of vision. She tilted her head back. "Where are you going?"

"To Bettenshire, without you if need be."

"Wait."

But he didn't. Ariel tried to push herself up, but her skirts had wrapped themselves around her legs, not to mention it was bloody hard to rise with one's hands tied behind one's back. In vain, she struggled, but it took her at least twenty long seconds to rise. When she stood, she scanned the ground for him.

He'd left.

But he couldn't have. He needed her.

Apparently, however, Nathan Trevain had momentarily forgotten that fact. So had she when she'd kicked the horse forward, but that was neither here nor there.

"Wait," she cried, turning in a slow circle. "Do not leave me."

"Too late," he called.

She turned in the direction of his voice, charging toward him, her lack of sight forcing her to use other senses to find him, which was probably why she didn't see the tree that came out of nowhere, why, she would wager, she bashed into it like a drunk on a binge. Her head hit first, followed closely by her breasts. For half a heartbeat there was a moment of shocked stupefaction, followed by a blast of sharp pain in her forehead. She felt herself tilting back as for the second time that day her breath whooshed out of her when she hit the ground.

Silence descended. She lay there, her nose throbbing. "Ohh," she moaned. She heard footsteps, was in too much pain to care.

"My, my, my," a silky voice drawled. "That was an interesting thing to observe. Was that some sort of gypsy ritual?"

She didn't move. Frankly, she wasn't sure she could talk just yet. If she did, she might howl loud enough to wake the dead.

"I've never heard of that ceremony before."

And was that amusement she heard tickling his voice? She turned her head and listened.

"It was quite . . . entertaining."

Why, that no-good bounder. It *was* amusement.

"You, sir, are an utter and complete black-guard." Humiliation filled her anew as she realized her voice sounded as high as Lady Pemberton's. Her nose was plugged from her collision with the tree. "You should be drawn and quartered for treating a lady thus." She struggled into a sitting position, wishing with all her might she could rub her stinging nose.

"I assure you, my lady, you are not the first person to wish me ill."

"Well, let me be the first to actually do you ill." She struggled to stand again. The bounder didn't even offer to help. When she finally managed to do it, she swayed a bit, the blood draining from her head. "What would you prefer?" she asked. "Pistol? Flogging?" If she'd had her hands loose, she would have placed them on her hips as she faced him.

Someone tapped her on her shoulder.

"I am behind you," said a voice, and blast it all, he sounded like he tried very hard not to laugh.

She swung around, titling her chin up, discerning beneath the blind that he was, indeed, standing where he said. "Well, bully for you."

And then he did laugh, a rollicking huge boom of a noise that made Ariel instantly still. Gracious, but he sounded odd. Like a human cannon that hadn't been fired for long time. She tilted her head and listened.

"You, sir, are a rogue," she said, when it appeared he wouldn't stop.

"So you've said before."

"Yes, well, I'm saying it again."

He laughed even harder. Ariel felt something within her snap. She charged. She wasn't sure she would hit him, but she gave it her best shot, hunching her shoulders low, hoping to run into him smack in the midsection.

She did.

With a satisfaction that would give her plea-sure for years to come, she heard his breath wheeze out, then felt his body tilt backward. Unfortunately, he took her with him, clasping his arms around her torso as he fell. But by then Ariel didn't care. She was too filled with victori-ous pleasure.

"Ha, sir. Now who is laughing?"

He didn't say anything right away, which caught Ariel's attention. She tilted her head, wishing—again—that she could see.

And then he said softly, so softly she had to strain to hear him, "I believe, my lady, that a les-son is in order."

And suddenly her laughter faded. Too late she realized she oughtn't have done what she did. The ridiculous attraction she felt to him flared to life. She gasped, caught off guard by the myriad sensations suddenly coursing through her. They seemed to double, then triple, almost as if her senses worked harder to under-stand what her eyes couldn't see. She felt him shift, felt him tighten his grip with one arm, felt him move. And suddenly she could see. The blind was lifted from her face to reveal his own face only inches away.

Her mouth formed a little O as she observed sinful silver eyes staring into her own. Her breath caught as she realized his gaze seemed transfixed by her lips.

"You should watch yourself."

"I should?" she breathed.

"I would hate for you to damage that pretty head of yours."

He raised his hand again, only this time it was to touch the knot on her head. Gently, almost kindly. Gone was Trevain the Terrible; in his place was Trevain the Thoughtful.

And suddenly she didn't care that he'd just laughed at her. Didn't care that he'd kidnapped her. Or that he'd intended to use her and then betray her. It was the first time in a long time a man had looked at her thus and really meant it, and her heart told her Nathan Trevain really meant it.

Thoughts of his kidnapping her, however, had her recalling who she was. She dipped her head in shame. The loss of eye contact seemed to break the spell. He set her away from him gently, his hands lingering on her waist longer than necessary. They didn't speak another word as he helped her up. To her utter horror, she found herself wishing for the contact again.

"I shall untie you if you promise to behave."

She jerked her head up. "You will?"

"Aye, if you promise not to try and escape."

He stared down at her, his hair still bound in that queue despite his brush with the ground. She nodded.

"And I shall leave the blind off, too."

He was being kind, she realized, a warm feeling suffusing her. And suddenly Ariel's heart softened toward him. She told herself she still hated him, but she knew it wasn't true. He truly was being kind to her, genuinely kind, and kindness was something Ariel had missed in her life.

Desperately.

13

It took them two hours to reach Bettenshire. The trip was shortened by the horse they recovered less than a quarter-mile away from where it'd bolted. Nathan was never more relieved to see the estate where Ariel had been reared.

" 'Tis a castle," he observed.

"Aye," his captive agreed.

They came at the estate from a higher elevation, but though its stone facade had aged over the years, the mellowed ivory color looked stark against the afternoon sky. Windows stretched along the bottom and top floors, sparkling in the sunlight. Green grass, meticulously scythed into a checkerboard pattern, lay across the grounds, trees that looked to have grown for ages framing the main building.

" 'Tis beautiful, is it not?"

There was no animosity in her gaze, no loathing, no fear, only pride. The sun, coasting high above them, cast a golden glow over her features, making her black ringlets look almost brown. Her eyes were the color of amber, sparkling with some emotion he didn't recognize. Relief? Comfort? He wasn't sure.

"My mother once told my father that she fell in love with the estate before she did him. Knowing my father, she might not have been jesting." She smiled over at him.

"How did they meet?" he surprised himself by asking.

"Her family had camped on the grounds. There." She pointed to a small rise to the right of them. "My father had just inherited the earldom and was very full of himself, not that that has changed over the years." Her smile turned wry. "When he heard there were gypsies on his land, he was determined to send them away." She looked up at him again. "Can you see my father, the future First Lord, racing up that hill, unarmed? The servants tell me she said she was surprised he didn't think to bring along his silver spoon as a weapon."

And Nathan stood, transfixed, as he watched the delight dance a waltz through her eyes.

"Who do you think he first saw?"

"Your mother?" he guessed, telling himself the last thing they should be doing was sitting atop this rise, having a conversation about her family. And yet he was helpless to turn away.

She shook her head, her eyes turning once again to the place where it'd all taken place.

"No. My mother's father. He had a pistol pointed directly at my father's heart."

Nathan found himself chuckling for the second time that day.

"The gypsies do not care whose land it is, you see. They believe the earth belongs to everyone. My grandfather was determined to hold his ground."

"Your grandfather?" For some reason, he'd not thought of the possibility that she could have gypsy relatives floating around.

She frowned. "Aye. My grandfather. He passed on these five years past."

She lapsed into silence. Nathan found himself wanting the enchanting urchin back.

"How did your father meet your mother, then?"

The sadness faded a bit, a small smile slipping back upon her features. "Well, when my father saw the pistol aimed at his chest, he turned to leave. That was when he saw her." Her smile grew. "She was coming up the hill, a basket of flowers over her arm. My father said when he looked at her, he felt the strangest urge to kiss her, so he did." She grew silent again, and then, as suddenly as a brisk wind, her smile faded. "He was never the same after she died." She looked over at him. "Do you believe in love at first sight?"

The question took him by surprise, most likely because one didn't expect to be asked such things by one's captive. "I do not know," he found himself answering.

She nodded. "I do not know either." She didn't look at him anymore; indeed, her expression had grown rather sad. "My mother is buried upon that hill. Father's family refused to let him bury her in her rightful plot. He could have gone against their wishes, he often says, but at the time he was too distraught." She grew silent for a moment. "He must have loved her very much. Sometimes I wonder if my father and I would be friends if my mother were still around. Do you suppose that is wrong of me? I mean, a daughter should love her father no matter how he treats her, isn't that true?"

The strangest urge filled him then, one that confused him with its intensity. She looked so earnest, yet so genuinely sad he wanted to lift his hand, wanted to place it against her cheek.

"Do you?" she repeated, her eyes never having left his own

"No. I do not think it's wrong."

"Thank you." She straightened a bit. "They still hate her, you know."

"Who?" he found himself asking.

"My mother. Society transferred that hate to me when I was ruined, I think. People think me just like her. Blood tells and all that."

Indeed they had. Nathan knew it. Worse, he'd believed it, too, when he first met her. Only now he wasn't so sure.

"People hate things that are different," he answered.

"Yes, they do." She took a deep breath, clutching the hem of her dress. "Well, enough of this. The sooner we arrive, the sooner you might locate your brother."

Her words took him by surprise. Why, it almost sounded like she wanted to help him.

"I know the location of my father's secret safe, you know." She smiled up at him impishly. "Indeed, I suppose I shouldn't tell you, but I'm feeling rather charitable right now."

He felt stunned by her revelation. "You know?"

She nodded.

"And you will tell me?"

She nodded again, her smile growing, and Lady D'Archer with a smile on her face, a slight breeze suddenly kicking up and tossing her curls around her face, was a sight Nathan knew he would never forget.

"I did a great deal of thinking while I was tied to that tree. Truly, there was not much else to do." Her expression turned wry. "But it was while beneath that tree that I came to a conclusion. You need to find your brother and quickly. On the other hand, I want to be released and quickly. It seems the most expedient way to solve both our problems is for me to help you."

He felt his mouth drop open.

"Only you must promise to release me should you find the information you need."

Was this a ploy? A trick to get him to lower his guard? He couldn't tell, but he found himself saying, "I promise," nonetheless.

"Good." She turned toward her home. "Shall we go?"

Nathan blinked, amazed by the sudden turn of events.

Don't let her fool you, Nathan. Remember what happened the last time you trusted a woman.

He gritted his teeth, forcing himself to concentrate, to remember his mission. She might appear kind now, but she was still the enemy.

One that was every bit as capable of betraying him as the woman who'd given him his scar had been.

They approached the house quickly, nary a servant about, no doubt because only a few of the staff had been left behind to care for the place. Ariel supposed that should distress her a good bit, but now that she'd decided to help Nathan—for his brother's sake—she truly didn't mind. She was too grateful to be home. At last.

"This was my mother's favorite room," she said, opening the door of the solarium. Thankfully, it was unlocked, although she doubted that would have stopped Mr. Trevain. A small hand rake lay on the bench, a pail of water nearby. The dank odor of freshly turned earth filled her nostrils, as well as the pungent scent of the flowers that grew within the glass building.

"Follow me," she said, motioning with her hand, touching favorite plants as she passed. A tea rose there, a lily here. All cherished, for they grew by *her* hand now.

They turned toward the oak door, hoping it, too, was unlocked. The servants frequently exited the house by this means. A sigh of relief escaped Ariel as the handle turned. Air from inside the house cooled her face. The view of the room beyond almost brought tears to her eyes. The Green Room. Her favorite. A room in which she'd spent many a day, contemplating her downfall.

Tall windows that overlooked the front of the property. Green and and white decor. Little touches that she'd added over the years such as a miniature portrait of her mother, which graced the fireplace mantel.

She sighed nostalgically, pushing the door wide and inhaling a deep breath of the rose potpourri she made, the smell so potent that it seemed as if a rosebush grew nearby.

"What is that stink?"

Ariel stiffened. "The pits of your arms, no doubt." She glanced back at him.

He'd scrunched his brows together, murmuring something about *her* armpits. Ariel ignored him. She was home. And not even he could spoil her mood.

Leading him forward, she kept to the part of the floor not covered by a green and beige rug, a childhood habit that she still adhered to.

You make noise walking on the hardwood floor.

And you will clean up your mess should you track in mud from the solarium.

She glanced back in time to see him glance down. As expected, large black prints marked his progress through the room. She stopped. Pointed. "Ooo. Just look what you've done."

The look on his face was rather sardonic. "Beg pardon, my lady. Next time I kidnap a woman, I will be sure to wipe my feet."

"I'm sure our servants would appreciate that."

He bowed mockingly. "Whatever it takes to please my lady."

She rolled her eyes, turned back to the room, then a moment later pushed another door wide.

John, a footmen, just about came out of his shoes. "My lady," he cried, his hands clenched to his chest, the rag he had carried fluttering to the ground like a lady's favor.

Ariel smiled, though she knew she must look a sight, with her wild, untamed hair and wrinkled burgundy gown. "John, I'm so sorry, I did not mean to startle you."

"You didn't, my lady." He frowned. "Well, you did, but I didn't expect to see you coming out of that room. When did you arrive?"

An impertinent question, one many mistresses would chastise a servant for asking, but not Ariel. The servants at Bettenshire were some of her few friends, and most of them had known her since childhood.

"We've only just arrived, John. Our, er, coach broke down on the lane. My companion and I walked the last few miles to the estate."

"Walked!"

She nodded, motioning Nathan forward. "This is Mr. Nathan Trevain, my fiancé."

The lie slipped off her tongue easily, Ariel having decided there was no reason to give the servants more fodder for gossip than necessary. And she'd dare say being accompanied by one's fiancé was not as bad as being accompanied by one's love, which is what the servants would inevitably think.

"Your fiancé," John said, surprise plainly evident. "Then congratulations are in order. We all knew it was only a matter of time before someone realized you're a prize worth plucking." He smiled at Nathan.

Ariel's own smile faltered. "Ah, thank you, John. Now, if you will excuse us, I'd like to show Mr. Trevain to his room."

"I can do that, my lady."

"No, no," she quickly answered. "I will do it." Truly, what she wanted to do was flee. How mortifying. The servants felt sorry for her. She'd never known.

"Should I send someone after the coach?"

"Er . . . ah . . . no. We've . . . ah . . . already sent someone after it."

"Very good, ma'am." He bowed as they walked by, Nathan, thankfully, having not said a word—that is, until they reached the main stairs.

"Well done, my lady."

She felt a blush of humiliation fill her cheeks. How she hated that he'd heard the exchange. "Thank you, Mr. Trevain. Your praise means the world to me."

If he noticed her sarcasm, he didn't comment upon it. Nor did he make his own sarcastic comments about her lack of marriage proposals. Instead he asked, "Where are we going?"

They turned left when they reached the first landing, a servants' staircase directly ahead.

"To the attic."

"The attic?" he repeated, sounding surprised.

"Yes. 'Tis there that the safe is hidden."

It was a long climb, entailing a trek through the family quarters—deserted—up to her childhood playrooms. And as they climbed higher, Ariel's mood lifted. Home. She was home. No matter that she'd been kidnapped. No matter that her clothes hung in tatters. Soon Mr. Trevain would release her, if he kept his word. All she need do was find the information he sought.

She refused to think about what would happen if they didn't.

"Here we are," she said at last, relieved. "The stairs are narrow. Watch your step."

She opened the door to the attic. It was dark. Her nostrils filled. Warm, stale air heated her lungs. Attic smell. Old clothing and musty house.

She lit an oil lamp kept in a recessed alcove. The brimstone match snicked to life, the small flame turning into a big one as the wick caught fire. Bright yellow light illuminated a narrow flight of stairs.

"You will note, sir, that our steps do not crumble beneath one's feet." She tested one for good measure.

He ignored her jibe, more's the pity. She'd actually beginning to enjoy herself. Lifting her skirts, the lantern in her left hand, she climbed, watching the steps carefully. When she was a child, she'd once used them as a makeshift hill. An old sled had proved to be remarkable fun. She'd climbed aboard it, bumping down to the bottom at what seemed breakneck speed. Her governess had caught her, she recalled, and her adventure had ended. Still, she smiled at the memory and at the gouges her adventure had left behind. When she was gone, evidence of her existence would mark her passage.

"Gracious, but I do miss being home."

"As do I," he said.

She stiffened, supposing he did. How horrible to have to leave your home in the hope of finding your missing brother. Truly, she hadn't given it much thought. She'd decided to help him for her own selfish reasons, even though a part of her had rebelled at helping a man who'd intended to use her so badly. She supposed she should feel marginally better that she was also doing a good deed, but the hurt she still felt at his duplicity made that difficult.

The lantern spilled a circle of light around them. Piles of old clothes were clumped on the floor. She breathed a sigh of relief when she spied what she sought: a massive oak closet that Ariel surmised must have been quite troublesome to bring up the stairs. Placing the lantern down—the circle of light instantly shrinking— she headed toward the wall behind it. Two-by-four planks were grooved together to form the wall. Ariel placed her hand upon the boards. They were loose, although not so loose as to come apart—unless you knew how to move them correctly, which she did. Lifting the uppermost plank toward the ceiling, she then tilted out the one below it. Instantly, the plank came loose. She set it down, then removed another board, which revealed the top of a metal object . . . a safe, Nathan realized.

"I'll be damned."

"Most likely you will, but we're not here to discuss your spiritual problems."

If she'd looked back, she would have seen the scowl Nathan gave her, a scowl that slowly faded as she pulled apart the wall to reveal more and more of the safe. Never would he have found the thing on his own. Excitement made his palms sweat. Pray God the information he needed was inside.

"Do you know how to work the tumblers?"

"Of course," she answered, demonstrating. With a click and a snap the metal door opened. Documents were inside. Only documents. No precious gems. No jewelry. Just documents. Hope made his breath still. She pulled them out.

"Give them to me."

"No."

He felt his brows shoot up. "What did you say?"

"I said no. I want to go through them first. After all, there is no need for you to see things that do not involve your brother."

He felt a moment's disbelief that she would defy him, then narrowed his eyes. "Give me the documents, Ariel."

"No."

"Ariel," he warned her with his voice, taking a menacing step toward her.

She shot him a look that managed to convey her loathing and pique all at the same time. "Oh, very well. Here." She shoved the documents in his face.

He grabbed them from her. "Thank you," he muttered sarcastically.

She ignored him, settling herself down on a trunk. Nathan ignored her, his excitement building as he looked at the first document. A list of names for promotion submitted by one of the admiral's officers.

But a flip through the rest of the documents

revealed nothing more than a financial accounting of the earl's holdings, some letters and a bag of gold.

He wanted to throw the objects to the floor.

"I can see by your face that you didn't find anything."

"No," he snapped.

She looked as disappointed as he felt. "Perhaps we should search his study."

They did, Nathan surprised Ariel actually helped him. He didn't know why she'd decided to assist him so completely, but he was grateful for her aid. Still, the search revealed nothing.

"Bloody hell," he snapped, turning away from her father's dresser.

"Nothing?" she asked in a small voice.

"Nothing," he repeated.

"Did you search our house in the city?"

"Thoroughly, except that one room." The room with nothing in it but wine. Bloody, bloody hell.

Wess, Wess, have I failed you?

Nathan didn't know, he only knew time was running out. With each passing day his brother's chances of survival decreased. He could be dead already, he told himself. The possibility was high.

He turned to the window. Night had begun to fall, the sun casting vibrant colors over the landscape. He wondered if Wess watched the same sunset. Or was he being held prisoner aboard a

ship somewhere, left to rot until someone remembered his existence?

Damnation.

"Nathan, oh, my goodness, are you alright?"

Only then did he realize what he'd done. He'd
smashed his fist into the wall. He looked at the
knuckles of his right hand. Blood dripped from
all five.

"Oh, my goodness," she repeated, "you're
bleeding." She reached his side. Her hands lifted
to his own. "Here," she instructed, leading him
by the elbow, then shoving him down upon her
father's bed. The fight had left him, so he let her
do what she wanted. He didn't care that she was
the enemy, that he would now be forced to take
her hostage again. Nothing mattered but how
the hell he was going to find out what had happened to Wess.

"Give me your hand."

Somewhere she'd found a cloth. She dabbed
at his cuts with it. He winced but welcomed the
pain. He deserved it. His payment for failure.

"Are you so very worried about him, then?"

She was on her knees before him, her dark hair
spilling over her shoulders. There was no need
to ask of whom she spoke. No need at all at this
point.

"Every day I do not find him is a day that he
could be put to death . . . if he isn't already
dead."

If she looked worried about her fate, she

didn't show it. "How can you be sure?" she asked.

"Because I've spoken to some of the men who've been released. As long as there was war, they would keep them alive. Now that the war is over, they will not care if he lives or dies. His usefulness is over. They don't have to feed him anymore. They will kill him."

She didn't say anything, merely stared up at him with sympathy shining from her eyes. He told himself he didn't want her sympathy, told himself he should push her away.

"Is it truly so bad?"

"Yes, Ariel," he sighed, wanting only to close his eyes. "British captains are brutal. The things I saw them do while fighting with the militia . . ."

She looked away, her voice husky when she said, "I know. I've heard the tales."

"Have you?"

She nodded. "Though I may not go out into society, my father receives visitors. I've heard how they treat the men they've pressed into service. I am ashamed of my countrymen for that."

He stared down at her in mute surprise. That she felt sincere there could be no doubt. That she was upset by her oversight there could also be no doubt. He stared, realizing he might have been wrong about her.

"I *am* sorry, Nathan, I truly am. You might be a fiend and a blackguard, but you don't deserve this. Nobody deserves this."

She looked up at him. And for the first time he allowed himself to wonder if she could be different from other women. Here he had used her terribly, kidnapped her, and yet she still knelt before him, sorrow making her eyes glint with tears. Tears.

For him.

"Come here." The words seemed to come from nowhere and everywhere at the same time. His mind, his body, his heart. Much to his surprise she obeyed, sitting beside him on the bed. He knew he should say something, knew he should do more than simply stare. Instead he used a finger to gently tilt up her chin, knowing what he was about to do was madness, pure and utter madness, but unable to resist doing so all the same. Perhaps it was the sudden loneliness he felt. Perhaps it was the understanding he saw in her eyes. He wanted to kiss her. The need was simple and irresistible.

He bent his head, saw recognition in her eyes of what he was about to do. Saw acceptance, perhaps even a touch of anticipation. And then his lips brushed hers. Kissing her was a cross between heaven and hell. Thoughts of why he shouldn't allow this to happen filtered into his mind, but he ignored them all, wanting only to give in to the sensations touching her evoked.

Yet even so the sane part of him bade him to be cautious. He drew away from her. "Ariel, Ariel," he murmured, "you're the most confusing woman I've ever met, but for some reason, I want you."

"Do you?" she murmured back, her sweet, hot breath wafting across his lips. He could smell her, the scent so distinct, so alluring, he was hard pressed not to close his eyes and simply breathe her in.

Instead he kissed her again. Madness, he told himself again. Madness to want her. Madness to crave the taste of her, madness to move his lips toward the line of her jaw.

"So smooth," he murmured, kissing the tender side of her neck. "So soft." And when he allowed his hands to tangle in her hair, he moved his lips even lower. "So tempting."

"Nathan?" she murmured, questioning, perhaps even pleading. "We shouldn't."

"We should," he answered, kissing her again just above the neckline, wishing he could remove the dress. Instead he trailed his lips across the fabric as if it were her flesh, nibbling, then lightly biting.

"Oh, Nathan. That feels . . . that feels."

"Good?" he supplied.

Wrong, Ariel thought. It felt wrong. And right. And so tempting she didn't know what to think. So she decided not to think at all, just closed her eyes, knowing she should push him away for her past's sake if for nothing else, yet wanting him to continue kissing her until he could kiss her no more. His lips moved lower, moved then sucked. She gasped, clutching his head to her breasts, telling him without words that she didn't want him to stop making her feel so—so wonderful.

No, she thought. *Beautiful*. He made her feel beautiful. Wanted. Desired. For the first time in years she didn't feel the pain of being an outcast, she didn't feel disliked. She felt needed.

And she needed him back.

She let out a moan, opening her eyes, staring at him, at his raven-black hair, at the scar on his face, at his lips as they kissed her. He must have felt her gaze, for he peeked up at her, his mouth still working the burgundy fabric turned almost black from the moisture of his mouth. Their eyes met. A need rose within Ariel to touch his face as he always did hers, to run her fingers down that scar or perhaps through his hair. She lifted a hand, watching his eyes narrow as she touched his cheek. The scar felt rough. And soft. She whimpered, a soft whimper, one born of sympathy at how much the wound must have hurt at one time. Tears rose in her eyes, too. Not tears of pity. Tears of pleasure when he lightly bit her again. Tears of wonder that he could do this to her with merely a touch. Tears of regret that he was Nathan Trevain and a spy, a man who might well be playing on her sympathy now to gain her support.

"Don't," she found the willpower to say. "Please don't."

He drew back, blinked, his gaze as cloudy as

her own. And perhaps it was the sight of her staring up at him so plaintively. Perhaps it was the pleading tone of her voice. But he did stop. And then slowly he straightened, pulling away from her.

"I'm sorry," she said, even though she didn't know what it was she was sorry for.

He scrubbed a hand over his face, then turned away from her, lifting himself off the bed to stare out the window of her father's room. "No, I am sorry. I shouldn't have kissed you."

She straightened her dress, thankful that he'd been willing to stop. And yet chasing the tail of that thought came the realization that had he truly meant to use her he would not have stopped. He would have seduced her, bound her to him in a way only a man could do. Goodness knows he could háve done it.

"Nathan, I—"

"No," he interrupted, holding up a hand. He had a wide scar on his palm, she noted. "Do not say a word." He dropped into silence, Ariel realizing he gathered his thoughts before he spoke. "I should never have kidnapped you," he said at last, rubbing his chin. "I should not have involved you in all this. It was wrong of me. I hope you understand why I did it."

"I do," she said. And she did. She would have done the same if she had been in his shoes. She might even have stooped to the same tactics of subterfuge.

"But that does not change the fact that I have

and that I need your help more than I've ever needed a person's help in my life."

She didn't say anything, knew he meant to say more.

She was right, for he turned to her, his eyes pleading. "I need your help, Ariel D'Archer. I beg you for it. Help me find my brother."

She felt a lump build in her throat. For the first time since meeting him she knew he was one-hundred-percent honest. It shone from his eyes, called to her.

At that precise moment Ariel knew she stood at a crossroads in her life. She could pretend to go along, have him taken captive at the first opportunity—and never be able to look in a mirror again—or she could help him to find his brother. The choice was hers to make.

But really, suddenly she knew it was no choice at all.

"I'll help you find him, Nathan Trevain. God help me, I'll help you."

PART FOUR

Better an open enemy than a false friend.

17TH CENTURY PROVERB

14

It was dark in the hold of the ship, the air so chill it ate at Wess's wounds like sand mites. Almost he was glad for that darkness, for Wess didn't want to see what he'd become. He knew just by the effort it took to sit on the floor, his back screeching in agony, that he'd be lucky to stave off infection another day.

"You alright, Cap'n?"

It took him a moment to gather himself from the pain, to realize someone had spoken, and even then Wess could barely utter one word, "Aye."

It was Jaime in the hold with him. Jamie with his bright green Irish eyes and equally bright red hair. Jamie, who'd gone to his aid when they'd started to drag him below. Jaime, who'd been dragged into the hold with him as a result.

God, how had he gotten them all in such a mess? He should never have gone after that frigate. But he'd thought the accompanying ship of the line had been sunk—why else would the frigate be floating in the Atlantic alone? Too late he'd realized why. A trap, one he'd sailed right into. The realization still filled him with rage, the same rage that had propelled him to escape, no matter how ill thought out the scheme.

"Word is that they expect to be in port soon." And Wess could hear the fear in his former lieutenant's voice. "Heard one of the crew members talking. Seems they think the court-martial will take place on land."

Soon, Wess thought. And how soon was that? Days? A week? Could he survive that long?

He didn't know. Infections were rampant aboard a ship. If you didn't catch one from a fellow crewmember, than you caught it from the vermin.

"Jaime," he managed to rasp out, his voice raw from his cries of pain. "If I don't make it, find my brother for me."

"No. Don't talk like that, Cap'n. We haven't lasted this long to have you die on us now. The war's over. We won. They can't hold us fer much longer."

Jaime, young, impetuous Jaime. The boy didn't understand that they would never let them go. The captain's bitterness at losing the war was a palpable thing. No doubt he would take out his anger on him. 'Twas the reason Wess had tried to desert. He knew they would kill him shortly. And though desertion was not a hanging offense in and of itself, they would hang him because a British officer had died trying to stop him from escaping. No matter that it wasn't Wess's fault that the man had died due to his own folly. He was dead. That was all the bloody Brits needed to know.

"Jaime," Wess tried again. "Tell my brother Nathan—"

But Wess's words were cut off abruptly by the sound of a door opening. A click and a snick later and their own door opened. Lantern light illuminated the gloomy inside of their makeshift cell. Wess caught a glimpse of Jaime's pale face before he turned to greet Captain Pike's stare.

"You're still conscious?" the man asked. "I must say I am surprised."

No matter that it caused excruciating pain to expand his rib cage, then release it to form words, Wess would rather have been pitched overboard than let the bastard see what he'd done to him. "Come here and give me your blade," he growled, "and I'll surprise you with the cold feel of it between your ribs."

Captain Pike's aristocratic face did not look well with a sneer. "I see your flogging has not improved your attitude."

"About as much as your good breeding has helped your manners."

The captain's eyes narrowed. He waved a man forward, the motion sharp, giving away his anger. Wess felt satisfaction surge through him, satisfaction that faded as a sailor came forward and grabbed Jaime by the arms.

"Cap'n?" his friend asked.

"Where are you taking him?"

"To be flogged. The young man will learn that his loyalty to you is severely misplaced. While he is aboard my ship, he will serve me. No other."

Wess wanted to shove himself to his feet, to wrap his hands around the insolent pig's throat. God, how he wanted to, but he could barely find the strength to sit there. To breathe in and out. To keep conscious.

"The boy was trying to protect me."

"He would do well to protect himself."

"Cap'n?" Jaime asked again,

Pike turned on him. "I'm your captain now, boy."

In response young Jaime straightened, drawing his shoulders back. "You'll never be half the man Captain Trevain is."

Wess thought Pike would hit him, but to his surprise, he didn't. Instead, he waved the boy away. Wess watched him go, never having felt so much pride in one of his crew. He looked at Pike, his fingers automatically flexing, then relaxing, then flexing again. He would kill the man one day. That he vowed. The bastard represented everything Wess hated about the British: power given by birth, not merit. Authority given by noble blood, not noble character. And with Captain Pike, that control was grossly misused.

When Jaime was gone, Pike turned to him.

Wess straightened up, though the motion brought fresh waves of fire into his mind.

"I thought you should hear at first hand that we should hit land soon."

Wess didn't let on that he already knew that.

"I've sent word out that a court-martial will need to be convened. Three days at most and you shall be hanged from the gallows."

"I look forward to it," he rasped, his strength fading quickly now, unconsciousness hovering nearby like a dark specter.

Captain Pike must have seen it, because his expression turned gloating. "Oh, no. I would never go against the Articles of War, much as it would please me to do so. No, I will adhere to the letter of the law, and the law states we must have five men ranked captain or higher to rule on your fate, no matter that the outcome is a foregone conclusion."

Wess didn't have the energy to answer, but Pike must have thought his silence deliberate.

"I should have let you sink along with your ship, Wess Trevain. And your men with you. You're a disgrace to the noble blood that runs through your veins."

Wess started, the motion causing him to gasp in pain, not that Pike noticed.

"Oh, yes. I know who you are. Your resemblance to your uncle is quite remarkable, and it is an unusual name." He took a step forward. "You disgust me with your patriot beliefs. And if I had my druthers, every member of your crew would be hanged. Instead I'll take great satisfaction in seeing you dangle from the end of the rope."

And with that, the bastard turned. Wess watched him go, vowing that it would not be he who dangled from the rope. No indeed.

15

Once Ariel had settled on helping Mr. Trevain, she would not rest until they'd arrived at a plan. Unfortunately, her newfound accomplice had a hard time agreeing to any plan she conceived. Bother.

"I've already broken into the Admiralty," he said. "No, there must be another way to find the information I need."

"But the information must be there, Mr. Trevain. It must."

Nathan shrugged. "No doubt it is, but we have no way of searching the place adequately." He paced to the end of her father's room, turned and paced back. Ariel watched him, feeling his kiss still burn upon her lips. But she tried not to think about that as she stared at him, tried not to feel a combination of both wonder and fear at her reaction to his touch.

"Perhaps there is a way," she forced herself to say.

He turned to face her suddenly.

"How?"

"Reggie."

"Reggie?" he asked.

"Phoebe's husband, my cousin. He is one of the secretaries at the Admiralty. 'Tis how they met, through my father."

He appeared to consider the notion, then shook his head. "No, I do not like it. We would have to trust this Reggie, and I do not trust British officers."

"He is not an officer, and really, we have no choice. As you said, every day you delay in finding your brother is a day he could die. Frankly, there is no other way to discover the information you need, short of waiting for my father to return. My father would tell us."

"So you think."

"No, he would. He may not like me much, but he is honorable. But 'tis neither here nor there. Reggie must be the one to help us. No one will question his presence at the Admiralty."

But Nathan Trevain did not seem impressed by her idea. He paced the length of the room again, his hands clasped behind his back, queue swishing back and forth like the tail of an irate horse. He looked dangerous in a sinister, darkly handsome sort of way. She found herself thinking things she oughtn't to think, given their circumstances, and forced herself instead to concentrate on the problem at hand.

"Come, now," she reiterated. "The idea is sound."

"Sound?" He whirled to face her, his queue all but hitting him in the face. "You believe it sound to ask Lord Sarrington to help me? Me, a man who's kidnapped his cousin?"

Ariel dismissed his argument with a wave of her hand. Men. Sometimes they did not see the logic of something if it hit them square in the face. "Reggie will do as I ask. That is all you need know." Especially once Ariel reminded him of the favor he owed her.

He paused in his pacing, arms crossed. "It's a ridiculous idea."

"No, it is not. All we need do is send him a note."

"A note? Asking what? For him to come rescue you?"

She got up from the trunk, placing her hands on her hips. "No. Explaining the situation."

He stared at her unblinkingly.

She turned away, feeling much better once she took her eyes off him. He didn't seem so . . . disturbing.

"Where are you going?"

"I am going below stairs to alert the staff, then send Reggie the note. We do not have time to argue."

"Since when did you and I become a 'we'?" she heard him mumble.

That, Ariel admitted, was a very good question.

* * *

John must have spread word of her sudden appearance, for the rest of the staff did not bat an eyelash when she appeared. Oh, perhaps they wiggled one or two. After all, she was a single female cavorting about the countryside with a man she was not married to. But they were well trained. And while Ariel was sure they clucked about it behind her back, they would never show their disapproval to her face, especially since she let drop the hint that she and Nathan had been trying to elope. No doubt they hoped this fiancé actually married her.

So now they stood in her favorite sitting room, Nathan by the fire, one arm resting upon the mantel in a typical male pose. They must teach them that at their clubs, Ariel thought. *How to Look Studious and Masculine While in the Presence of Female Company.* And he did look masculine, she admitted. He'd cleaned up after they'd shared an evening meal. So had Ariel, her full wardrobe still in the family quarters. She'd changed into a light green dress, but whereas she knew her hair looked to be in total disarray—after all, it always looked in total disarray—Mr. Trevain's hair was newly slicked back into its queue. His coat looked cleaner than before, though still a bit worn. She admired the way it hung across his shoulders.

Gracious, but his kiss had disturbed her, though she was hard pressed to understand why. Certainly he'd kissed her before, but never with such complete and utter . . . what?

Kindness, she realized. He'd kissed her with kindness and genuine desire.

Heaven help her.

He began pacing again. "Will you stop that?" she asked. "You are making me nervous." Actually it brought attention to his masculine physique, something she didn't need to be reminded of right now.

"He should have been here by now."

"I know."

"No doubt he's been delayed fetching the magistrate," he offered, stroking his chin.

She shook her head. "No. He will not bring the magistrate."

"I wish I had your confidence."

"Nor will he bring a pistol to shoot you with."

"That remains to be seen."

Yes, it did, Ariel admitted, not sure if her reminder of a promised favor would sway Reggie into doing as she asked. Worse, with each passing moment, she grew more and more nervous. Gracious, what if Reggie really did arm himself? What if right at this moment a group of men bent on taking Nathan captive headed toward the estate?

Almost as if her mind conjured the sound to go along with the mental images, Ariel heard hoofbeats on the drive.

She stiffened.

So did Nathan.

They nearly collided as they headed toward the window and peered out at a moon-soaked

drive. A lone horseman rode hell-for-leather toward them, the white flecks of foam on the
horse's chest visible against its black coat.

" 'Tis Reggie."

"How do you know?"

"The horse. 'Tis his gelding." She turned toward the door.

"Where are you going?"

"Why, to greet him."

A hand on her arm stopped her, although his
touch was truly gentle for the first time. "Stay,"
he ordered.

She swung toward him. "Why, I—oh," she
gasped, the pistol in his hand catching the glow
of the fire. "Where did you get that?"

"From a servant," he answered.

"What are you doing with it?"

"While I seem to be temporarily cursed with
trusting you, my lady, I have no such affection
for your cousin by marriage. He might have a
similar pistol or a group of armed men waiting
down the drive to take me hostage."

"So you propose to hold me hostage whilst you
wait to find out? That will go over well with him."

"I am not a fool, my lady. I will not jeopardize
my freedom or risk your being taken away from
me."

Oddly enough, the words made her feel
needed. His eyes did, too. She warmed up in the
oddest way, but then all thoughts vanished as
the door suddenly burst open.

Reggie's small form stood in the doorway, his

body illuminated by candlelight, brown hair swept to one side. His traveling cape swirled around him like waves around a pier. His familiar brown eyes instantly spied her from behind his small spectacles.

"Ariel," he said. "Thank God you are well."

She had just enough time to shoot Nathan a see-I-told-you-so look, noting the pistol was now hidden, before rushing into his arms.

"Reggie. Thank you for coming."

He pulled back. "What have you gotten yourself into?" he asked, shaking her shoulders. "First Phoebe tells me you're engaged to this man, and then she tells me she fears he's kidnapped you, for you didn't return home last eve."

She glanced at Nathan. Reggie followed her gaze. She felt him stiffen, saw his face tense.

She pulled out of his arms, turning toward Nathan. "Reggie, this is Mr. Nathan Trevain, lately of the American colonies."

Neither man moved. Ariel clasped one of Reggie's hands and pulled him toward Nathan, who, thankfully, had hidden his pistol. She halted a few feet away.

"Mr. Trevain, this is my cousin by marriage, Reggie Whittfield, Lord Sarrington."

Nathan bowed. Reggie tensed. He drew back his fist and punched Nathan square on the jaw.

"Oh, my goodness!" she cried.

"That," Reggie pronounced, "is for scaring my wife, a woman I happen to love rather fiercely."

Nathan never moved an inch, even though she could plainly see where Reggie's fist had connected with his jaw. A livid red mark marred his skin. The sight intrigued her, for by all accounts, Nathan should be on the floor.

Instead he said, "I see manners haven't improved for British noblemen."

"Manners, you bloody bastard," Reggie gritted out, shaking his fist again. "You kidnapped my wife's cousin. I should take a pistol to you, except Ariel asked me not to."

"Enough," Ariel interjected, stepping between the two. "This is ridiculous. Reggie, you are here to help us, not incite a duel. Nathan, Reggie is quite within his rights to be angry, if you will but take a moment to admit it."

Both men admitted nothing, each glowering at the other. Truly, she was rather fond of Reggie and growing fonder by the moment. To think he loved Phoebe so much he would punch a man in the face for her. She almost sighed. Oh, to find a man like that!

"That is better," Ariel said, when she realized the two of them would end up staring at each other all night if she didn't say something. "Reggie, thank you for coming."

Reggie pulled his gaze away to look at her. "You're welcome, though I should take a birch to your backside, too, for what you put Phoebe through last eve. She was afraid to call the magistrate, afraid because she thought you might have actually run off and married the man."

Ariel bit her lip, trying not to wince at the expression on Reggie's face. She'd seen that look before, when she'd complied with Phoebe's wishes and accompanied her back to London. Reggie had known she would not be accepted back. Reggie had been right.

Silence filled the room. Ariel wondered who would say something next.

It was Reggie. "Ariel, I would like to speak to you in private."

She shot Nathan a glance before saying, "Whatever you have to say you may say in front of Mr. Trevain."

"Actually I would be happy to leave you alone."

Ariel turned toward him again. "You would?"

He nodded. "Were I Reggie, I would want to speak to you privately, too."

But she didn't want to be alone with him. She shot Nathan a look that told him so, a look that the wretch ignored, for he gave them a bit of a bow, then turned and left. " 'Twill serve you right if he does abscond with me," she called out.

Nathan paused at the door, lifted a brow, then turned away. Cad.

"That was easier than I thought. Come. I've men waiting outside."

Ariel started, turning back to Reggie, who had a sudden look of urgency on his face. "You do?"

"Aye. Now, we must hurry, for they've orders to storm the house if they do not hear from me soon."

"Oh, Reggie, you haven't!"

"Of course I have. You didn't think I'd believe that nonsense about wanting to help him."

"But I *do* want to help him."

"Impossible."

She shook her head. "I do, Reggie. What is more, I will not move an inch until you agree to help him, too."

An unblinking stare was his response. "You're mad."

"Indeed I am."

"But you can't help him."

"Why not?"

"Because the man has kidnapped you, Ariel. Or did that escape your notice?"

"No, Reggie. It did not. Now, tell your men to go away, for I shan't move an inch." She took a step toward the door.

Reggie spun her around to face him, his expression livid. "Ariel, I do believe I could throttle you."

She lifted her chin, deciding to brazen it out. "You will do no such thing, Reggie, for I know you love me too much to harm a hair on my head. 'Tis why you will help Nathan and me."

"I will agree to nothing."

"You will, just as soon as you tell your men to leave."

He didn't move.

"*Now*, Reggie." She crossed her arms.

She thought he might do the same, instead he

spun on his heel, stomped toward the window, then opened it up. He let loose with a whistle. A few moments later, she heard a man's voice say, "You all right, sir?"

"I am well. It appears my cousin was embarking upon an elopement."

Silence, then the voice said. "Well, then, glad she's all right'n tight."

By now Ariel had moved behind Reggie, blanching at the sight of three men, all of whom held pistols.

"Gracious, you were serious."

Reggie leaned back, closed the window and turned to face her. His glare made all moisture instantly evaporate from Ariel's mouth.

"Bow Street Runners. I paid them ten guinea to ride ahead of me and help me apprehend your kidnapper."

Gracious, she'd heard of the late Henry Fielding's Runners, though she'd never seen one before. "Let me see."

Reggie caught her about the arm. "No, Ariel, this is no time for curiosity. What the devil have you and my wife gotten yourselves mixed up in?"

"Well, certainly not an elopement." She quickly outlined the events of the past two days. "Granted, Nathan has not behaved in the most admirable way, but he is the victim of an injustice, and though I toyed with the idea of having him hauled to the local magistrate and incarcerated in a gaol, I no longer wish for that to happen."

"Nathan is it?"

She blushed. Gracious, she'd been doing that more and more of late, calling Mr. Trevain by his Christian name. She really should stop. There could, of course, be no future for them. Not with all that stood between them now and in their past. "I meant Mr. Trevain."

"Mmm hmm."

She held her tongue.

"And you would help him despite the way he fooled you into thinking he wanted to be your friend?"

She colored. Truly, Reggie had a way of picking at open wounds. "While I haven't exactly forgiven him for that, I've decided it would not be Christian of me to turn my back on his needs . . . and he needs our help."

Reggie crossed his arms.

"He does, Reggie."

"Oh, I've no doubt."

She didn't think explaining the look on Nathan's face when he'd begged her to help him would help her cause, and so she kept quiet.

"The man cannot be trusted."

"Perhaps, perhaps not. But what I *do* know is that his brother is missing. Would you not do whatever it took to find Phoebe if she were missing?"

He didn't like the question, she could tell. "This is different."

"How?"

"His brother was a naval officer. He knew the risks he took when he went aboard his ship."

"And that makes it all very nice and neat in your mind, does it not? Let the man become a slave. He should have expected as much. How utterly convenient."

Reggie's eyes narrowed. She crossed her arms again. When that failed to sway him, she drummed her fingers as she waited for his response. It was his turn to swing away from her, his back stiff as Lady Pelton's wig. He was grappling with his moral self. She recognized the signs. Clenching hands, tense jaw.

"How do you propose to help him?"

Ariel released a breath, crossing to his side in an instant. "Thank you, Reggie."

"Do not thank me yet, for I've yet to agree."

But he would, she was sure of it. "We need access to the Admiralty."

"No." Reggie held up his hands. "I will not risk myself or my family being branded a traitor for a bloody patriot."

"But you must."

"No."

"Then I will tell my father about the papers you lost, the ones I helped you find that day. You remember, the list of troops and their positions? The *secret* papers—"

"Silence," he interrupted. "I remember."

"Then you remember your promise to me when I found them for you. You are a gentleman, Reggie, I would hope that you keep your promises. I am calling in the favor you owe me now."

His face tightened, his lips compressing. "I am not so dishonorable."

"Then help us, Reggie. That is all I ask."

16

So it was that the three of them found themselves on their way to London less than a hour later, Reggie looking mutinous as they rambled down the road in her father's carriage.

Ariel didn't care. She was quite pleased with herself. The day had turned out quite fine, she noted, one of those sparkling days when the sky and leaves and grass look fresh and new.

They arrived earlier than anticipated. Or perhaps Ariel's thoughts had not marked the passage of time appropriately. She stared out the window as they crossed over the Thames, her thoughts of Nathan Trevain fading as she grew more and more tense. What if they couldn't locate his brother? What if they searched the Admiralty and were caught?

What if . . . What if . . . What if . . .

Gracious, the challenge of finding Nathan's brother seemed too monumental to embark upon.

So when Reggie asked, "When do you want to leave for the Admiralty?" Ariel tensed as she waited for Nathan's answer.

"Today."

Ariel gulped. Today!

"Very well. I shall get started on locating a disguise for you the minute we arrive," Reggie answered, for they had decided to accompany him. His eyes swung to Ariel's. "Ariel, you will stay behind."

"Oh, no, I will not," she answered immediately.

"Yes, you will."

"No, Reggie, for if you do not let me go, I shall follow on my own. Would you not rather have me safe by your side?" She lifted a brow.

His eyes narrowed. She smiled. His hands clenched. Her smile grew.

"Well, if you will not stop her from going, I shall."

Ariel's gaze swung to Nathan's. "No, you will not, Mr. Trevain, for if you will not let me go, I will stop Reggie from going. I'm sure he would be only too happy to comply with my request, wouldn't you, Reggie."

Her cousin by marriage didn't answer, just frowned, clearly not liking either of his options.

"Do you both understand?"

Neither of them answered.

Ariel felt supremely pleased with herself. "Well," she sighed, leaning back in her seat, her hands plopping onto her lap. "Now that that is settled, I think it would be wise for you, Reggie, to find me some boys' clothes. I can pretend to be a lackey or some such nonsense. Nathan, of course, will have to dress as a naval officer . . ."

And on and on she prattled, Nathan wanting to throttle her. Damnation, but she had them both by the balls. It was not a feeling he particularly liked. Judging by the looks of things, neither did Reggie. He was almost tempted to suggest to the man that they band together to overpower her, but he discarded the notion. Without Ariel D'Archer he could not guarantee Lord Sarrington's cooperation, and without Sarrington he had nothing.

Clever chit had them outwitted.

He pressed his lips together, a part of him applauding her cunning, the other part wanting to throttle her and a small, small part of him wanting to kiss her. But just a small, ridiculous part.

So when they arrived at his lordship's residence, neither of the two men was in very charitable spirits. They were greeted by Phoebe, Lady Sarrington, bounding down the stairs and into Ariel's arms.

"Ariel D'Archer, where have you been?" she asked, drawing back.

"I was kidnapped, Phoebe, if you will believe that. Mr. Trevain took me hostage to help expedite finding his brother—"

"Ariel, not out here," Reggie chastised her.

Nathan saw her gaze shoot to the groom. She seemed to blanch. "Er . . . ah . . . yes. Let us go inside, and I will tell you all about it."

Nathan and Reggie were left upon the pavement.

"How long have you known her?" Nathan found himself asking.

"Ariel or my wife?"

"Ariel."

"Since she was seventeen."

"And does she always raise within you this uncontrollable urge to strangle her?"

Reggie looked startled, then amused, though it was a reluctant amusement at best. "Always."

"Hmm. 'Tis as I thought."

Two hours later all was in readiness for their departure. Reggie had made good on his word to secure an officer's uniform, though where he'd obtained it, Nathan had no idea. The blue, short-waisted jacket with gold buttons fitted a bit snugly. Nathan left it open, exposing the white sash beneath. White breeches and shiny black boots—his own—completed the outfit. Having worn such disguises before, Nathan knew he looked the part of a captain, only he refused to wear the black *chapeau bras*. In his opinion, the half-moon-shaped hat looked better carried beneath an arm than perched atop a head.

"Well, how do I look?"

Nathan swung toward the sitting room door,

his gold epaulets swinging, only to take a step back at the sight of Ariel.

"Is the transformation not amazing? I confess myself rather pleased."

And it was amazing, but not for the reasons she surmised. Bloody hell. Every curve she possessed showed. Her ankles were covered by stockings rather than skirts. He felt himself stare at those ankles, at the delicate curve of the calves above them, then her thighs. By the time he reached her waist, he found himself as hard as cannon iron. Bloody, bloody hell. With her brown jacket open, he could see her breasts protruding beneath her white shirt. "Phoebe helped me, though she was not best pleased. I suppose my cousin and her husband regret ever inviting me to London. Gracious, but it has been an adventure, has it not?"

And all he did was gawk. If he hated wearing his own pilfered uniform, he hated what Ariel wore all the more. But whereas he hated his clothes because of the war they represented, he disliked what Ariel wore because they revealed far, far too much.

And that bothered Nathan.

A lot.

"You need to change."

She lifted black brows. "I do?"

"Yes." Into a habit. A multilayered cape. A chastity belt. Nathan didn't care. "Something that isn't quite so—"

"Revealing?" she supplied.

"Exactly."

She straightened, the white shirt she wore tightening over her breasts. "I'm glad you noticed."

Their eyes met. Suddenly the room stilled. The amusement in Ariel's eyes faded. Nathan stared. God, but she was beautiful, even with her hair beneath a boy's cap. That she had agreed to help him still amazed and confused him. After all he'd put her through, after he'd treated her so ill, after their kiss . . .

"Nathan?" she asked, her head tilting at the currents that swirled around them.

He felt the urge to go to her, to tip her chin up, that damnable urge he didn't seem to be able to stop. Instead he held himself erect, hands clenching then unclenching.

"Change," was all he said.

She shook her head. "There is no other choice but this."

"Can you not cover yourself a bit more efficiently?"

"How?"

Good question. Just then Reggie entered the room, looking crisp and professional in his standard secretary's garb of beige breeches, black coat and dark gray waistcoat. But when he spied Ariel, he stopped, looked at her over his spectacles, then turned to Nathan.

"I see the clothes fit her as well as the ones I secured for you."

"They do, but I am not pleased with the attire."

He turned back to her. "Whyever not? It looks quite effective to me. I would not know her for a woman had I seen her on the street. Phoebe tells me you bound your breasts. That was quite good thinking."

Not know her for a woman? Was the man blind? Could he not see as clear as day that the exotic, slanted eyes, thick brows and luscious lips belonged to a woman? The way she blushed at the mention of her breasts. Bloody hell, her wonderful breasts.

"She needs to wear something else."

"No time."

"There is plenty of time."

Reggie looked at his pocket watch. "We need to get there as the guard changes. There is no time."

Nathan wanted to protest further. Bloody hell, how he wanted to protest.

"Are we ready?" Ariel asked. "For if so, I would like to say good-bye to Phoebe first." She shot out of the room before Reggie had a chance to protest.

"She should change," Nathan immediately complained again.

Reggie peered over at him with a look of impatience. "Mr. Trevain, let us get something straight. I am helping you under duress. What Ariel is wearing is her best chance of getting in and out of the Admiralty without being detected. I may be angry with her. I may want to throttle her. But I love her like a sister, and I do not want to see her get caught. Now, shall we leave?"

He didn't wait for Nathan, much to his disgruntlement. Yet oddly enough, as he watched him go, Nathan wasn't angered by the speech. Instead he found himself almost liking the man.

The office of the Admiralty was located in Whitehall, a bustling street with three- and four-story buildings blocking the afternoon sun. Ariel had never been inside the offices before, although she'd been in front of them often enough, usually when her father stopped on his way out of town.

Now her pulse leaped as they pulled up in front, the red-coated guards on either side of a nondescript door making her instantly nervous.

"We will start in the records room," Reggie said. "Follow me."

The records room. It sounded so official, Ariel thought, squirming upon her seat. The door opened, emitting the smell of mud, sewer and horses. None of it fazed Ariel as she gingerly stepped down, Nathan following in her wake. She did tense, however, as they passed the guards, but no cry of "Halt, who goes there?" stopped them. Thank goodness.

Inside were narrow halls with numerous doors lining them. The air felt dank and smelled of paper and men, not surprising, since there were men in abundance around. It was a Thursday, most of the Admiralty staff in attendance, though probably not as many as had occupied the place in time of war. Still, Ariel felt intimidated by the blue-and-gold-jacketed officers, despite her familiarity with everything Navy.

And nobody spared her a glance.

She felt a bit miffed about that. After all, it wasn't as if she looked *that* boyish. Then she reminded herself that she should be grateful no one gave her more than a passing glance. The realization caused her steps to become more bold, the freedom the breeches provided feeling rather scandalous and wonderful.

"Turn here," Reggie instructed.

They turned left down a hall with doors on either side of it—some open, some closed—then climbed up two flights of steps to the third floor. Apparently, no one thought it odd to see a secretary, a young lad and an officer, though more than one person gave Nathan a passing glance. 'Twas the scar, no doubt, Ariel thought. The thing made him look rather dashing and dangerous, like an officer just come back from war, the hat beneath his arm completing the image.

"Here," Reggie said, stopping before a door.

Her heart sped up again. They stood in a long hall, windows to their left, a row of doors to their right, all of which were closed. It appeared deserted and little used, dots of dust dancing upon lazy air currents, the windows dull for lack of cleaning. Reggie felt inside his pocket, and when that turned up nothing, searched the other.

"Damnation, I forgot my keys." He faced them. "Let me fetch another set from my office. You two wait here." He took a step, stopped, turned back to them. "Do not move. And if anyone asks you a question, Ariel, you stay quiet. Mr. Trevain, you say you're waiting for me."

Ariel nodded, Nathan did nothing more than cross his arms. Reggie kept his gaze fixed upon him for a long moment, shooting him a look of warning, before he swiveled on his heels and left, his steps angry on the hardwood floor.

"We should go with him," Nathan said.

"No," Ariel contradicted him, reaching out to stop him. "He will be back in a moment."

Nathan looked at her hand. She dropped it, though she had to force herself to do so. Suddenly she felt a bit intimidated by her surroundings. Or was it the look on Nathan's face? It had hardened since their arrival. His demeanor was that of a callous soldier. Gone was the lover who'd told her he'd wanted her; in his place stood a man who looked the part of a warrior.

"I do not trust him," he said.

"Whyever not?"

"Because he is British."

"So am I."

He met her gaze, his eyes a smoky gray. "Yes, you are."

They lapsed into silence, Ariel feeling her pulse beat faster as she garnered the courage to ask a question she'd never dared ask before. "Nathan, why do you hate the English so?"

"One of your captains stole my brother."

"Yes, I know, but there is more than that. Your hatred runs deep. I can tell."

"Oh? Are you a soothsayer? Did you, perhaps, inherit gypsy skills from your mother?"

She stiffened at the mention of her mother. "You are being rude."

"And you are being impertinent in asking such a question."

"Yet I notice you have not answered it."

His jaw tightened, so did his lips. His eyes grew as tough as steel.

She touched his arm, the urge uncontrollable. His muscles were stiff beneath the wool jacket. "What is it, Nathan? What has hurt you so?"

He drew away. "You imagine things, Ariel."

"Do I?" she asked. "I wonder. And I wonder why you will not answer the question."

"I have already answered," he snapped, his face turning more hard, more cold, his eyes warning her away. "I told you 'tis because of my brother."

"And I know 'tis more than that."

"You know nothing—"

A door closed at the end of the hall. Both Nathan and Ariel stiffened. A man came toward them, the sound of his boots echoing off the floor. He gave them a curious glance before passing. Ariel breathed a sigh of relief.

"You were saying?" she asked.

"I was saying you'd best drop the subject."

"No," Ariel found herself disagreeing. "You owe me an explanation, Nathan Trevain. I have put *everything* aside to help you. Everything. My integrity. My honesty. My loyalty to my country." She suddenly found herself angry. "You intended to use me, then you went and kidnapped me. You have been mean to me, rude to me, threatened me. And still—*still*—I put aside my prejudices to help. You could at least tell me why it is you refuse to do the same." She turned, stomped to the window. The street below was a long way down.

A hand upon her shoulder startled her.

"You are correct," he said.

She refused to face him. He turned her around, and she was surprised to see he looked genuinely contrite. "I am a cad and a bounder and all those other things you've called me."

"You are," she agreed, looking into eyes gone silver in the afternoon light.

"Sometimes it's hard for a man to forget the past."

She tilted her chin, refusing to let him see how much he'd hurt her by not answering.

Hurt her? As if he had the power. He did not, she told herself.

"As hard as it is for a woman to forget, no doubt," she said.

His eyes softened. "No doubt."

She turned back to the window. Where was

Reggie? Gracious, but she wished they could leave.

"I was betrayed by a woman."

She stiffened.

"An English woman. A spy, sent from London to track me down." His hand dropped to his side. His voice was low as he told her the tale. This time it was his turn to stare out the window. "She came to Virginia in 1778. I'd been performing my duties as a spy for two years." He shot her a glance. "My ability to mimic a British officer is exemplary."

She had no doubt it was. Even now he looked every inch the part.

"I had no idea that my reputation had reached across the ocean or that they would feel threatened enough by me to send someone to stop me." This time when he turned to face her, he touched his scar. "She almost did."

She gasped. "She did that to you?"

"Aye."

No wonder he had been so angry on discovering her deceit. No doubt he'd thought her cut from the same cloth.

"But that is not the worst of it."

She searched his eyes, looking for a clue as to what could possible be worse.

"She'd gotten close to me by becoming more than a"—he searched for the right word—"friend."

"Did you love her?" she asked, obviously understanding what he meant. Though she didn't look shocked by the admission, she was obviously repulsed.

"I did."

"You did," she repeated, turning away to stare out of the window. "I'm sorry for that, Nathan. I know how it is to think someone loves you only to find out they don't love you in return."

Aye. She must, but she had become a better person for the betrayal, he thought, whereas he had become bitter and hard.

"She left the colonies, thinking she had killed me."

"And you let her go on thinking that?"

"I let the English go on thinking that. It served my purpose. She was after information I had in my possession. With the British thinking me dead, they no longer pursued me. I ended up taking the information to my superiors, information that ultimately resulted in the your countrymen's defeat at Cowpens. But the ball she struck me with ended my career as a spy, for I could not effectively disguise my face. So I suppose in the end they got what they wanted. I wasn't dead, but my career was over."

"And that angered you," she stated matter-of-factly.

"It turned me bitter," he found himself admitting. "I wanted revenge against your kind. I joined the militia, fought in hand-to-hand combat. That is where I truly learned to hate everything British, for the tactics were brutal. Women and children were killed, houses burned. I did my best to take out as many of the bastards as I could. 'Tis where I got the rest of my scars."

If she seemed repulsed or upset that he'd killed her fellow countrymen, she didn't show it. Instead she turned toward him, her face unreadable. He found himself unable to look away from those golden eyes. Found himself wanting to pull her into his arms, to hold her as the images of war and what it'd been like to fight faded.

"You did what was necessary, Nathan. War is never pretty, never black and white, never cut and dried. That people must die sometimes in their fight for freedom is a fact that cannot be denied. I applaud your country for taking the steps necessary to become independent."

He stared down at her in shock, in utter disbelief, in wonder. She amazed him with her total honesty.

"Ariel, I—"

His words were cut off by the sound of footsteps. Many footsteps. They both turned. Nathan stiffened.

"Do not move," said a uniformed man, pointing a bayonet at his chest. Two more men stood behind him.

Nathan froze, disbelief holding him immobile. And then he spied Lord Sarrington standing behind them. "What have you done?"

"I've caught you, you bloody patriot. Now, step away from my cousin."

But rage propelled Nathan's legs forward. The hat fell to the floor. One of soldiers raised his musket. Nathan prepared to be shot, wanted to be shot, anger and disappointment near choking him.

"Nathan, no!" Ariel screamed.

He hesitated just a fraction of an instant, but it was enough. Instead of firing at him, the soldier raised his weapon higher. He swung it.

Blackness claimed him.

17

"How could you?" Ariel accused him. "How could you do this to me, Reggie?"

"I did it for the family, cousin. What would your father say if he found out we'd helped a known enemy?"

They were back in the sitting room they had left less than an hour ago, only this time Nathan wasn't present. Ariel felt tears come to her eyes at the thought. Heavens, the way he'd fallen to that floor . . .

"He is my friend," she cried.

"Ariel, calm down," Phoebe said, wringing her hands. She raced forward, the hoops of her emerald-colored gown swaying. "What Reggie did he did for your own good. Can you not see that?"

"No," Ariel gasped, turning to the window, tears escaping. "No, I cannot. Nathan will think I was involved. You do not understand the man as I do. He does not trust easily, and now he will never trust again."

Phoebe's blue eyes clouded. "Ariél, please. Only remember. The man fooled you into thinking he wanted to be your friend. How could you trust *him?*"

She recalled the way he had looked at her as he begged for her help, the way he'd stared down at her so earnestly as he'd told her the story of the woman who'd betrayed him. "I trust him because no matter what you might think, the man is desperate to find his brother. That fact cannot be denied. And now he can no longer search for him."

"Where are you going?" Phoebe asked.

Ariel hadn't even realized she'd turned. "I have an errand to run."

"Dressed like that?"

She stopped, looked down, her vision blurring once again as she recalled the look on Nathan's face when he'd seen her in the clothes. She was not a total innocent. He'd found her attractive.

"You're correct. I should change." She moved again.

"No, Ariel," Phoebe pleaded. "Don't go. It can't be wise to go out alone."

"Will you go with me, then," she asked.

"Ariel," Reggie warned her.

"No," Ariel said to Phoebe, "I thought not. Truth be told, you should probably stay here. 'Twill be safer."

Phoebe stared up at her intently before turning to her husband. "Reggie, say something."

"I'm sorry if things did not go as planned," Reggie offered.

She whirled on him. "Sorry are you? Sorry for having a man captured for doing nothing more than wanting to find his brother? Or sorry for not telling me of your plan to make me look a betrayer in that man's eyes?"

He didn't say anything. Ariel wouldn't have cared if he had. Fifteen minutes later, dressed in a primrose-colored gown, she left.

But it took hours to track down the magistrate, the man with the power to set Nathan free. The lateness of the day when she arrived at his office had ruined her chance to see him. When she finally found him at his home, the sun had disappeared from the sky, the evening air was heavy with foggy moisture. She'd forgotten a cape in her haste to leave, had neglected, even, to pile her hair atop her head. The curls fell down her shoulders now, wild and in disarray. But Ariel cared little for her appearance. Nor did she care that it was highly inappropriate of her to visit a single gentleman on her own. Given her past, she thought, she had very little reputation to uphold. But as a footman led her into a study, the magistrate rising from behind his desk, she felt distinctly nervous.

"What did you want to see me about, Lady D'Archer, that is so important you would interrupt my dinner?"

Was it dinner time? She hadn't noticed. He glared at her from above double chins. His blue eyes were cold, his wig had very obviously been put on in haste, for it listed to one side.

"I beg your pardon, my lord, but this could not wait."

He settled himself in his study chair. The desk he sat behind was littered with paper. "Very well, then, what is it?"

"Nathan Trevain," was all she said.

The magistrate looked at her as if she'd escaped from one of his goals. His wig dipped down practically to his eyebrows. "What of Nathan Trevain?"

"I want him released."

"Surely you jest."

"No, sir. I am completely serious."

The wig was drawn back up his forehead. His watery eyes filled with disapproval. "Mr. Trevain is a prisoner; as such he will not be released."

"But he is Davenport's heir. Surely that must count for something."

"We are well aware of his lineage. 'Tis the only thing that has saved him from a hanging."

"He is not to be hanged, then?"

"No, as tempting as the thought may be. Frankly, we are not sure what to do with him."

Her relief was so great, she almost melted into the plush, green armchair she stood next to. "May I see him?" she asked.

"No."

"But why not—"

"Because," he interrupted, "the man is a criminal and a traitor. He is not fit for the presence of an earl's daughter."

So he recognized her name. She should have known he would. "Let that be up to me."

"No, my lady. I will not allow it."

"But, I—"

"No," he repeated, standing up from his chair. Ariel realized he'd never asked her to sit down. "Now, if you do not mind, I shall get back to my dinner. My footman will show you the way out."

She wanted to protest, truly she did. Instead she gritted out, "Thank you, my lord, for seeing me."

He nodded, motioning for her to precede him. She felt his eyes on her back as she entered the hall, her spine stiff to disguise the disappointment she felt.

Nathan, I've let you down twice today.

It was a downhearted Ariel who entered Phoebe's carriage. Her thoughts ran pell-mell, so much so that she couldn't think where to tell the driver to go. She didn't want to go home, for facing Phoebe and Reggie was more than she could take.

Gracious, if only she could have convinced the magistrate to release Nathan. But, obviously, that would take someone with more power than she. Someone like her father. If only he weren't still out of the country. Sometimes Ariel wondered if he didn't leave on purpose. An attempt to avoid her company, she conjectured. It was not the first time she'd thought such a thing, for a person in her father's position did not need to make voyages. In fact, most of the other admirals elected to stay at home.

She stiffened.

Most of the other admirals.

Oh, gracious heavens, how perfect. How utterly perfect. 'Twas Thursday.

"1570 Knightbridge Street," she called to the driver, her stomach knotting with anticipation, anxiety and dread.

Pray God they would see her. But if they refused, she would give them no choice.

It was near ten o'clock when Ariel arrived at her destination. She could see the carriages waiting outside Lord Parker's elegant home: Lords Hamilton, Vincent, Gordon and Howell, she recognized. All were present for their Thursday night card game.

The footman who opened the door looked startled to see her. She gave him no time to protest as she barreled past him.

"Beg your pardon, miss, but—"

"I will just be a moment," she answered. The room they used was on the right, the house familiar to her eyes. Lord Parker's daughter had once been a good friend, until her ruination of course. One of many such "friends" she had lost.

"Miss, really—"

She felt the footman tug at her arm, his hand sliding off the satin fabric when she pulled away and opened the door. She entered the room, the footman at her heels, a heavy cloud of cigar smoke almost choking her.

"I'm sorry, my lord. I tried to stop her—"

Lord Parker laid down his cards in shock. So did the other gentlemen. The scent of male sweat filled the air, as did the smell of brandy.

" 'Tis all right, James. Let her stay."

The footman bowed. Ariel watched him go, turning back to the room with an artificial smile upon her face. "My lords, how good it is to see you again."

Five faces, all of which bore a striking resemblance to the others, stared back.

"Lady D'Archer," Lord Parker greeted her, half rising, a lock of gray hair falling down his forehead. "Might I ask what we owe the pleasure of this visit to?"

"Nathan Trevain," she said with narrowed eyes. She waited for their reactions. There were none. That more than anything convinced her they'd already discussed him this night.

"Have you nothing to say?"

"What do you want with Nathan Trevain?" asked Parker, the senior officer there.

She came into the room further, feeling their

eyes bore holes in her. "I want him released and failing that, to see him. I would also like the location of his brother."

"Impossible," Lord Howell cried.

"No, it is not, Uncle George." If he minded the old endearment she used to use prior to her becoming a social pariah, he didn't show it. "Each of you has almost the same power as my father. Each of you could release Nathan Trevain if you so desired. And each of you could also tell me where his brother is. In fact, I would wager you all have that information in your head."

None of them responded. Smoke from their smoldering cigars rose toward the ceiling. A clock tick-tick-ticked in the room.

"Not going to tell me?" she asked.

"According to our sources in the colonies, he is a criminal and a traitor," Howell snapped. "He belongs in the Tower."

"He is guilty of nothing more than defending his country. If that makes him criminal, my lords, then you are criminals, too."

"You are wrong," Parker contradicted her. "What is more, if you do not leave my house this instant, I will see to it your father hears of your activities."

She laughed. "I would wager he will hear of it whether I leave or not."

"Yes, but you can be certain of it if you do not heed my warning this instant."

"You cannot order me out, Lord Parker. I am not one of your ensigns."

"No, you are the daughter of a trusted friend, a daughter who should have been married off or sent out of the country long ago. That your father did not do so was considered a bad mistake by us all, his lack of judgment showing its effects now. You are a disgrace, Ariel D'Archer, a woman it shames me to admit is the daughter of our First Lord."

His words hit her like tiny rocks, though she told herself it was silly to let his barbs affect her so. She tilted her chin, telling herself Lord Parker only said aloud what everyone else thought. It shouldn't hurt. It shouldn't.

"Leave, please, before I have you forcibly removed."

She looked at them all. Each one was staring at her with identical looks of icy coldness and disgust. "So you will not tell me?"

"No," Parker said with impatience, others murmuring no along with him.

She struggled to keep her chin up, fought to stand there without letting them see how much they'd disappointed her. That her fellow countrymen—nay, men she'd once considered friends—could treat a fellow human being this way . . .

"Very well, then, I shall leave." She held herself erect, let her loathing shine from her eyes. "But when each of you looks in the mirror this night, ask yourself one question. Can you live with yourself if you cause the death of a man who was forcibly removed from his ship, made to serve aboard another vessel against his will, then not released once the reason for capture was over?" She let her eyes linger on each and every one of them. "If you can live with that, gentlemen, then you are sadder than I thought. Good evening."

She turned on her heel, barely seeing her surroundings. But when she reached the carriage, it all came undone. Her shoulders slumped, her eyes filled with tears. She stood there trying to get her breath. Failed. Again.

"Lady D'Archer?"

Ariel stiffened.

Lord Gordon had followed her from the house. "A moment, if you please."

She turned, stared, damned if she would be the first to talk.

"You should not have come," he said after a lengthy pause.

"I had no choice."

His aged gray eyes looked disturbed. "It will go ill with you and your father."

"I know that, too, but it does not stop me from doing what is right."

He didn't answer, just glanced back at the house. Light shone through the windows. Ariel thought it looked remarkably serene, considering the tumultuous words that had just been spoken. Gordon turned back to her. The war had aged him, she realized. Well, the war had aged them all. For the first time Ariel understood what that meant, for she felt a different person since meeting Nathan Trevain. Older. Wiser. Less naive.

"I never agreed with the navy's unspoken approval of press gangs. 'Tis a deplorable practice for a nation that prides itself on civil liberties."

"As I recall, my lord, 'tis exactly that right which the colonist fought for."

He grew silent again. Ariel didn't know what to do. Hold her tongue? Plead Nathan's case again?

She did what came naturally, reaching out and placing her hand on his jacket. "If you know where his brother is, at least tell me that."

His blue eyes stared at her with unwavering consideration for a long moment. Then he seemed to nod to himself. "Very well. He is being held aboard Captain Pike's ship, HMS *Destiny*. It's due into Portsmouth any day now. A court-martial is convening."

Ariel stared up at the man, speechless. When the words finally penetrated, she spun on her heel and entered the carriage.

There was no time to waste, not even on a good-bye and thank you to Lord Gordon.

18

The acrid smell of urine and sweat filled Nathan's nostrils as he awoke. Bits of straw clung to his white shirt and breeches, the guard having stolen his naval jacket. It was cold, though Nathan didn't feel it. No, he burned inside, burned as he had never burned before.

Betrayed.

Again.

By a woman.

How could she do it? he asked himself. How could she stand there and seem so sincere, all the while plotting his capture? He stood up from where he leaned against a cold, hard wall. Muted gray light shone in from a window high above him. He stared at it, his jaw tight with bitter anger. He would escape from this hellhole, he silently promised, escape and then find his brother. Then he would leave this godforsaken country and its treacherous people.

But as he looked into the cloudy sky, a pair of golden eyes haunted him.

Damnation. Why could he not get her off his mind?

Because you'd started to like her, Trevain. More than that, you'd started to care about her.

Yea, he'd cared about her just a bit too much. Fool. Imbecile. He'd almost done it again, fallen in love with the wrong woman.

He clenched his fists, felt the scabs on his knuckles begin to crack. The realization only brought back memories of her.

I'll help you, she had said.

And she'd looked so damn earnest, so damn heartfelt. So damn beautiful.

But as the memory of her beauty splintered apart his heart, so did his trust. He choked on that trust, surprised to feel himself unable to breathe for a moment as he tried to get his rampaging emotions under control.

"Well, my bloody patriot. Time to move you to yur new 'ome."

Nathan spun to face the door, his dirty sash flaring. He welcomed the interruption, for with it came the opportunity to think, think about something other than Ariel D'Archer.

" 'Ave you 'eard? Yur ta be taken to the Tower this mornin'. First-class 'ccommodations, they are. Like it there you will, I'll wager. They've got more mice than we 'ave."

The man opened his mouth, a loud guffaw emerging past his cankerous-looking gums. He clutched his gut, squeezing out the words, "Come along, then, let's put these chains on ya."

Nathan tensed, thinking he could take the man on, but two more guards entered the cell. One of them pulled out a pistol, the other came forward to put on the chains. Nathan forced himself to calm. Time enough to fight later . . . when he wasn't so outnumbered.

The light outside his cell seemed bright after the dimness of his former quarters. Two more guards stood outside, these with muskets, the muzzles pointed at the sky. Nathan followed the first two out, his wrist and ankle chains rattling as he walked up a flight of stairs, down a narrow hall and out a door.

Be patient, he told himself. *Bide your time.*

He emerged into a courtyard of some sort. A prison transport with a single draft horse stood impatiently pawing the ground. The horse's breath steamed in the chill morning air. Nathan felt a shiver race up his spine as they led him toward the vehicle. Big wheels, high, wooden walls and a thick roof. A small door had been cut into the back. A square window with iron bars over it was the only adornment.

"Get in."

He did as instructed, using the steps they provided. The inside of the cart smelled as horrendous as his cell. He settled himself on the grimy, dank floor, his lip curling in disgust. The light faded as the door closed. The carriage tipped as someone climbed aboard—the driver, no doubt.

" 'Ave fun in the Tower," called the gaoler. "Try not ta lose yur 'ead while yur there."

Again a loud guffaw rang out. Nathan closed his eyes, leaning his head against the wooden sides.

Would this day never end?

But unfortunately, it would, without Wess's location discovered. Without even a clue as to if he was still alive. Bloody, bloody hell.

The streets seemed to be deserted. The sound of the carriage was the only thing Nathan heard besides the persistent beat of his thoughts. That they used no soldiers as escorts showed their contempt for him as a prisoner. They would realize their mistake soon enough. Not for nothing had he fought in hand-to-hand combat for a year.

The carriage picked up speed. The road became bumpier as it flew over cobblestones, then bumpier still as it rounded a corner.

"Bloody hell," he heard the driver yell. The cart tilted abruptly. Nathan placed his hands against the walls to avoid being tossed about. The cart swayed in the other direction before stopping suddenly with a *thunk*.

"Bloody, bloody hell. I could have been killed," he heard the man mutter.

"Do not move," a female voice said a moment later.

Nathan froze.

"Step down from the carriage and let the prisoner out."

Ariel.

And if he didn't miss his guess, she was—

"Now," she added.

Staging a rescue. He shot up, his chains rattling as he flung himself at the door.

" 'Ere now, lad. I can't be doing that."

"You will do whatever I say or I will use this pistol to put a ball through you."

Silence as the man obviously contemplated his options. And then he felt the carriage tip, heard keys jingle as they were pulled out.

Nathan closed his eyes in relief. Demme, it wasn't a lad . . . it was Ariel. She was rescuing him. And though he told himself what he felt was simple gratitude, he knew it was more than that.

Much, much more.

The door opened, a hooded figure stood behind the same guard who'd put on his chains, a figure disguised as a boy yet unmistakably Ariel.

"Take them off," she ordered, her voice low, obviously in an attempt to disguise it.

He could barely see her face in the early-morning light, for she wore a cloak over her boys' clothes, a hood shielding her face.

"Quickly," she added.

The man's eyes narrowed at the order. Nathan saw his intent before he had time to do it.

"Ariel—" He flung himself at the man, the pistol the guard reached for flying to the ground. They both landed hard. The breath rushed out as Nathan flipped onto his back.

But his chains turned out to be a blessing, for when the guard drew back to hit him, Nathan swung his arms, one of the iron bracelets he wore catching the man square in the head. He collapsed like a broken tent.

"Nathan, oh, Nathan, are you all right?"

He didn't answer. Truth be told, so many of his bones ached from his collision with the ground he doubted if he could have talked if he'd wanted to. He lay there, eyes closed.

"Nathan?" Small hands shook him.

Reluctantly he opened his eyes. Wonderful, beautiful golden eyes stared down at him. They were filled with concern and something else? Relief? His hand lifted automatically, only to fall back to his side as he winced. "I am well, Ariel."

"Oh, thank goodness. That means you can get up."

No, pray God, don't make me move.

She nudged him with her hand. "Hurry, Nathan, before someone comes upon us."

She had a point. He hated to admit it, but she had a point.

"Find the man's keys. We'll need to unlock my shackles."

She nodded, doing as instructed. Slowly Nathan pulled himself into a sitting position, watching her search, wanting to reach out and clasp her to him, wanting to kiss her, wanting to do so many damn things he was hard pressed not to touch her.

"Here."

She made short work of the locks, her hands shaking, her eyes darting behind and around them numerous times. When the last chain dropped away, he clutched at those hands. Her gaze immediately went to his.

"Thank you."

She nodded, her eyes filling with heartfelt emotion. "You're welcome," she answered softly.

The urge to kiss her overcame him, but she spoiled it by pushing herself to her feet, the gray cloak she wore flaring as she turned toward two horses tied nearby.

He turned toward the cart.

And gawked.

The horse was gone. All that butted up against the side of a deserted building was the cart.

"I worked the pin loose this morn," she explained. " 'Twas a difficult task, let me tell you. And then I must have followed you for a mile before it finally worked its way all the way out. Gracious, this made forging those documents with my father's seal seem easy. Of course it was easy to copy my father's hand and cancel the order for an escort for you this morn."

"Ariel, I do believe I could kiss you."

"Save it for later, Nathan. For now we must hurry."

She took his hand, leading him toward the horses. They stood in the middle of a street with buildings on either side, some dilapidated, some not. 'Twas only a matter of time before someone spied the broken carriage and called the Watch, if they hadn't seen it already.

"Take the black," she instructed, mounting her own bay horse.

"Where are we going?" he asked as he mounted.

"Portsmouth."

"Portsmouth? Why?"

"Your brother's ship is due into port there."

He stared at her in mute shock. And then he gave in to the urge that had plagued him since first hearing her voice. Pulling his horse abreast of hers, he leaned over and kissed her—quickly, lest his body embark upon other ideas.

"I am in your debt, Ariel D'Archer."

"Yes, you are. And so I will settle for you moving that horse."

He smiled, then did as asked. Suddenly the day didn't look so bad.

19

They left London at top speed, Nathan turning his horse off the main road once traffic cleared. Ariel followed, wondering where he was going. Apparently to a stand of trees, tall oaks whose gnarled limbs reached toward the sky. He stopped in a dappled patch of sunlight. The smell of oak leaves and rich earth filled her nostrils.

"Why have we stopped?"

"Tell me what ship my brother is on."

"Why?" she asked suspiciously.

"Because you are staying behind."

She stiffened. "No, I am not."

"Yes, you are, Ariel. 'Tis too dangerous for you to go any further."

"So you would have me ride back into town alone?"

"It is the lesser of two evils."

"Evils. Why, I—" She released a huff of air in mute belligerence. "I've just rescued you, you fiend. In broad daylight. And yet you worry that a ride to Portsmouth will be dangerous?"

He frowned. "The ride concerns me not. It is what awaits us in Portsmouth that I fear."

"Fear not, sir, for I shall be perfectly safe." She turned her horse to go.

"Ariel, wait—"

But she ignored him. Silly man. Did he not see there was no way to stop her from accompanying him?

Apparently he didn't see for one minute she was on the horse, the next he pulled her off it. They both landed on their feet.

"How in heavens did you do that?"

She pressed up against him. Her cape had parted. Without the mounds of petticoats and hoops, she could feel every hard muscle in his legs. Gracious.

"A trick I learned in war, my dear." And did his voice sound strained, too?

Her body began to warm in the most lovely way. Not in desire. No, not really that. In something else, something that felt wonderful and sweet.

" 'Tis a good trick," she admitted.

He still held her, his arms around her waist. "Yes, it is," he answered back.

He would kiss her, she was sure of it. That was good, for she felt quite willing to be kissed. But instead he put his nose next to hers. His face was a blurry blob. All she could see were his eyes. No scar, no forehead, just his eyes. She didn't move. Truth be told, she felt rather curious about what he intended to do.

"What are you doing?"

"I am trying to tell you with my eyes that you are not going." His breath whispered over her skin. She liked the smell of that breath, which was rather odd, for she couldn't ever remember thinking such a thing before.

"Is it working?" he asked.

If she tilted her head back just a bit, just a tiny bit. "No."

"Then listen to me. You are not going."

His breath wafted across her lips again, his body snuggled next to hers: hip to hip, chest to chest. "Yes, I am," she answered, moving even closer.

His eyes grew heated. "Please, Ariel, do not argue with me."

Gracious, but his eyes were amazing. So many colors all mixed into one: green, blue and silver gray. "I am not arguing, Nathan, I am merely stating facts. We are going together."

"No, we are not."

She drew back, hating the loss of contact but beginning to grow piqued. "And what will you do if I do not comply? Tie me to that tree there, like you did before?"

"Yes," he answered, crossing his arms in front of him.

"And how will you tie me?" she asked sarcastically. "With the ribbon that holds back your queue?"

"No, with your horse's reins."

She placed her hands on her hips. "Bully for you."

"Yes, it is rather a good idea."

Her eyes narrowed. "Nathan, we don't have time to argue. Your brother's ship will arrive shortly—"

"The name of that ship, Ariel," he interrupted.

"I am not telling it to you, so you will just have to take me with you."

He took a step, pulled her back into his arms, his eyes so suddenly earnest her breath caught, "Please, Ariel, do not be stubborn. 'Tis too dangerous."

She swallowed, opened her mouth, swallowed again and said, "You need me, Nathan. I am the First Lord's daughter. I can help. Or have you forgotten that?"

He let her go, his arms falling to his sides, his eyes dimming. "Of course I have not forgotten that."

"Then you should know this, too." She reached out and touched him, not wanting to make him panic but knowing she would have to tell him about his brother sooner or later.

His silver gaze intensified. "What?"

She took a deep breath. "The captain of your brother's ship, a Captain Pike, is coming into port for a court-martial. I believe he has men he needs to try, for what I do not know, but if he is coming into port so that this is done as per the Articles of War, then it must be serious indeed."

He spun away from her.

Bullocks, she knew that would happen. "Where are you going?" Even though she knew well and good where.

"I am leaving," he said, clutching the reins, his ring glinting in the sunlight. "There's no time for us to argue."

Isn't that what she'd just been saying?

He mounted his horse, looking down at her. "Are you coming?"

She stiffened, thinking some men were truly idiots at times. "Yes."

"Then hurry."

Portsmouth, Britian's only island city, had changed little since her last visit, Ariel noted when they arrived nearly five hours later. The moats and ramparts which encircled the town still gave off a rank odor as they crossed through one of the two gates which gave access to the city. As usual, the Navy's presence was everywhere. A group of mounted, blue-jacketed men passed them by, one of them studying her intently as they turned onto High Street. Ariel sank back farther into her hooded cloak, relief flooding her as she spotted the harbor directly ahead.

"He could be on one of those ships."

Ariel started at Nathan's words. Aye, she thought, following his gaze, he could be. There were several three- and two-masted ships moored in the harbor, but of course there would need to be. Not for nothing was she the First

Lord's daughter. As such she knew the workings of a court-martial. Between five and thirteen officers had to be present in order for it to conform to naval law. Held for those crimes that required more than thirty lashes, such as desertion, and for those crimes that required the death penalty, such as murder or cowardice, it was usually an unpleasant affair. If Wess Trevain was alive and he'd tried to desert, then he would be court-martialed here.

If he was alive.

"We need to find out when the court-marital will be convened," Nathan said in a clipped voice.

"Let us ask someone."

Nathan nodded. Ariel slowed her horse. They asked the first person they came across, a small man who had the look of the sea about him with his leathery skin and wiry frame.

"Court-martial?" the man repeated Nathan's question. "Aye, I heard about it. Convened already, it did. Ships got ta port early, so they did it this morn."

"No," Ariel gasped, clutching the reins.

The man glanced at her. Ariel tensed as she waited to be identified as female. But the man must have seen what she wanted him to see, a young lad dressed in a too-large cape.

"Are the ships still in port?" Nathan asked.

The man shrugged. "Aye, three of them are."

Ariel's breath caught.

"Captains Hillis, Crane and Bantry, but that

be all. Pike left port like 'is ballast were afire."

Ariel could do nothing more than stare, first at the little man, then up at Nathan. His jaw had grown tight, his knuckles as white as her own as he gripped the reins.

"Thank you, sir," he said tightly.

The man nodded, then moved on. Nathan still sat atop his horse, looking, yet apparently not seeing anything.

"He could still be alive," Ariel said, moving her horse alongside his.

But he wouldn't meet her gaze. "He could be dead, too."

She shook her head. "No. I do not think so."

But he didn't look interested in arguing the point. She watched as his hands clenched even tighter, his fingernails digging into his palm.

"We will find him, Nathan. I promise."

"How?" he asked, finally meeting her gaze. "Hire a sloop? Chase after him on an ocean that leaves no trail?"

"That is one possibility."

"Do not be absurd. We would sooner find a needle in a haystack."

Something inside her cringed at his raised voice, something that made her feel both hurt and sick at the same time.

"Nathan," she began again, "we can at least try. I am the First Lord's daughter. Surely there is something I can do."

"Yea, just as you've done already."

His words stabbed at her with hurt. She

watched as he clucked his horse forward, stopping in front of an inn a few muddy blocks later. Ariel followed, feeling helpless and hurt and so sorry for him she could barely think.

"What are we doing?"

"Securing rooms for the night."

"Should we not ride back to London?"

"No. My best chance of finding Wess starts here."

His best chance. So he didn't want her help anymore.

"Nathan, please—"

He refused to look at her, just entered the building. Not even as he talked to the innkeeper did he pay her heed. Not even as they climbed the stairs. Instead he gave her a key, turned and entered his own room, slamming the door behind him.

Ariel stared at the scarred oak door, wondering what to do.

Leave him be, Ariel. He needs time.

But she didn't want to leave him alone, she wanted . . .

What?

To comfort him. She wanted to comfort him.

She went to his door, stared at it, knowing what she did might change her life forever. She lifted her hand, only to drop it back to her side again. Fiddlesticks. He would not welcome her attention. She knew this, yet she lifted her hand again, only this time she knocked.

No answer.

Almost she gave up. Almost. But that same perverse desire that made her want to comfort him, that same emotion that made her care when she knew she shouldn't made her lift her hand again, and when he didn't answer a second time, to try the handle.

The door opened.

"What are you doing?" he snapped, turning to face her.

He stood by the window on the opposite side of the room, a fireplace to her left, the bed opposite. Nathan stared at her, his face as rigid as the hardwood floor.

"We should talk."

"There is nothing to say."

"I want to help."

"Help? Haven't you helped me enough?"

He said it as if his brother's disappearance was all her fault. She swallowed back a pinch of hurt. He felt wounded. Aching over the loss of his brother. She knew this. If only she could convince him of the fact that Wess Trevain was not dead, not yet.

"Nathan, please. Try and believe me when I say—"

"No, Ariel. I will not listen. Leave." He swung away from her, his queue swishing angrily, his scar more pronounced as he turned toward the window.

She followed him, knowing it was tantamount to cornering a wolf in his den, but determined to do so anyway. "Nathan, please," she tried again, stepping around in front of him, her words dying in her throat.

He cried.

No. Not cried. A single tear made its way down his cheek, but for a man like Nathan Trevain, it was as good as a bucketful of sobs.

Men like Nathan Trevain did not cry. They blustered. They yelled. They did not cry.

"Oh, Nathan," she soothed, placing her hand against his jaw, just like he always did to her when she was upset. Something inside her shifted as she stared up at him, something that made her feel breathless and frightened. She looked into his silver eyes, eyes that had stared at her with so many emotions in the past. Loathing. Anger. Gratitude. Now they simply looked down at her with sadness and resignation.

"Leave, Ariel."

She shook her head. "You need me."

"I need no one."

"Shh," she soothed, touching his lips with her hands. "Just shh." She slipped into his arms, expecting him to thrust her away.

I love you, she thought. *I love you Nathan Trevain. Don't push me away.*

She pulled back before he could, stunned. Her eyes searched his intently.

And she knew.

She knew with an absolute certainty that the words were true.

Somehow, amazingly, she'd fallen in love with

the man. It didn't matter that he'd kidnapped her. It didn't matter that he'd tried to use her. He was as different from Archie as sun was from rain, his motivation for doing as he did one Ariel wholly understood.

"Nathan," she hoarsely, a throat full of tears suddenly choking her. She reached up again, stroked his cheek.

He didn't move, his silver eyes staring into hers.

"Kiss me."

"No."

"Yes," she contradicted him. "Let me help you forget." She lifted herself up on tiptoe, drawing his head down, forcing him to do as she asked. He didn't move at first. She nibbled at his lip, sucking on it.

"Demme," he moaned, trying to push her away. But she wouldn't let him. Instead she held him tighter, her lips working his own more fervently. She thought he might turn away from her then, thought he might pull back. Instead he suddenly jerked her to him. Ariel gasped at the suddenness of it. His tongue plunged into her mouth.

Yes, she thought. Yes. This was it. This was what she sought. The way he angled his mouth just perfectly. The way he smelled. Why hadn't she realized it before? She wanted to taste him. Wanted to feel his tongue inside her mouth. Wanted to suck in the essence of him as he did her.

"Ariel," he said, cupping the back of her head, his hands warm against her scalp. She tilted her head into those hands, the gold from his ring cold against her cheek. She let him kiss her deeper and then deeper still. Blood rushed to places that suddenly warmed, then began to burn. She knew the feeling, had been kissed enough times to know that the feeling promised something else, something wonderful, and that she wanted.

And then he pulled back, both of them gasping for breath in the wake of their passion.

"Ariel," he moaned again, staring down at her a second before kissing her again, but not on the lips. On the cheek, then on the forehead. She sighed in relief, having thought he might stop, but he didn't stop. Oh, no. He began to kiss her in a whole new way, biting, teasing kisses. On the temple. The line of her jaw. In places she'd never been kissed before.

"Oh, Nathan," she answered back.

His hands moved away from the back of her head to her cloak, parting it, his fingers slipping beneath it to flick it off her shoulders as he continued to kiss her, only now he kissed her neck. Oh, gracious heavens. Her neck. Her vision blurred, the world slipping away at the dizzying feel of his lips sucking at her flesh. Heavens, she didn't want it to stop. Didn't want the feelings that began to build inside her to end. She wanted . . . she wanted . . .

What?

Gracious, she didn't know, only knew she didn't want to stop being enchanted by his kisses. Ever. And then he shifted, air cooling the wetness where his lips had just been. She felt reality begin to return, only to fall away again as his mouth found her ear. She closed her eyes, groaning at the feel of his tongue.

"Ariel," he breathed, pulling back. "I want you. And if you do not leave, I will have you."

"Then have me."

"No. Not tonight."

"Yes, tonight," she answered, boldly touching his white shirt. She felt him tense beneath her hands. "I want this, Nathan. More than I've ever wanted anything in my life."

I love you, she silently added, more certain of it now than ever. She loved him, there was simply no use denying the way he made her feel. She loved him more than she'd ever thought it possible to love a man who had treated her thus. She'd loved him for asking for her help. She loved him for trusting her right back. But most of all, she loved him because he stood here kissing her, loving her, even though she must seem more an enemy tonight then ever before.

"Why are you crying?"

Was she? She hadn't even realized. "I'm crying for you, Nathan," she said softly, touching his cheek again. "I'm crying because I know you must think your brother lost. But he isn't. I promise you this. We will find him. You need only believe."

He stared down at her, his silver eyes so beautiful. "Show me how to believe, Ariel. Show me."

She knew what he meant, though she didn't know how to do as he asked. "Kiss me, Nathan."

He didn't immediately. Ariel never looked away as he weighed his decision in his mind, and she could tell that he weighed one.

"We shall both regret this."

"No," she answered. "Never."

And then he did kiss her, only this time there was a frantic edge to his touch. His hands fumbled at her shirt. Ariel did the same to his shirt. She pulled on the fabric, Nathan doing the same. He undressed her. Ariel knew they were approaching the point of no return yet wanted what lay beyond that point with a desire such as she'd never craved. He ducked down, letting her tug off his shirt. She held still as he pulled her own shirt loose. They both paused at the binding that covered her breasts, and then a new rhythm began. A slow one. His hands lifted bit by bit, his gaze never leaving her own, as he gently, seductively began to unwind the fabric.

"Lift your arms."

Ariel did, she closed her eyes. She felt each brush of his fingers, each tug on the fabric, until at last she knew only one layer remained.

"Do you want me to stop?"

It was the last time he would ask her that question. She knew this. Now or never.

"Don't stop," she breathed.

He tugged on the fabric. Her breasts sprang free. She heard him gasp, though she might have been imagining it, but then he said, "God, but you're beautiful."

She stared up at him, for the first time seeing herself with his eyes. "I feel beautiful," she answered.

And she was, Nathan realized. More beautiful than he'd ever thought it possible for a woman to be. Her skin was as white as sunlight on pure silk, her shape as perfect as God ever intended it to be, and he wanted . . . how he wanted . . . Thoughts of his brother faded. He allowed himself to get swept up in the smell of her, the taste of her, the feel of her, the enchantment of her.

He reached out a hand, touching the top of her breasts, then dipped lower, finding her nipple.

"Nathan," he heard her moan.

He rubbed it, making it hard, as hard as he was for her. He could feel himself straining against his breeches, felt his own answering moisture for her, and he knew that if he didn't take her soon, he would lose himself.

Still, some perverse desire made him continue to stroke her, watching as she tilted her head back, her dark curls falling almost to her waist. He didn't seem to be able to stop touching her, his craving for her such that he wanted to hear her moan again. He closed the distance between them, leaned down and kissed her. She opened immediately, moaning, just as he'd wanted. He sucked her, rubbing his thumb around her nipple in time with his tongue.

"Touch me, Ariel," he ordered.

And she did. She touched his chest tentatively at first, and then with a growing desperation that made his desire erupt in a way that made him almost lose control. God, she knew how to touch him. Almost as if she'd been doing it all her life. He lapped the taste of her with his tongue, using his other hand to tug the fabric of her breeches. They were so big on her they fell the moment he released the rope holding them around her waist.

He pulled back and looked.

Perfection. He needed no lust to heighten his appreciation of her. She was everything he'd fantasized she would be. He reached out a hand, touching her shoulder, moving his hand lower toward the top of her breast. He skated around one round globe toward her side, feeling the bumps of her rib cage, then the smooth feel of her abdomen. Her muscles contracted beneath his touch, her flesh dotted with goose pimples. The fine, fine hairs that covered her skin felt soft to his touch.

"Nathan," she whispered as his hand moved lower, her head tilting back.

He stared at her, marveled at her, even as his hand moved lower, until at last he touched the softness above her thighs.

"Oh, Nathan," she sighed, her head moving from side to side, long hair sweeping almost to her waist.

He stepped closer, making sure to keep his body out of contact with her, even as he fought a longing to pull her toward him. His body was so hard for her, his erection throbbing in anticipation of being inside her. He ran his hand through her soft curls, using his index finger to skate the folds of her womanhood.

It was then that she moved closer, pushing into his hand, forcing him to cup her slick wetness. His eyes drank in the sight of her. Her nipples tiny little buds, her skin glistening with a fine sheen of sweat. She kept pushing into him, moving her body in a way that spoke of a freedom Nathan had never seen before. He felt her moist valley, let her seek the climax her body craved. She moaned again, then again, seeming to be lost in a world all her own.

"Nathan," she said, clutching at his forearms, her eyes opening. They were foggy, unfocused. Confused. "Oh, Nathan."

"Let it come, Ariel."

She shook her head, continuing to move against him. He bent, captured her lips with his own, dipping his tongue into her mouth with the same rhythm he used below. His hands shook as he touched her, showing her how to touch him likewise. And she did, Nathan groaning as she stroked the length of him.

So lost were they that he didn't even realize

he'd somehow moved them to the bed. Not until he began to gently lay her down did he realize what he'd done. There was only one thought. *Make love to her*. It was a need that rose within him with such a fierce longing he could barely contain the shaking of his limbs as he settled her back. Firelight cast its flickering spells across her body. A shadow here, the glow of flesh there. But always, always there were her eyes. So intense the look in them. So filled with a need that matched his own. There was no hesitancy. No shy innocence. There was only want, want and something else, a something that filled him with hunger and had him capturing her lips with his own. Then her tongue, their dueling fueling a fire of its own. Somehow he was lowering his breeches. Somehow, without knowing quite how he'd gotten there, they ended up naked in each other's arms, Nathan alongside of her, Ariel half beneath him, one leg drawn up, knee bent.

Not once did she resist, not even as he stroked his hand down the side of her, awed by the softness of her flesh. She wanted him as badly as he wanted her. He could see it in her eyes, feel it in the way her body pressed into his hand, touch it in the wetness of her desire. And though Nathan sensed there was something deeper to her need than just desire, he didn't dwell on the matter. He was past the point of wanting. He needed only to take.

"Nathan," she whispered his name again.

He closed his eyes, the husky sound of her voice the essence of everything he craved. At that moment he wondered if she was a virgin, for she seemed a woman of the world, one who knew what she wanted in a man and wasn't afraid to take it.

But if a man had been there before him, did he really care?

For an instant sanity returned. And then she reached up and touched his face. A simple gesture, really, but the feel of her fingers stroking the side of his jaw, the way her eyes burned into his own, the way, God, the way she lifted her head off the pillow and captured his lips with her own, it was all his undoing. And he realized he didn't care. There was no going back, there was only going forward now.

He returned her kiss gently and then, as he realized she didn't want it gently, with more pressure, the pleasure in his own body building to a point that beckoned him like her amber eyes. His hand stroked her breasts, then moved lower, dipping to a silky-smooth belly that jerked against him in response to his touch. He moved lower, felt her arch into his hand as he palmed her again. Bloody hell, but she was wet for him. He groaned, stroking her, dipping his fingers deeper and deeper. She moaned, her hands lifting to cup the back of his head. He felt her work the leather that tied his hair back, felt the first locks of it fall forward around his face. Her eyes seemed to grow even more gold as she stared up at him.

It became a kind of pain to hold back. And yet he was determined to do so.

"Please," she begged.

He knew what she wanted, so he stroked her deeper. He could feel her climax begin to build in the way she clenched around him. It was then that he covered her. At last. There was a moment, a brief one, when he weighed what he was about to do against what he knew he should do. Stop. But his body's craving for her, his need for her wouldn't allow him to hold back. He held himself steady at her entrance, his manhood replacing the hand he pulled away.

Still, he found himself saying, "Ariel," in a husky groan that was part question, part plea.

"Shh," she soothed, reaching up to touch his face, telling him without words that she wanted this as much as he. She spread her legs wider. He groaned at the feel of her doing so.

"Ariel, we can't go back once this is done. Do you understand?"

She swallowed, nodded, her eyes languid with desire. "Do it to me, Nathan, please." She lifted her hips.

His restraint broke. He pushed himself into her slowly, oh, so slowly, for she was a virgin, and he didn't want to hurt her. She was slick for him, so slick it was hell to keep from thrusting all the way. He began to pant, began to tremble.

"No," she said, as he started to back out.

"Wait, love," he soothed. He moved into her again, only deeper this time. He wanted to kiss her, knew to do so would break his control.

"Yes," she whispered. "Oh, Nathan, yes." She closed her eyes, tilting her head against the pillow.

He pulled out again, then slowly moved into her again, deeper still.

"Hold me tight, Ariel," he instructed her. "Hold me."

She did, crossing her legs behind his own. He moved out of her again, teaching her how to move, how to use him so that he didn't have to move. And she learned quickly, her hips rising and falling, rising and falling, faster and faster. And then, to his amazement, he felt the barrier of her maidenhead break. The realization drove him over the edge. He heard her gasp once, knew he'd broken through, then began to move deeper, the possessiveness he felt on realizing he was the first filling him with raging desire.

"Nathan," she cried. "Oh, Nathan."

Their movements grew more frantic. Nathan plunging in and out of her, Ariel moving with him. Their mouths found each other. They sucked, Nathan moving, moving, moving until he felt himself began to give, felt her answering moan. *Yes. Yes*, he thought. *Come with me. Come now*.

And then she cried out, her body clutching his

own, then releasing in sweet abandon, throbbing around him, milking him of the seed he gave her.

"Ariel," he sighed against her lips, pouring himself into her, feeling the heat of his seed within her. "My sweet Ariel."

"Nathan," she whispered back into his ear. "My darling Nathan."

20

If Ariel loved Nathan before, the act they'd committed made her love him all the more. Ariel's body still hummed from the last time they'd made love. Embers from the fire glowed, casting muted light on his form. He slept. Yet even in sleep he still looked the hardened warrior, for he still carried the scars of his past. The one on his face. The one on his back. And the one on his chest. She wanted to kiss all of them. But most of all, she wished she could heal the only scar that mattered.

Wess Trevain.

She closed her eyes, trying to think of a way to find him. But the only solution she came up with, the only chance they might have was through her father.

The thought filled her with dread.

Dealing with her father on a normal basis was difficult enough. Asking him to help made

Ariel cringe. She'd rather set her toes afire.

Yet what choice did she have? She loved the man beside her. And his life would not be complete without his brother by his side. So she needed to get that brother back. If he was alive.

Nay, she would not think about Wess Trevain being dead and the obstacles to her and Nathan's relationship if Wess'd been killed. Nathan would never blame her. To do so would be like blaming her for the war between their two countries.

Still her thoughts made her restless. She got up from the bed, careful not to disturb Nathan. It was dark outside and foggy, the kind of night when mist seems to creep through doors and permeate your clothes. It felt dank and cold, so much so that she longed for a bath to make her warmer. Bother that, she *would* take a bath, although in her own room so as not to disturb him.

Dressing quickly and quietly, she went across the hall, ringing for a servant when she got there. She'd donned her gray cloak. Her face was in shadow as she waited for her call to be answered.

"Lady Ariel D'Archer?" a masculine voice asked when she opened the door.

She started, but not because of the use of her name. No. It was his attire.

An officer stood there, his gold tassels and shiny gold buttons proclaiming him a high-ranking one. He looked young, perhaps not much older than herself. His face and hair were powdered, blue eyes slightly wrinkled at the corners from time spent aboard a ship.

"I have orders to bring you with me, my lady."

"Orders? From whom?" And more importantly, how had he discovered she was here?

"I was told to say nothing more than that, my lady. Will you come?"

Ariel almost told him no. She looked across the hall at Nathan's door, but as she stared at him she realized the only person who knew she was in Portsmouth was Lord Gordon. Had the man decided to help her further?

It could be. "Did Gordon send you?"

"Yes."

She closed her eyes in relief. Oh, thank goodness. "Then, yes, I will come with you."

Hastily she followed the officer, for he had already turned and left. Only once did she think to go back for Nathan. But what if they did not know he was here? Nay, better to keep his presence a secret.

Outside the air felt heavy with moisture, little droplets clinging to her face and eyes. He helped her into a hired hack, then settled on the seat opposite.

"Where are we going?"

"To the docks."

Her heart sped up. Had Gordon found Wess Trevain? Would this man take her to Nathan's brother? She clenched her hands in the folds of her cloak, wanting to find Nathan's brother so badly she could barely breathe.

They arrived at the docks quickly. Unfortunately, they smelled just as she remembered them. Fishy. The sounds of the ocean were just as she remembered, too. The booming roll of breakers offshore. The sound of nearby waves as they broke upon the legs of the pier. She clutched her cloak tighter, for the fog seemed thicker here, the chill increasing as the officer helped her into a shore boat crowded with rowers. He sat down next to her, his body affording little protection against the cold ocean air. The boat tilted as they both settled down.

Nervous energy made it hard to sit still, and as they rowed across the bay, that energy grew harder to bear. The fog and the darkness made it impossible to see the ship they headed toward, until suddenly they were next to its hulking mass. The thing was huge. Like a ghostly building it rose from the water, at least four stories high. A first-rate warship, no doubt, Ariel thought, the kind her father served on.

Her father.

She stiffened, her heart suddenly stopping in her chest before kicking back into action, if possible, at twice the speed.

It couldn't be.

"We're not here because of Gordon, are we?"

She could barely see the man as he glanced her way. "We are here because of Admiral Gordon, but 'tis not him you are going to see."

She closed her eyes. Oh, dear God, no. Not her father. But she was afraid to ask.

Still, did she need to? A court-martial had been convened. Only the highest-ranking officers were allowed to preside over courts-martial. If her father was near shore, he would have had to attend. And what if Lord Gordon had known that? What if he'd sent word to her father of her expected arrival last eve? What if this was Gordon's way of getting rid of her?

Her mouth turned dry, her body grew clammy. In vain she tried to make out the name of the ship, but it was too dark and too foggy to see anything but the shape of the vessel.

"Ship ahoy," called the watch on board deck as they pulled alongside, the boat rolling even closer on the crest of a small wave. They bumped into the side.

"Let me give you a hand, my lady," the officer said.

Ariel nodded. She had climbed aboard a ship before, though not in boys' clothes. Breeches and boots would make it much easier to move, no doubt. Taking a deep breath, she stood up. If she wanted to turn back, now would be the time. But if it was her father who was aboard, she had a feeling these men had their orders to bring her to him.

Bring her to him.

As if she were one of his crew, not his own flesh and blood.

Now, Ariel, you don't know 'tis your father aboard.

But she knew. It had to be. The officer treated her with too much respect for it to be anyone else. A lady in boys' clothes did not as a rule lend a man to behave with good manners.

"Are you ready?" he asked.

She nodded. He put his hands around her waist, lifting her, then holding the ladder steady. 'Twas one of the hardest things she had ever had to do, and not because of the physical effort. No, 'twas difficult because she knew if her father had ordered her presence, it could only bode ill. That meant he'd heard about her attempt to help Nathan Trevain. It meant, too, that he might suspect that she had become his lover.

The memory of the lovemaking acted as ballast. It steadied her, gave her courage, as a crew member helped her on board. Lantern light spread a muted, foggy glow over curious faces. She searched those faces anxiously.

"So Gordon was right. You have turned traitor."

She spun.

And there he was. Her father. She stiffened, telling herself she had nothing to be afraid of. She'd done the worst possible thing a daughter could do, ruin herself, and he hadn't beaten her or threatened her or sent her away.

No, he just stopped caring for you.

But she refused to think about that. "Father," she acknowledged him with a nod.

"Where'd you find her?" he asked the officer who'd just climbed up behind her.

"At the Boat and Anchor Inn."

"Was she alone?"

He nodded. "But Trevain was across the hall."

So they knew. They knew he was here. She felt her hands clench in sudden fear.

Her father nodded, his eyes shards of ice as he stared at her.

"Bring her here."

"I can follow on my own," she told her father, but he'd already turned. The officer took her elbow. She tried to pull away, but he wouldn't let her. The men on deck stared, then looked away. Ariel wondered how much her father had told them. But did she care?

No, she admitted. She did not.

They followed in her father's wake, the smell of hemp and salt water filling her nostrils. Tall masts rose up on her left. The sails were furled now that the ship was in port. Cannon squatted in specially carved holders along the rail. The gun ports were closed. She thought of the battles this ship had fought, of the men who'd lost their lives because of it.

Opening a door beneath the poop deck, her father ducked inside. She knew his cabin would be at the back of the ship down a narrow gangway with smaller cabins on both sides. By the light spilled by small lanterns, she could see his stiff back. He wore no wig, like most of the officers when aboard a ship, including the one who had escorted her with such aplomb.

Without looking back, her father opened the door. The officer paused before the same door, holding it open for her as she passed.

"That will be all, Phillips."

The officer nodded, shooting Ariel a look of sympathy before closing the door. The look surprised her, helped to steady her. Not for nothing had she faced her father before. She gave Phillips a small smile before turning to face her father with her body held straight, her eyes level, her hands relaxed at her sides.

Inside she trembled.

Slowly, so slowly she knew it was a calculated move, he turned to face her. His right hand rested upon a small desk, the papers that rested there moving a bit as his fingers caught the edges of them. She knew beyond the door behind him lay his personal quarters. She also knew that he would never let her into that private world, and though the notion did not wound her—not after all this time—she would still have given much to know why.

"Gordon sent me word that you are helping the traitor Nathan Trevain find his brother. Is this true?"

His voice was low, yet booming all the same. A trick of having to yell over the sound of wind and surf. And in his blue and gold admiral's attire, he looked every inch the commander.

"Aye, Father, it is true."

He merely stared. And as always Ariel wondered how she could possibly be his daughter. He was so unlike her in so many ways. His hair was silver, but it'd been blond before that. His face was long, his nose autocratic, his jaw hard and unyielding. A portly body stood upon short legs. That her mother's traits had been passed on to her there could be no doubt. That she looked nothing like her father there could also be no doubt.

Finally he gathered himself. She could see it in the way his hands flexed by his sides. The way his jaw tightened a bit. The way his eyes narrowed. "You are a deep disappointment to me, Daughter."

She tried not to react to his words, tried not to let him see how much they hurt her despite the fact that they were expected.

"Only a deep disappointment, Father? I'm sorry to hear that, for I've always struggled to be a huge disappointment. I see I have failed in my aim."

His eyes glittered. Ariel wondered why she always felt the need to bait him in situations like these. They were like two weather systems, warring with each other until thunder and lightning stuck. She knew it would be that way tonight.

"I should have married you off," he snapped.

"What? And missed out on the fun of ignoring me my entire life? Of making me feel less worthy than one of your officers? Or going away so often I feel as if I was born an orphan?"

He stiffened his stance. "I have a job to do at the Admiralty."

"Most admirals stay in town, father, do not try to bamboozle me. I know the truth. You want to avoid me." She stepped further into the room, her boots tapping on the wood floor. His eyes swept down, obviously noticing her boys' attire for the first time. His gaze turned even more disgusted. "And what I want to know, now, tonight, is why that is." Lord help her, she didn't want to cry, but suddenly she felt tears come to her eyes. Ridiculous tears, for she'd realized long ago that her father didn't love her, she'd just never had the courage to ask why.

"I don't wish to discuss our relationship, Ariel. We're here tonight to discuss Mr. Nathan Trevain."

"What have you done with him?" she asked, for suddenly she knew he had done something. There was a look on his face, one of smug satisfaction.

"Nothing . . . yet."

"What do you mean?"

"Surely you realize that as the daughter of a

First Lord, I cannot have you associating with the man? He has been taken into custody, again. But I will release him if you promise to never see him again."

"Impossible," she cried. "Father, I—" She struggled to find the right words, settled on the simplest ones. "I love him." She opened her mouth, couldn't speak for a second through the clog of emotions, swallowed again and said, "I know it sounds improbable, but I truly do. He is a good man, one who fought for his country as proudly as any of your men. If you would but meet with him—"

"Never," he slashed her with his voice. "To do so would be political suicide. My position is appointed, or have your forgotten that?"

"Is your career so important, then, that you would sacrifice your only daughter's happiness?"

"Are you such a poor daughter that you would sacrifice your father's career? Again? Already I have weathered one storm for you . . . barely. But this, this promises to be worse. What am I to say to Howell and Parker and the lot of them? Sorry, sirs, but my daughter seems to have fallen in love with a bloody patriot?"

"Would that be so difficult?"

"Not difficult, impossible. They will wonder if a man who cannot control his daughter is fit to run the navy."

"You do not need to control me, Father. Just let me marry him. I will go away. You will be rid of me forever."

"And you think he will want to wed with you after already sampling your wares? Did Archie teach you nothing?"

She felt as if he'd slapped her. "Archie was different. He had no character. Nathan Trevain is the most honorable man I know."

"So honorable that he would kidnap you? Use you whilst you pretended to be engaged to him? Oh, yes, I know it all, although how Phoebe could let you do something so foolish, I have no idea. Imagine, your going back into society."

"I only went to appease her. And what Nathan did he did out of necessity. Surely you, as a man of war, should understand?"

"I understand better how a man would pretend to love a woman in an effort to cajole her into helping him."

"Is that what you think he has done?"

"Of course."

"No. You are wrong. He loves me. I know it here," she placed a hand on her chest. "In my heart."

He didn't look appeased by her words. "Well, you shall not have the opportunity to find out if he truly does or not. He is to be taken to the Tower the moment I give the signal."

"I am surprised you have not done so already."

"I have not because I wish to make you an offer of sorts." And here her father's eyes turned crafty.

"An offer?"

"I will let Nathan Trevain go free if you agree to cut off all relations with him."

"No," she immediately said. "I already told you. I will not do it, Father. I love him, and he me."

"That is my offer. Take it or leave it."

"Then I will leave it. I will find some way to be with him, even if it means never seeing you again."

His face became pinched. "You would not dare to cut off relations with me. Think of the scandal."

"Scandal?" Anger had her taking a step forward, had her flexing her fingers. "As if I care. You may be my father, but you do not act it. You could have arranged a marriage for me years ago, a marriage that would have helped to salvage some of my reputation. But you did nothing, just as you promised. You left me in Bettenshire to rot. I have nothing to gain by staying under your control and everything to gain by following my heart."

"There is Wess Trevain."

She all but flinched. "What about him?"

"He is on board this ship."

"No," she gasped.

Her father's expression turned unreadable. " 'Twas a simple matter to have Trevain's brother transported to this ship."

"Release him, Father. Release Wess Trevain." Her pulse pounded at her neck. She held her breath as she waited for his response.

"No," he said.

She closed the distance between them, grabbing his cold, hard hand. "Please, Father. If I mean anything at all to you—anything—do this for me."

His lips tightened. He pulled his hand away. "No," he repeated. "We will use the man as a way to get information out of Mr. Trevain."

"Information? But the war is over."

Her father shrugged. "To some it is, but the political war is far from over. There are still battles being waged, but they are not of the physical kind. Nathan Trevain can help us shed some light on the climate back in the colonies. His brother will serve as the perfect impetus to do so."

She stepped back, felt her face drain of color. "Have you no heart? The man has been through enough already."

"The man is a traitor to the Crown and a former spy. Ah, yes. I know he is Helios, though I see by your face you are surprised. I've always known. 'Tis why I choose to take my time helping him. 'Tis the least I can do to repay him for the damage he caused us in the war. And now his recapture will only enhance my position with the Board by showing them that my foolish daughter's actions were the result of a broken female mind."

"You bastard."

He lifted one side of his mouth. "I am a man of war, Ariel. It is time you realized that."

"Please don't do this."

"You have only to give the word and I will not. I will let him go—and Wess Trevain—if you promise to have nothing further to do with the man—and if you promise to have Dr. Anthony Addington examine you."

She jerked in surprise. "Dr. Addington? Why, that is a mental physician."

"Aye, it is, and the perfect way for your behavior to be explained."

Her temper flared. "So you would sacrifice my reputation even further? You would now have me branded mad as well as a harlot?"

"That is the deal, Ariel. You may take it or leave it."

No. She would leave it, for what he suggested was so heartless, so cruel, she could barely fathom his loathing for her.

"Why?" She found herself croaking. "Why do you hate me so?"

He gave her a look of impatience. "Ariel, I do not hate you. For all your faults, you are still my daughter—"

"Am I? I begin to wonder."

The impatience turned to anger. "You are my daughter, and as such, I will do what it takes to insure that you behave in a manner befitting your station. A mental imbalance is the only explanation to my peers of your recent behavior. Imagine, parading about town as if nothing had happened. That in itself speaks of madness. And it is the only deal I am willing to give you. Give yourself over to Dr. Addington and never see Nathan Trevain again, or do your best to make a life with him in the Tower, his brother left to rot somewhere else. The choice is yours."

She lifted her head, a tear of frustration and disappointment escaping. "You truly mean to make me decide?"

"Be grateful I am giving you something to decide on at all."

"Ah, but you do so for your own political gain, not for me."

"I do so for both our sakes. The D'Archer name has been synonymous with government since Henry VIII was on the throne. That will not change with me simply because I have had the misfortune to sire a daughter without an ounce of common sense in her head."

She wanted to hit him of a sudden, even found herself leaning forward to do so. But the fight drained out of her. She would not give him the satisfaction of seeing how he'd stripped away whatever love she'd felt for him.

"Well?" he asked.

"I need time to decide."

"Time? What is there to think about?"

"There is much." She turned.

"Where are you going?"

"On deck." She paused, looking back. "Do not fear, Father, I will not do something truly mad, like toss myself overboard in an attempt to swim ashore."

"Just the same, you will be escorted."

She almost balked, almost told him to go to the devil. But again she refused to react. "As you wish."

If her father was surprised by her easy acquiescence, he didn't show it. He called out to Phillips, who apparently stood right outside the door. Tightening her cloak about her, she didn't give her father another glance as she left his quarters. She ignored Phillips, too, preferring instead to seek the company of a black night and foggy air. Moisture clung to her face. No, not moisture, she realized, tears, instant tears of anger and frustration and hopelessness.

What to do?

Truly, she didn't seem to be able to think straight. She turned left, climbed the steps of the poop deck, then headed for the back rail. 'Twas quieter up there, the men who inhabited the main decks going about their evening business of stowing ropes and sails.

What to do? she asked herself again and again.

She closed her eyes, grateful that Phillips gave her a bit of distance.

If she left the ship now, her father would have Nathan taken to the Tower. Worse, he would do so before she could reach him, for the only way off this ship was to jump or be rowed ashore. And on such a dark and foggy night, finding shore would be a lucky guess at best, not to mention she could drown in her clothes or suffer from the cold to the point at which she lost consciousness and drowned. The possibilities were endless, even though she knew the shore lay less than a quarter-mile away. Dare she risk it?

"I wouldn't if I were you, my lady."

She jumped, surprised that Phillips had moved in so close.

"Wouldn't what?"

"Jump," he said.

"What makes you think I shall jump? My father runs this ship. If I wish to go ashore, I shall simply ask."

"I am your father's second in command. I know the offer he presented you with."

She straightened in surprise and hurt before turning back to the rail. Though she could barely see his face, she could feel his presence like a shadow of her father's will.

"Then you know of my relationship with Nathan Trevain?"

"Yes, but jumping will do you no good. If you

made it to shore, there would be nothing you could do to help him—*if* you made it. You could lose your way in this soup. Find yourself swimming toward France before you realized what you'd done. 'Tis not worth the risk."

She clutched the rail, the dank wood sinking into her nails. Closing her eyes, she took a deep breath. "But I cannot do it, sir. I cannot make a decision like this." Sudden tears choked her throat, tumultuous emotions pooled in her stomach and made it ache. Or was that her heart? "I love him, you see."

He didn't answer. Truly, she didn't expect him to. He was her father's ally, one who'd been sent to keep her doing something foolish. A decision must be made and made tonight, yet never had she felt more confused and more incapable of one in her life.

"You need to understand that your father will do anything to protect your reputation."

"Have I truly damaged it then? Have I plunged the D'Archer name into scandal again."

"Aye. Only this is much worse than ruining yourself."

So he knew of that, too? She should not be surprised. She would dare say every man on board knew of her scandalous behavior.

"What I have done I have done to right a wrong. Mr. Trevain is not a traitor for serving his country any more than you are."

"Not in the colonies, but here on this shore he

is. That your father is willing to let him go free is a risk I am surprised he is willing to take."

"Oh, I've no doubt he will spin it into a political move on his part. He will claim to be restoring relations between the two countries or some such nonsense. 'Tis how my father is. Nothing is done unless he stands to gain."

She felt a hand fall on her shoulder. For some reason the contact nearly shattered her control. More tears slid down her face, tears she been valiantly trying to hold back.

"Sometimes, my lady, one must give the ultimate sacrifice in order for the greater good to be done."

She stared down into the black water. "But how can I let him go?"

"The way we all let go of our loved ones when we step aboard this ship, many of us never to return to shore. Say good-bye."

"He will not let me. I know it."

"Then send him a note, fabricate an excuse, but do what you must."

Do what she must? But did she have to do this? Was there not some other way to resolve it all?

Yet she knew there wasn't. 'Twas why her father had brought her aboard the ship. The waters around her acted as a prison. He knew she might try to flee when faced with such a decision. He'd also known she'd elect to stay with Nathan, as his wife or as his lover, she didn't care. Only now she knew that would never happen. If she told her father she cast her fate with Nathan, then he would take him to the Tower. Wess would be kept a prisoner, too, for how long Ariel had no idea. Short of pleading her case before the king, her hands were tied.

She closed her eyes again, feeling tears squeeze through her lids. God, but could she do it? Could she let him go?

Taking a deep breath, feeling as if she were about to splinter apart inside, she turned to Phillips. "May I see Wess Trevain? I wish to give him a message to take back to Nathan."

"I'll see what I can arrange." He patted her shoulder. Ariel wanted to tell him to go to hell, wanted to yell at him for doing her father's bidding. But most of all, she wanted to curl up into a little ball. God, she didn't think she could do it. She just didn't. For so long she'd hoped to find someone to love her. So long . . .

She faced the sea again, wondering how uncomfortable a death it would be to drown. But no, she could not think that, for she needed to face Nathan's brother, needed to find a way to break Nathan's heart, for that would be the only way he would leave her side. Of that she was sure.

She shook her head, feeling the pain of what she was about to do as a physical ache in her chest. It took her a moment to catch her breath, took her a moment to stop the tears she hadn't known she'd been crying from flowing down her face. She blindly stared out to sea, knowing what she was about to do would be the hardest, most difficult thing she'd ever face.

For how did one break a loved one's heart? How did one *live* with a broken heart?

21

Nathan stared at the four midshipmen and one officer who stood in his room, wanting to lunge at them all, to grab them about the throat and scream at them the one question they refused to answer.

Where was Ariel?

He'd woken a half hour ago to find her gone, had sat up in bed looking for her when the men had burst in, muskets leveled. Their orders for him to get dressed were hastily obeyed. And though a part of him had wondered if Ariel had somehow aided in his capture again, the other part of him knew she had not. If she'd wanted him captured, she'd have left him in London. There was nothing for her to gain by bringing him here to Brighton.

Nothing but her love.

And she did love him. Though she had not spoken the words aloud, he could see the reflection of how she felt in her eyes. She loved him, and, God help him, he loved her, too.

A click and his bedroom door opened. He turned, hoping it was Ariel, shocked nearly into speechlessness at who he saw there instead.

"Wess!" The name escaped in a gasp.

"Nathan," his brother said. His body was held between two officers. Then his eyes rolled back in his head, the two men on either side of him having to act quickly to keep him from falling. And when he did slump to the ground, who stood behind him but Ariel?

Ariel, his wonderful Ariel.

Love such as he'd never known filled Nathan. How the hell had she found him?

"Put him in the bed," she ordered softly.

They did as she ordered, Nathan rushing to his brother's side. It was then that he saw them. The bruises. The cuts. God, they were everywhere. Wess's shirt was ripped from the force of them.

"I'm sorry, Nathan," Ariel said softly, having come up behind him.

He turned to her.

"They have beaten him rather badly."

"Who?" he clipped.

There was no need to explain who he meant. "Captain Pike and his men."

He would kill them. He turned toward the bed again. They had laid him down on his belly. Nathan saw why in an instant. Cuts, hundreds of them, crisscrossed his back, his shirt stained red with the blood from them.

"Leave us," Ariel ordered to the room at large.

"My lady," said a man Nathan hadn't seen before. He must have come in with Ariel, a young officer who looked at her with warning.

She shook her head in so small a movement as to be nearly undetectable to anyone but the man. But Nathan saw it, wondered at it.

"I will be safe here," she said. "You need only wait outside the door."

The man's eyes shot around the room, clearly uncomfortable with her request. But then his eyes settled on Wess, then Ariel. He nodded. "As you wish."

"Please have someone fetch a physician, too. And we will need bandages and water. Lots of water."

Again the man nodded. Nathan's gaze shot between the two. His brother groaned, and all was forgotten but the need to help him. Wess. Wess who'd been beaten to within an inch of his life.

He heard the door close, heard Ariel approach the bed, but she went to the other side.

"They made him run the gauntlet while he was at sea." she said, pain evident in the husky timbre of her voice.

"Why?" he croaked, looking back at his brother, at all the blood, some of it black around the edges, some of it still oozing.

"He tried to escape. He was put on trial for

desertion. They were going to hang him, but my father stopped them."

His gaze snapped to hers. "Your father?"

She nodded. "He is here . . . in port."

The news stunned him, as he was sure it had stunned Ariel. She must have reacted quickly, however, going to the man to plead for help. Never was Nathan more grateful to someone in his life, never more in love.

"How can I thank you?"

She looked away. The door opened without a knock. The same officer said, "Water, my lady. And clean cloths."

"Put them here." She motioned next to her.

One of the men who'd guarded Nathan carried two buckets.

"One is cold water, the other warm."

Ariel nodded again. "Thank you, Phillips."

The man called Phillips stared down at her. Nathan felt an instant of jealousy as he watched him touch her shoulder. "An hour, my lady. Nothing more."

"I understand and I thank you for what you've done so far. I know you take a great risk."

The man nodded. " 'Tis the least I can do."

Nathan listened to the exchange, wondered about it. He was about to ask what would happen in an hour, but Ariel had turned back to the bed. She dipped one of the cloths in a bucket, handing it across the bed to him. "Here. We need to bathe him. I fear he may suffer from an infection."

The moment Nathan touched his brother's body, he knew her words to be true. He could feel the heat rise off his body. Working together, they removed his shirt, then his breeches, Nathan's anger at the men who'd done this to Wess increasing with every revealed scar.

" 'Tis awful," he heard her say.

Yet she did not flinch, not even when they began to wipe away the blood. Not even when Wess cried out in pain. Nathan bade him stay still, but a few minutes later nature took care of the matter for him. His brother lost consciousness again. He and Ariel worked quickly in tandem then. She would remove a piece of shirt, he would wash the wound, his brother's blood spilling on his hands, his clothes, the bed. Yet she did her work silently, efficiently. Nathan's admiration for her, if possible, increased even more. And when they were finished and she came over to the basin that stood upon a dresser to wash her hands, he marveled at her cool reaction, even as he followed in her wake to do the same.

"The doctor should be able to tell you more about his condition."

Nathan glanced back at the bed. "If he dies of his wounds, there will be hell to pay."

"He will not die," she said, turning to face him at last, touching his arm before pulling her hand away. "I will ensure that he receives the best care possible."

He nodded, touching her chin as he had on that longago day when they'd met in the garden. "Ariel, I can't thank you enough. You have given me something I never thought to have back. How can I ever thank you?"

She closed her eyes as if in pain. "Nathan, I—"

Someone knocked on the door. They stared at each other for a second before she said, "Just a moment," then turned. And had he mistaken it, or were there tears in her eyes?

"Five more minutes, Phillips, please," he heard her say.

He heard a low, masculine voice respond, too low to make out the words.

"I know."

More softly muttered words.

"I will tell him."

She closed the door, her hand lingering on the door handle for a long moment.

"Ariel, what foolishness is this? Why does it sound like you must leave?"

"Phillips said the physician will be here shortly. He was out on another call when they arrived, but word was sent. He'll be here soon."

Her voice sounded odd, muffled, as if she spoke through a cloth or—

Cried.

"Ariel," he said, crossing to her in three quick strides, turning her. "What is going on?"

Tears streamed down her face as she met his gaze. "Oh, Nathan, I cannot do it. I cannot."

"Cannot do what?"

She wiped away her tears, only to have more replace them instantly. "I was going to tell you a lie. I was going to make up a story about how I've been working for the Admiralty. That I'd been told to help you escape so that I could gain your trust, but I cannot do it. I just cannot."

"What are you saying?"

She stared up at him, searching his eyes, her hand half rising as if she meant to touch his face, only to fall back to her side. "You are going back to the colonies, Nathan."

"Of course I am, with you and my brother, once he heals."

"You would have me?"

He nodded. "Of course. I love you. After what has happened between us, did you think anything else?"

But his words caused more tears. She glanced over at the bed, her eyes filling with pain and something else. Hopelessness?

"I could not be sure, but it changes nothing."

"What do you mean?"

She seemed to brace herself, took a deep breath. "I am not going with you."

He stared down at her, unable to speak for moment. "What nonsense is this?"

She grabbed his hand, stemming the flow of angry words he'd been about to snap. "Listen to me, Nathan. I cannot go with you for a reason that you must understand—"

"What do you mean I *must* understand?"

"My father—"

"What has he to do with this? Is he forcing you to stay?"

Aricl knew she needed to be careful in how she answered the question. If Nathan knew the truth, he would be furious and likely want to confront her father. Then he would know that both of them had no choice in the matter. He was to be sent back to the colonies with his brother. She was to remain here, alone, without the man she loved. Should he refuse to leave, he would be incarcerated again, his brother suffering the same fate. She couldn't let that happen.

Wouldn't let that happen.

She took a deep breath. "No, Nathan," she said firmly, though the words all but stuck in her throat. "He is not forcing me to stay here. The decision was mine to make."

He looked incredulous. "But why? Don't you love me?"

Oh, aye, she silently answered, *if you only knew how much.* Instead she looked him in the eyes and said the only words she could say. "No, Nathan, I do not."

He drew back. "Then what was all this nonsense about being honest, for I know as surely as I breathe that you *do* love me."

"I thought that by fabricating a story I could make you hate me, but it is not in me to do that. No, I must tell you the truth."

The truth. If only she could.

"I do not love you, Nathan. Please believe me

when I say that I desire you, there can be no denying that. But love? Impossible. We are from opposite worlds. My father helped me to see that."

He looked down at her in disgust. "Your father is trying to poison your mind."

"No, my father helped me to see we have no future together. My family is here, your family is in the colonies. You could never come back to England once you leave, so I would never see my family again."

"You would like it in the colonies."

"Not if my family is not there with me."

"But you love me." He grabbed her by the arms, almost as if he wanted to shake her. "You do. I will be your family."

"No, Nathan, I do not love you. For how could I possibly love a man who turns his nose up at his own uncle? And a title, too, no less."

He looked like she'd struck him. "Titles are important to you?"

"Of course they are, Nathan. If you knew me better, you would know that. Despite my checkered past, I have still been raised to be a nobleman's wife. What we shared was nice, and"—she searched for a word—"enlightening, but if we are honest with each other, we must admit that love does not happen quite so quickly."

He drew back. She knew she'd finally gotten his attention, knew he was taken aback by her words.

"You cannot be serious," he said.

"I am."

"This was all a game to you?"

"Game? No. I would call it more of an adventure, one that ended better than my affair with Archie. Of course, my father interrupted Archie and me at the wrong moment. Pity, for it would have been nice to have someone to compare you to."

He drew himself up. She thought she might have gone too far, that he would see through her lies. But too many years of not trusting women had apparently taken their toll. She saw the emotions flit across his face. Disbelief, anger, and worst of all, pain. An answering pain rose in her throat.

Nathan, Nathan, she wanted to scream, *can you not see that I lie? Has our time together taught you nothing of me?*

He stepped back from her, his face turning cold. "Then I wish you well, my lady. Since you are set on leaving, you may as well go now."

She wanted to fall at his feet and cry, wanted to fling herself into his arms and never let go. Instead Ariel stepped back, amazed at how calm her voice sounded when she said, "Then I bid you good-bye, too, Nathan Trevain. And God speed, for despite what you may think, I do care for you." Heavens, if only he knew how much. "Have a safe voyage."

But he'd already turned away from her, crossing to his brother. Thus he didn't see her lift a

hand in mute agony, didn't see the tear that escaped.

Escape.

Aye, she needed to escape. Now, before she
did something foolish like ruin it all by telling
him the truth.

On feet heavy with sadness, she crossed to the
door, forcing herself to take every step, forcing
herself to breathe, to walk away without shed-
ding a tear.

I love you, she silently said, looking back at
him one last time.

His face was in profile, the scar vivid by
lantern light. He stared down at his brother, not
even looking up when she turned the handle of
the door with a click, not even when she didn't
move for a second, hoping, nay, praying, he
would look her way one last time.

But he didn't.

With blurry eyes, she stepped through the
doorway and toward her future.

A future without Nathan Trevain.

22

Ariel had no memory of the journey home, her wounds making it hard to see anything but her misery. Her father remained silent the whole way, and for that she was grateful. Even when they reached the outskirts of London and she had broken down in tears, he remained silent. So she cried most of the way to Bettenshire, cried away her despair and anguish and grief.

When she reached home, she wanted only to sleep. Sleep so that she could forget about the lies she'd been forced to tell. And sleep she did, but if one must sleep, one must awaken, too. She did, her childhood room coming into focus, though at first she didn't know where she was. Then memories assailed her. Nathan. His brother. What she'd done. A stab of misery so acute it made her long to close her eyes again hit her in the heart, but she didn't close her eyes. Instead she turned her head, spying a figure in profile by the bed.

Phoebe.

"Arie?" her cousin said.

She ignored Phoebe's voice, wanting only to curl up with the pain of her loss.

"Arie, thank God. I thought you would never wake."

Would that she hadn't, for now that the pain had begun to hit, she could barely breathe. Her throat tightened up, her breath quickened, her eyes filled with regretful tears.

A hand reached out and stroked the hair from Ariel's eyes. The tears began to break free.

"Oh, Arie," Phoebe soothed. "Come here."

Ariel didn't want to go. She wanted to tell Phoebe to leave, Ariel just wanting to be left alone with her misery. But she didn't have the strength to say even that. And when Phoebe moved to the edge of her bed, the mattress tipping with Phoebe's weight, then collected her into her arms, Ariel's control broke. Ariel sucked in air, felt the damn burst, then began to sob in Phoebe's arms. She cried for the loss of Nathan, cried because she knew she'd never see him again. Cried because once again she'd loved a man and once again she'd lost him.

"Arie," Phoebe soothed. "I'm so sorry."

Ariel blinked away tears. "Oh, Phoebe," she choked out, her voice raspy. "Is he gone?"

"Nathan?" she asked.

Ariel nodded.

"Aye, Ariel. Your father said he set sail the morning after you spoke with him."

Oh, Nathan. You didn't. But he had. She'd known he would, had seen the pain in his eyes.

"You fell in love with him, didn't you?"

Fresh tears rose. She gasped out the words, "I did," and the realization made her begin to sob all over again. "Oh, Phoebe, I did. And I made him leave me. I made him think I didn't love him. And he believed me. He left."

"Arie," her soft voice answered. "I'm so sorry." She hugged her tighter. Rocking her. "So, so, sorry."

She held her. Ariel let her, crying out her pain on her shoulder. But the pain would never go away, she realized. It would be a part of her forever, something she would carry around for life. And just when she thought she couldn't shed another tear, more came. Phoebe continued to rock her and hold her and murmur soothing words in her ears.

It was a long while later that the crying slowly stopped. She knew the tears were still there, hovering beyond the edge of her lashes, but she contained them. For now. Phoebe pulled back, looking down at her again, her face filled with so much sympathy she wanted to cry all over again.

"Can I help?" she asked.

A small tear leaked out at her question. Would that she could. But there was nothing anyone could do. She would live with the loss of Nathan for the rest of her life. "No, Phoebe. You cannot help. What's done is done, thanks to my father."

"Is he the one who made you do this?"

She nodded. "In exchange for Nathan's freedom and his brother's."

Phoebe inhaled deeply. " 'Tis not a very nice thing to do.

Ariel shook her head. "Where is he?"

"I do not know. He has been keeping to himself for the past few days."

Days? "How long have I been asleep?"

An edge of worry filled Phoebe's eyes. "You arrived four days ago."

Four days! She didn't know why the realization should make fresh tears rise. Perhaps because there was no hope that she could watch Nathan's ship set sail. He was gone. Back to the colonies. She to stay here.

The realization brought a desperation to her soul so hard to combat she could barely breathe.

"Do you want to see him?"

"See who?" she asked in a monotone.

"Your father."

"No, Phoebe. Not yet. In time."

Phoebe nodded. "I will let you get some rest." She rose from the bed.

"Phoebe, wait." Ariel reached for her cousin's hand. Her eyes burned again with tears. "Thank you for coming."

Answering tears rose in Phoebe's eyes. "Where else would I be?"

Where else indeed?

* * *

But it was days before she would deign to see her father, not that he asked to see her. Or even stopped by. Phoebe said he'd been engrossed in his work. Engrossed. Hah. Likely he plotted how best to look the hero by releasing Nathan Trevain.

"Father," she said. The skirts of her lemon-colored dress flew behind her as she entered his study.

"Ariel," he replied in a clipped voice, looking up from the papers he'd been studying. He sat behind his desk in a deep leather chair, his wig firmly in place. The sterile interior seemed to fit her father's personality perfectly, even the stack of papers to his left piled in perfect, precise order. "I see you are feeling better."

"Am I?" she asked, coming to stand before him. Morning light reflected off the surface of his cherry-wood desk. It showed both their images. He looked small when viewed from such an odd angle. And older. Or perhaps it was her loathing for him. He looked different to her, perhaps more repugnant and well-used. "And how would you know that, Father, when you have visited me not even once?"

His eyes narrowed. "I kept tabs on you through Phoebe."

In a smooth motion she settled herself on a brown leather chair in front of his desk. "How very fatherly of you, Father."

He sat up straighter. "Ariel, what is it you wish to see me about?"

"Perhaps nothing. Perhaps I merely wish to

see how you fare. Did you receive a knighthood from the king for your brilliant recapture of Nathan Trevain?"

His lips tightened.

"No? How about a promotion of some sort? Oh, but that's right, you can rise no further in your career, can you? There is only one place to go from here, and that is down."

He stared up at her, a look of mistrust suddenly entering his eyes. Well, good. As she'd lain in bed the past days a thousand thoughts had gone through her mind. Had there been something different she could have done? Had she done the right thing? Would Nathan be happy without her?

Bother that, would she be happy without Nathan?

And the answer to that was always no, she would not be happy. She knew that as surely as she knew the sun would rise. And then everything seemed so simple. If she loved him, she would go to him. He was a free man now, out of her father's reach. She would go to him and explain, leave England, never to return again. And though she would miss Phoebe, she would miss little else, most especially the man who sat before her.

"Ariel, what are you plotting?"

She smiled, a smug smile, one to set him on edge with worry. "A voyage, Father."

"A voyage? To where?"

But surely he must know. "Why, to the colonies, where else?" She settled back in her seat, enjoying the moment. "It dawned on me whilst I lay in bed that I am no longer a little girl. I can do as I wish, and that includes leaving a country and a man who have done nothing but hurt me. Frankly, I am surprised the idea has not crossed my mind before."

"You wouldn't dare."

"Oh, yes, I would."

He shot up from his chair. Ariel thought he might come around the end of his desk and grab her. His face had turned red, a vein popping out on his forehead. That he'd gone into a sudden, instant rage there could be no doubt.

Oddly enough, she felt no fear. Just a deep, wonderful sense of satisfaction.

"What, Father, no threats?" She lifted a brow. "Oh, but that's right, you've nothing left to threaten me with, have you? Already you've done your worst." She slowly stood. "Now let me do mine."

She placed her hands on his desk, leaning across it. "I am leaving, and nothing you might say can stop me. The carriage is outside, and in a matter of hours all of London will know that the First Lord's daughter has left England to become the lover of a patriot spy." She straightened, standing before him proudly, daring him to say something. When he didn't, her smile turned a bit sad. "Good-bye, Father. Though you never did tell me why you hate me so, know that despite what you've done, I *do* love you."

She turned, paused, swiveled back to face

him. "And do not worry, sir, for I'm sure you can have it put about that I've lost my mind. Your career should not suffer too much." She turned back to the door.

"Ariel, wait."

She almost didn't listen, but some urge, some long-forgotten compulsion that dated back to childhood, made her turn again.

"Do not do this," he begged, his blue eyes boring into hers.

She gave him a sad smile. "Begging, Father?"

"No, appealing to your loyalty as my daughter."

"Just as I appealed to your loyalty as a father. Oh, wait. 'Twas not your loyalty I begged for, 'twas your love. But I should have known better than to do that, shouldn't I? You haven't loved me from the start."

"How could I when you took the one woman I ever loved away?" And the words came out as a rasp.

She felt her mouth open in shock. So that was it. That was all it was. She'd been responsible for her mother's death, and he held it against her. How could he be so selfish? A sadness overtook her. Didn't he realize she would rather she had died being born than live with the responsibility of causing someone's death? That she felt like an orphan without her mother and without her father's love.

Apparently not.

"Then we are even, Father," she said. "For you

took away the only man *I* will ever love." She turned to the door.

"Don't go," he repeated.

She ignored him.

"Ariel, please."

Something in the tone caught her attention, something that tugged at her in a way she would never have thought possible. Slowly, reluctantly, telling herself she was a fool for opening herself up to more of his hateful words, she turned.

He cried.

She'd *never* seen her father cry.

"I loved her desperately, Ariel," he said in a low voice. "You do understand that, do you not?"

"Aye. As much as I love Nathan," she answered proudly.

He stared at her a long, long moment, Ariel's breath quickening with every moment that passed. Something was changing in his face, something she hardly dared believe.

"I'll need to send a note to Lord Dunsmeer. He runs the harbor in Portsmouth and can tell you which ships will be the fastest to the colonies." He was straightening, once again becoming the First Lord, even though his eyes still shone red with tears. "I'll send him a note straightaway."

Ariel stared at her father in disbelief. "Oh, Papa," she murmured, his face growing blurry through her tears. "You're going to help me."

He nodded, though he didn't look at her. "I would rather have you gone than live the rest of your life with half a heart, as I have done."

Tears fell down her cheeks. "Oh, Papa," she gushed. As if in a dream she found heself racing into his arms. He didn't hold her at first, but then she felt his arms slowly move around her. They tightened, then tightened even more.

"Go, Ariel. Be happy. Goodness knows you've earned it."

Her tears came harder, and it was then that Ariel D'Archer, daughter to the earl of Bettencourt, realized she was not an orphan after all.

23

The ship crashed through the wave, sea foam hitting Nathan in the face with an icy slap. But Nathan didn't care, for with each bob of the prow he traveled further and further away from her. Further away from the black-hearted bitch he'd fallen in love with.

A woman who gave you your brother back, said a voice.

Oh, aye, she'd done that. And for that he was grateful. Her parting gift to him. How touching.

"Sir?"

Nathan turned, having to pry his hands away from the rail.

"Come quick, sir. He is awake."

Nathan jolted alert. Wess awake? Could such a miracle have happened?

Judging by the smiling look on the doctor's face, it had.

He followed quickly along the rail of the deck, then down some stairs to the private quarters below. He'd been fortunate to find a doctor willing to set sail with them, though Nathan had wondered at the necessity of it—especially since his brother had made little improvement since they'd left Brighton. He'd needed a physician, and the good doctor was the only one willing to go. But Nathan would pay him double his wages if his brother was indeed awake.

He was.

Nathan could see it the moment he entered their brightly lit cabin, lantern light seeming to illuminate every corner.

"Wess?" he called out. His brother's face was still bruised, even after two weeks at sea. But his cuts looked better. For that he could thank the good doctor, too.

"Where is she?" his brother rasped.

Nathan stared down at him in surprise. "Where is who?"

"The angel who rescued me from the bowels of that hellhole, HMS *Destiny*. I wish to thank her."

Nathan drew back in shock. "Lady D'Archer?"

"Aye, that is her, for I heard the naval cur who came to get me call her so. Where is she?"

Nathan's face suddenly felt frozen. Any joy he felt at having his brother awaken temporarily faded. "She is not here."

Now it was Wess's turn to look confused. "But she must be."

"I assure you she is not."

"But how can that be when I heard her tell that naval scum of a captain how much she loved you?"

The words were slow to sink in. "She *what*?"

Wess motioned with a shaking hand for water. Nathan hurriedly complied, helping his brother drink. When he finished, he looked a bit better.

"Wess, you must tell me what you heard."

His brother nodded, seeming to understand the urgency of the situation. "I was barely awake," he murmured. "They'd starved me of food for days. It seemed like it all happened in a dream. But it was when we were in the carriage on our way to you. She was thanking the man who accompanied her for letting her go along. She said she was grateful that he knew what it was like to leave a loved one. I assumed she was talking about you."

Nathan sat there, stunned, the breath knocked out of him.

"She was crying, too, I seem to recall. I couldn't understand why, if, as she said, you two were in love. And then the man said something about a deal she'd made with her father. A deal that she could not break if she wanted to see you escape with your life."

"Damnation!" Nathan exclaimed.

Is he forcing you to stay? he had asked.

No, the decision was mine to make, she'd responded.

It had been her choice. Her choice to sacrifice her love so that he could have his freedom and his brother back. Her choice to live her life, knowing she'd made him hate her. Her choice to never know love again, for as surely as he knew what she'd done, he knew her love was true.

"Damnation," he repeated, shock, hope and amazement forcing him to his feet.

"Where are you going?"

"Back to England."

"To *England?*"

"Aye, to the woman I love."

24

The streets of Portsmouth were more crowded than the last time Ariel had visited. Or perhaps it was simply that she was more aware of them. Ariel stared out of the carriage window, observing the myriad colors the ladies wore as they walked by store fronts. Her own off-white gown with black trim would hardly make a splash against the colors she saw. Even the gentlemen looked colorful. 'Twas the last time she would ever see these streets, Ariel thought, feeling melancholy, for when she left on this afternoon's tide she would never return. Even now her father was waiting for her at an inn while she gathered some last-minute supplies. And though she should look forward to her future with Nathan, there still remained the question of whether or not he would forgive her.

Pray God he would.

The coach passed more shops. A sudden urge made Ariel tell the coachman to stop. She'd

planned on sending Phoebe something from the
colonies, but she would send her cousin something now, too, something that begged Phoebe's
forgiveness for refusing to take Phoebe with her
to Portsmouth. Two weeks she'd had to wait for
a ship to take her to the Americas. Two weeks of
knowing she'd have to say good-bye. Two
weeks of dreading that good-bye. How could
she explain to her kind-hearted cousin that saying good-bye in Portsmouth would have been
harder than in town, especially since saying
good-bye to her father would be hard enough?
Phoebe had been hurt, Ariel hurting along with
her. She would miss her darling cousin more
than any other person in England, even more
than the father she'd come to know in the past
weeks.

"Come back for me here in one hour," she instructed, as she was handed down from the carriage.

The coachman nodded, Ariel adjusting her
gown as she stepped upon the pavement. The
shop she'd spied prior to stopping lay across the
street. A sweet shop, something Phoebe was
never able to resist. She would send her something from there.

She turned, her carriage blocking the view for
a moment. Sunlight blinded her, too, for the sun
shone on that side of the street; her own side
was in shadow. That was why she probably
didn't see him at first, though it was obvious
that he'd seen her.

Nathan.

Her heart froze. She blinked, wondering if it could be a trick or the light, for it could not possibly be . . .

"Nathan?" she called out.

Another carriage passed between them, but when it moved on, he still stood there looking as wonderful and as handsome as if he had stepped out of her dreams. Wide, muscular shoulders stretched beneath a trim, dark gray jacket. Angular face with intense silver eyes, the scar hardly noticeable in the bright sunlight.

She moved as if in a dream. He didn't come to her. And as she drew nearer, she realized that it wasn't a dream. He was here. Before her. His wonderful silver eyes gazing down at her enigmatically.

"It is you, isn't it?" she asked, coming to stand before him.

"It is."

And the sound of his voice. Never had something sounded so wonderful.

"What are you doing here?"

"I had to come back," he answered, still not moving.

"Why?"

She held her breath as she waited for his answer.

"My brother."

She felt a disappointment so keen, she could barely breathe. But then she reached out. Of its own volition her hand touched his arm. The contact made her breath catch, made her ache in a way that almost hurt. "Has he taken a turn for the worse?"

"No. He is actually doing quite well."

He didn't return her touch. Ariel supposed that would be asking too much. He hated her. He must. Why else would he stand there as if nothing had ever happened between them? She pulled her hand away.

"I am glad to hear that, Nathan. Truly, I feel ashamed at what my countrymen did to him."

He nodded. They both lapsed into silence. A cart laden with hay rumbled by, the horses' harnesses jingling.

"And what of you? What are you doing in Portsmouth?" he asked.

She stared up at him, letting him see all the love she felt for him. "I came for you." And suddenly there were tears in her eyes. "I came for you, because I love you, because I couldn't let you think I didn't love you, because today I was to set sail for the colonies."

"Oh, Ariel," he said, pulling her into his arms. "I cannot believe what he said is true."

Ariel closed her eyes, feeling his big arms circle her, knowing she had a future she had only dared to dream of. She felt his breath sigh across her ear. Or was it she who sighed? She didn't know.

"What who said?" she asked.

He pulled back, stared down at her. "My

brother. He told me he'd overheard you tell that officer that you loved me."

Wess had overheard the conversation? She'd thought he'd been unconscious. But did it really matter? "I do love you, Nathan." She placed her hand over his heart, feeling the heat from the sun warm her. People walked by, many of them stared. She didn't care. "I love you with all my heart."

He didn't move. Neither did she.

"My darling Ariel," he said softly staring down at her in wonder, in awe.

She closed her eyes. "Oh, Nathan, Nathan. When I made you leave—"

"Shh," he soothed, resting his fingers against her lips. "I understand, Ariel. Truly, I do. I put it all together while we sailed back. Your father forced you to choose, didn't he? Give me up, or I would be taken prisoner again."

She didn't answer, just burrowed deeper into him. Gracious, but she'd missed his smell. Missed the sound of his voice. Missed *him*.

"Is that what it was?"

She drew back, looking into silver eyes filled with all the love in the world. It shone from his gaze, warmed her, made her realize that miraculously he wasn't angry with her.

"Aye, Nathan. 'Tis what he did."

"Bastard," he accused.

"No, Nathan. Do not be angry, for he realized his mistake soon enough. 'Twas he who helped me get here, my father sacrificing the right to even see his grandchild in order to help me."

"Child?"

"Indeed, for I could be carrying our son right now."

"Our son," he murmured, an odd smile lifting his face. "Our son. Aye, I like the sound of that."

"Me, too," she sighed, tears blurring her vision again. "I like the sound of it, too."

He bent his head toward hers. Their lips met. Neither of them cared that they were in the middle of the pavement, that the people inside the sweet shop stared, some with envy, some in shock. They cared only for each other. And that, Ariel realized a long while later, was all that really mattered.

Epilogue

England, 1803

Sixteen-year-old Lady Caroline Trevain stared at the smooth surface of the lake and contemplated love—a tricky subject at best, she'd oft been told by her mother. Of course, her mother the duchess was something of a legend where love was concerned. 'Twas said she had been ruined in her younger days, a situation that filled Caroline with an odd sort of envy. There had also been rumors that she'd been kidnapped by her father, but those she dismissed as the ramblings of an old man—her grandfather, the earl of Bettencourt.

But if her mother had been wild in her youth, she was now something of a stick-in-the-mud.

Bother that. She was a veritable tree in the mud, Caroline thought.

She threw a small pebble in the water. It sank with a plop, small, circular ripples that turned to larger ones spreading from where it'd disappeared.

Why her mother was so strict with her when she herself had been wild Caroline would never know. All she wanted to do was go to a party. Just one dance before they left England. Just one, that was all she wanted. She sighed, feeling suddenly so melancholy and so upset she could hardly keep from crying.

"What is it, little one?"

She started, surprised to see her father standing over her.

"Good evening, Papa."

He stared down at her, his tan face filled with question, his hair windswept. Hair as black as her own and her mother's. That she looked like her father there could be no doubt, but she had her mother's eyes.

"May I sit?"

She patted the pebbled ground next to her, moving her pink skirts aside. "Of course."

"Well?" he prompted again, tugging at the white shirt he wore.

She almost didn't answer, but they had a special bond, she and her father, one her mother said was as different from her own relationship with her father as a young woman as a rose is from snow.

"I am upset about leaving England."

"Upset about leaving, or upset about not seeing Lord Robert one last time?"

She looked over at her father in surprise, her curly black hair bobbing in her face. She swiped it away. "Am I that obvious?"

"As obvious as a boil."

She cringed. "That is a revolting analogy, Papa."

"But true."

She smiled. "Aye."

"So you want to go to the soiree to see Robert again."

"I do, Papa. I really do."

"But there will be other soirees. Other young men to meet."

"But Robert is leaving to fight against the French. This may be my last chance to see him."

"I assure you, my dear, you will see him again."

"But how can you be so sure?"

Her father gave her a smile. "Because at this very moment he is at the house, cooling his heels with your mother in our drawing room."

Caroline shot to her feet. "Oh, Papa, why didn't you tell me?"

"Because I wasn't supposed to, so when your mother chastises me, you'd best defend me."

She reached down and gave him a hug. Nathan closed his eyes, realizing that he loved his only little girl more than he'd ever thought it was possible to love someone other than his wife. She was exactly like Ariel, and never had a day gone by when he wasn't grateful she'd been born.

"Thank you, Papa," she said with a kiss, turning away to all but run back to the house.

Nathan watched her go, his thoughts traveling through the past to the time when she'd been born, then to before that, to when Colin had been born back in the colonies. That he'd been born a free man was a source of pride for Nathan, the wounds of his past having long since healed, thanks to the love of his very British wife.

"I thank you very much for telling our daughter her true love is here."

Nathan looked up, his wife of twenty years standing over him. She had her hands on her hips, the amber-colored dress she wore nearly the same color as her glittering eyes. That she had lost none of her beauty in the past twenty years there could be no doubt. Men still stared, it seemed to Nathan, even more in recent years than in the past. She still had her thick black hair, but now it had a wide, gray streak on the left side, something she had acquired after the birth of their first son.

"I know you wanted me to tell her exactly that, else you would have dismissed Robbie from the house the moment he arrived."

Her lips pursed. "And how do you know that?"

"Because, my dear, you, like me, would rather she see him in the privacy of our home than at some inn somewhere. You know how dangerous inns can be."

Her eyes narrowed. " 'Tis not very sporting of you to remind me of my past."

"Ah, but it has been a good past, has it not?"

The teasing glint in her eyes faded. They softened as she sat down next to him, her high-waisted dress a pretty contrast to the scenery around them.

"Indeed, it has," she answered. "We may not have wanted to return to England when your uncle died, but it has been good for the children. One day this will all belong to Colin, and my father's earldom, too."

"Speaking of which, when is the old battleship supposed to arrive?"

"Tomorrow," she said with a smile.

"Tomorrow? What a sad coincidence. I find I need to go into town tomorrow—"

She hit him on the arm. "You do not."

"No?" he teased.

"No," she answered.

He smiled, losing himself in his thoughts again. "It has been good, hasn't it?" he murmured after a while.

Ariel nodded, smiling up at him. "Aye. And if our children are half as lucky as we, they will find what we have. Still."

A wobbly smile tilted her lips. Nathan was surprised to see tears enter her eyes. He tilted her head up, just as he had a thousand times, just as he would go on doing until the end of their days.

"I love you, Ariel. You are the woman of my dreams."

She smiled, sniffing. "The woman of your dreams, am I?"

He nodded. "And of my fantasies. You enchant me with your kisses, my darling wife, you beguile me with your smile, and never has a day gone by when I don't thank God we found each other."

Her smile could light up a room, Nathan admitted, surprised to feel his own eyes mist up.

"Enchanted by my kisses?" she asked. "I think I rather like that."

"Oh," he said. "What say I show you just how much they enchant me?" He bent, kissing her as he longed to do every time he saw her. Kissing her as he had for the past twenty years. Kissing her as he would go on kissing her for the rest of their lives.

"Well?" he asked a long while later, drawing back, his hands on her face.

"Well, indeed," she said, placing her hand against the side of his face, her gaze filling with tenderness. "I think, my love, that 'tis I who am enchanted by *your* kisses."

The WONDER of KATHLEEN E. WOODIWISS

America Loves Lindsey!
The Timeless Romances
of #1 Bestselling Author

Johanna Lindsey

Nationally Bestselling Author
CHRISTINA DODD

"Christina Dodd is everything
I'm looking for in an author."
Teresa Medeiros

The Governess Bride series

RULES OF ENGAGEMENT
0-380-81198-7/$6.99 US/$9.99 Can

RULES OF SURRENDER
0-380-81197-9/$6.99 US/$9.99 Can

And Don't Miss

RUNAWAY PRINCESS
SCOTTISH BRIDES
(with Stephanie Laurens,
Julia Quinn, and Karen Ranney)
SOMEDAY MY PRINCE
THAT SCANDALOUS EVENING
A WELL FAVORED GENTLEMAN
A WELL PLEASURED LADY
CANDLE IN THE WINDOW
CASTLES IN THE AIR
THE GREATEST LOVER IN ALL ENGLAND
A KNIGHT TO REMEMBER
MOVE HEAVEN AND EARTH
ONCE A KNIGHT
OUTRAGEOUS
TREASURE IN THE SUN